Paul Hirons

Paul was born and raised in Engl… Black Country. His academic pror… was hot-housed through school w… eventually burned out and then dropped out. After a few false starts, he put together a successful work career of sorts.

He retired early (twice). After studying art history, he changed tack and did some creative writing courses at Oxford University, picking up a diploma in the process. Armed with an early draft of his first novel, he set up as an author and blogger.

Since then, he's published a couple of novels and both are available on Amazon. His first, *1997 remembered,* is a comedy, a faux memoir about an ordinary man's journey through an extraordinary year. *The Good Russian* is his second novel. He's currently writing his third novel, a dystopian story in which a dead billionaire seeks revenge for the murder of his husband. Watch out for this in 2025.

When he's not writing, he plants trees for a local charity, watches cricket, reads other people's books – scandi-noir mainly – and goes to art exhibitions. He wastes too much time wandering around the internet.

You can contact him at **pahirons.com** or email him at **paulh.books@zen.co.uk**

The
Good Russian

Paul Hirons

ISBN 978-1-7398697-1-7

Cover Design by More Visual Ltd.

The Good Russian

Chapter 1

Robert Smith stands proudly on his bedroom balcony, shamelessly naked. With his legs and arms splayed wide and his mop of greying hair grazing his shoulders, he brings to mind Da Vinci's Vitruvian Man. He basks in the early morning rays, gradually warming himself as a reptile might. He's not usually around at such an early hour but sleep is out of the question – there's far too much rattling around his head for that. He's tempted to linger outside but thinks better of it, forcing himself back to the bedroom. He walks into his dressing room and scans the serried ranks of clothes, spoilt for choice. There's plenty of time to get suited and booted later so he settles for black Levi's and a plain, white tee shirt.

Leaving the bedroom, he walks quietly along the corridor in his bare feet. His destination is the kitchen on the floor above. It's as good a place as any to start the day, especially if Joanna, their dour but undeniably efficient housekeeper-cum-cook, is up and about.

The door to his wife's bedroom is closed but he can hear sighs and snuffles within. He's unable to tell whether they belong to

Pamela or her latest girlfriend, whose name he ought to know but can't recall.

Moving on, the door to his fiancée's bedroom is slightly ajar and he can't resist a peek inside. The bed looks made, so he can't be sure she slept there last night. He's not overly concerned by Varvara's absence as she usually rises early to start her punishing fitness regime. He reckons she spends at least an hour in their gym most mornings and evenings, followed by a swim. She might still be down there or she might by now have moved across to her workshop.

The bedroom at the end of the corridor is occupied by Monty, who doesn't do girlfriends. Or boyfriends for that matter. Knowing Monty, he's probably curled up in bed with an empty bottle of champagne. Thank God he's not snoring right now – when Monty gets going, he emits a deep bass rumble equivalent at its peak to a low-flying Lancaster bomber.

Robert has lived in this house for upwards of five years and still doesn't know how most of the stuff works in the state-of-the-art kitchen. He's content to leave that sort of detail to Joanna, and through sheer indolence has become reliant on her for basic necessities. He knows how to work the coffee machine, but only the basics, so conjures up a double espresso of sorts. When its cooled sufficiently, he'll down it in one gulp. He looks around in vain for somebody to fix him some toast or something. Sadly, he's much too early for that.

He's about to tackle the coffee when Desmond shuffles in, introducing himself with a lacklustre croak. He's Robert's slightly older half-brother and they've been looking out for each other since they were kids. He slumps down at the table, a dishevelled, dreadlocked mess, clad in the same crumpled clothes he wore yesterday. He's brought his smoking paraphernalia with him in a battered tin case but a look from his host is enough to stop him in his tracks.

'No smoking, bruv. You know the rules. Includes weed, in case you're wondering. Over by the garages if you want a smoke. And pick up your rubbish as well. You don't want "Herself" on your case, do you?'

The term could apply to any of several women in the house right now, although he had one in mind when he said it.

'I seriously resent your hectoring tone, bro. Gimme a break.'

There was six months between them. They'd both been sired by the same wayward, feckless piece of shite whose only favour to his progeny had been to die early. Don't feel too sorry for them though as, in very different ways, they've built successful businesses and become seriously rich on the back of them. Desmond's a TV producer and him and his actress wife Lizzie are up from London for the launch party, staying in one of the guest bedrooms. Lizzie's parents are looking after their young kids.

'Listen up bruv, Joanna will be turning up soon.' He's a bit intimidated by his housekeeper, so lowers his voice. 'She's a miserable bat at the best of times but I'm sure she'll do some breakfast for you if you ask her nicely.'

'Thanks, bro.'

'I'm going for a walk around the estate, check it out before the hordes turn up. Join me if you like.'

Desmond looks longingly at the battered baccy tin.

'Thanks, but no thanks. Think I'll just chill 'til the breakfast lady turns up.'

'Fair enough. Whatever you do, don't forget the rules on smoking.'

*

'Do you want it to come with outline planning permission?'

'Yes, ideally.'

Whatever that was. The bloke mentioned a figure and when he'd done the mental arithmetic it turned out to be far less than he'd been expecting.

'Sounds interesting. Could you send me details of anything that might fit the bill?'

'Of course.'

The man gave him his business card and jotted down Robert's contact details – he didn't carry business cards then. Their team lost the match, cementing them in their usual spot, around halfway in the league. Call it tenth. The bloke said he'd send him an invitation to his company's hospitality box at the stadium. He'd politely refuse this on principle, the principle being that he never wanted to be in a position where he owed something to somebody. Or anything to anybody.

*

Within six months he'd acquired a piece of land – an abandoned, tired-looking farm called Highfield – and, within twelve, the rundown farmhouse and ramshackle outbuildings had been bulldozed and removed. He'd obtained permission to build a substantial new dwelling on the site and had appointed an architect. After discussing a few ideas on the phone and agreeing an outline specification, he'd arranged to meet him on site to assess the potential. The architect was a local man, Michael Foster, who'd developed a thriving practice producing 'cutting edge designs for modern living'. He didn't come cheap, but he had an impeccable reputation and a stunning back catalogue. When Robert arrived at the appointed time the architect was already on site, judging the lie of the land as it were.

Foster had the look and feel of a BBC *Top Gear* presenter about him – pinkish-white, wealthy and middle-aged. Robert was shaken by a large mitt, festooned with gold rings. The handshake hurt but he tried not to show it as Foster carried on squeezing and pumping. After what seemed an age, he let go.

'Hello, Michael, good to meet you.'

'Call me Mike. It's always good to get out of the office and see what we've got to work with. This site has fantastic potential, believe me. Stunning views as well – we need to make the most of them, for sure.'

'So, er, Mike. We discussed my requirements on the phone.'

Yes, they had. During the call he'd deferred to what he thought was Mike's better judgement, unwittingly ceding control of his own project. After much agonising, he'd plumped for a suite of reception rooms and a whole floor dedicated to bedrooms – number 'tba' but at least eight, reasons unknown. Plenty of space for entertainment, sport and leisure, including a gym and a cinema. Lots of garage space for his collection of cars, although he'd only managed to collect one thus far. A sweeping driveway and fully landscaped grounds. He wanted good security, but he'd see to that himself via people he knew and trusted. He didn't want the house overlooked by anybody or anything. That was about it.

'I'm fully au fait with your requirements, Robert, and we'll be able to meet the spec in any number of ways, no worries. There is something, though.'

Mike moved in a bit closer and lowered his voice. He was puzzled by the lowered voice as there was nobody around.

'With respect, my friend, we'd be missing the point, big time. The most important aspects in the architect's playbook are style and setting. In other words, what sort of statement do you want to make with this building? Without that, it's merely a dwelling.'

He had to think long and hard about this. Style and setting. He wasn't entirely sure he wanted to make any sort of statement.

'You're going to have to help me out, I'm afraid.'

Luckily, Mike had his laptop with him. He balanced it on a nearby tree stump, eased himself down and swept through some examples from his back catalogue. Greatest hits, more like. Regarding style, the consensus was they should go for a scaled-back – remember those words – classical design with tasteful pillars and porticos, perhaps an ornamental fountain or two. A few modern follies were suggested to complete the look but he didn't want any of those on the quite reasonable grounds that they were a waste of space. Mike had some interesting ideas regarding setting, which he shared. To illustrate what he was thinking, they climbed to the highest point on the site, by which time they were both gasping for breath.

'You see how the land drops away from this elevated piece? Where the farmhouse used to be? If we build the house here, we can have an imposing, three-storey property that almost disappears into the landscape. The main entrance would be at the top of the house and you'd access the bedrooms via the floor below. There would be a large basement area for the sports and leisure facilities.'

'I see. A sort of upside-down house.'

'Exactly. Designed to take maximum advantage of these fabulous views. Big windows, a large terrace and plenty of balconies. I can send you some provisional outlines to show you what the house and grounds might look like. Would you like me to factor in a helipad?'

'Yes please.'

He was getting carried away. He hadn't the faintest idea why he needed a helipad. Or an indoor swimming pool for that matter but he was getting one of those as well, a big one. He didn't swim all that well and had a pathological fear of water since a traumatic experience when he was young and in care.

Mike sneaked a glance at his watch. Inevitably, it was a hefty Swiss-made sports chronometer.

'Shall we leave it there for now?'

'That'll be great, Mike. D'you know, I'm very much looking forward to working with you.'

*

In less than a year, the house was ready for him to move in, although work continued for a while on the extensive grounds. When he did move in it was just him, a suitcase and an overnight bag. He felt very small and utterly alone. He was also hungry but despite having a kitchen the size of the Starship Enterprise's bridge, he ordered a pizza. When the pizza turned up, he didn't know how to open the main gate and it had to be left there. By the time he got it back to the house, it had gone cold. He consoled himself with a warm beer before rolling out his sleeping bag on one of the many beds and climbing inside.

Chapter 2

The house and grounds are looking their best for the launch party and Robert makes a mental note to congratulate Simon when he sees him. Now, he must find Varvara. When she first came to the UK and moved in with him, she'd been keen to continue her interest in making jewellery. Since then, she's built up a small but thriving business based on making and selling it. High-end, high margins. He's very much in love with her and is keen to do everything he can to make her happy. With this in mind they've converted one of the garages into a workshop, equipping it with the best tooling and machinery available. As her business builds, she's spending increasing amounts of time in the workshop, producing the goods and pushing the online sales and commissions through her new website.

Right now, however, Pamela is hurrying across the lawn, dressing gown flapping, determined to intercept him. She doesn't look particularly pleased so he stops, assembles the various components of his face into what he hopes is a look of concern and braces himself for the impact. When she arrives, it takes her a while to get her breath back, hands on knees.

'Desmond said ... you'd be out ... here.'

A significant pause. She's really struggling.

'I've just read ... your so-called ... Souvenir Brochure.'

She pauses to gather in some more air. He maintains his fixed look of concern.

'You never mentioned ... the fackin guided tours.'

Another pause. His look of concern is still present and correct.

'Guided by yours truly. Thanks for asking.'

As she takes another deep breath, he relaxes and replaces the concerned look with a smile.

'C'mon Pamela. I thought they'd be a great idea. Nobody's better qualified than you to lead them. You know more about my collection than I do and you have a profile. I don't.'

'So, I'm over a barrel again. Great. Just 'cos I'm still married to you, it doesn't mean you can take the piss.' There's a brief pause. 'How many?'

She was making a fuss but he was sure she'd be pleased to lead the tours, even though he'd forgotten to ask her about doing them.

'Oh, about three or four. No more than an hour each. Maybe a bit more for the press.'

'Great. That means I've got to stay reasonably sober for most of the day. Thanks very much.'

'You'll do it?'

She turns away and walks back to the house but a waft of her hand probably means she will. He and Pamela still have an understanding despite everything that's happened since they first met.

*

By the spring of 2012 he'd been away from the workplace for a couple of years and after drifting around rudderless for a while, he was finally getting some of his mojo back. The new house was underway, his charity work was going well and he was devoting more of his time to a burgeoning interest in art. He'd enrolled in some art history courses at Oxford University and was edging closer to starting a collection. He was uncertain about what sort of art he might collect but was leaning towards modern and contemporary. He'd taken a few tentative steps into the rarefied world of fine art and during one of them he'd collided with the force of nature who'd eventually become his wife.

He'd been invited to an exhibition preview in London and thought he'd give it a go. He could make a weekend of it, visit some galleries, perhaps take in a show. The venue was memorable – Two Temple Place was a splendidly over-the-top, neo-Gothic fantasy on the Victoria Embankment. The event, however, was unmemorable, as was the name of the artist. After standing around like a spare part for a while, he'd failed to interact with any of the guests and was experiencing the first unwelcome symptoms of imposter syndrome. Nearly everybody around him, male and female, seemed to be channelling their own excruciating version of Brian Sewell's arty-farty voice – ridiculously posh, borderline effete, studiedly bored and impossibly condescending. He kept shtum, painfully aware of how his flat, Midland vowels would go down in a place like this. Despite the preview being pitched somewhere between pretentiousness and exclusivity, somebody must have been counting the pennies. As a result, the canapes and prosecco, dispensed by disinterested, minimal-wage staff, were well below par.

He was on the brink of leaving when he heard an incredibly posh yet grating female voice rising above the general hubbub in the gallery. For the voice, think of a circular saw that's somehow been calibrated to speak beautifully modulated Queen's English. From what he could pick out, the voice was delivering a critique of one of the paintings. On turning a corner, he happened upon the source.

According to the catalogue, the voice belonged to that rarest of beings, a successful artist. In addition to her creative work, she'd developed a successful sideline in art consultancy and criticism. Her role at this particular event was as a critic, a job she took very seriously. She knew what she liked and if she found something she didn't, her criticism was both withering and entertaining. Based solely on the voice, he'd been expecting a pocket battleship of a woman, a bit like Margaret Dumont out of the Marx Brothers films. Instead, the toe-curling diatribe was being delivered by a pretty, birdlike creature who was holding sway in front of one of the exhibits. She was immaculately turned out. Her elfin face was lightly made-up and her dark hair was swept back into a tight bun. She wore an elegant, sleeveless dress and matching black pumps. She'd chosen to wear a light drizzle of tasteful jewellery, pearls mostly. Think Audrey Hepburn in her pomp, when her publicity people had been persuaded to stop describing her as 'gamine'.

He'd caught her in full flow, delivering a disparaging excoriation of a sorry-looking daub to a couple of bystanders who clearly didn't want to be there. Having skimmed the catalogue earlier, he recognised one of the bystanders as the artist and the other may well have been her agent. Interest piqued, he joined the small group and tuned in to the continuing tirade. To be fair to her, he thought the piece thoroughly deserved the opprobrium being heaped upon it. It struck him even then as indistinguishable from the sort of scribbly splashes the likes of Cy Twombly churned out back in the day. As she turned away to draw her audience's attention to yet another appalling aspect of the painting, the couple seized their chance to escape and quietly melted into the crowd. When she turned back to hammer home her latest point, accidently knocking away a large piece of impasto from the unfortunate painting, it was only him standing there. She stopped talking mid-sentence and scrutinised him as if he was an exhibit in a museum. A coprolite, perhaps.

'And who the fack are you when you're at home?'

The same jagged voice albeit a little quieter, this time compelling him to give a full account of himself. He wasn't sure why but as he did so, he felt the need to tone down the less couth aspects of his voice. Call it an inferiority complex, if you'd prefer.

'Me? Oh, I'm just one of those random people who fetch up at these events, drink the cheap wine, scoff the M&S canapes and leave without a trace.'

'Hmmm, presumably without buying anything either. A "hanger on" in all senses of the word.'

'Got it in one, erm ...'

'Pamela. Pamela Atkinson-Hayes.'

There was a brief pause – for effect, most likely.

'R. A.'

She offered him a slim, delicate hand and he thought for a moment that she meant him to kiss it deferentially. Instead, he gently shook the proffered hand, trying not to break it. She was a proper artist, the short, grubby fingernails a dead giveaway. Try as he might though, he couldn't place the name or the reputation of Pamela Atkinson-Hayes, RA.

'Do you agree?'

'I'm sorry?'

'Do. You. Agree. With. What. I've. Been. Saying. About. This. Piece. Of. Shit. Masquerading. As. A. Serious. Painting?'

This was the first time he could remember Pamela talking to him as if he was an imbecile and it wouldn't be the last, by any means. He should've pulled her up on it straight away but something held him back. He didn't want to get on the wrong side of her, that was for sure. He was also starting to feel attracted to her, although he would have struggled to explain why at that moment.

'Well ...'

'Well, what? Come on man, spit it out.'

'I don't like it.'

'You don't like it?! Why don't you like it?! Fack me, this is like drawing teeth!'

Her attempt at a stage whisper hadn't worked. In fact, it had created an uneasy silence right across the exhibition space. He blundered on, trying to conjure up something telling and pertinent from his paper-thin knowledge of art.

'I think she's taking the mick.'

'Gooood. Very good. What else?'

That was it. He felt unable to dredge up anything that wouldn't be met by a look dripping with contempt. He suggested they move on instead.

'Very well. To be honest with you, I've seen more than enough of this nonsense. I'll find Monty and think up an excuse to leave. Monty actually likes this stuff.'

'Who's Monty?'

'He's an old friend of mine. Fine art auctioneer, based in the Cotswolds. He's a top man when he's sober, which isn't often. Even nicer when he's had a few. A bit rough around the edges. You'd like him, I'm sure, despite him being from Yorkshire.'

She seemed distracted by something. Her eyes darted around the room.

'Do you smoke by any chance?'

'No. I've never smoked.'

'Good for you. Filthy habit.'

With that, she scrabbled around in her clutch bag – a beaded, slightly distressed vintage item – and produced a squished pack of menthol cigarettes. She waved it at him and asked if he minded joining her outside. He agreed, his interest in her outweighing his profound dislike of smoking. They made their way to an ornate, illuminated inner courtyard. She produced what looked like a gold cigarette holder from a faded velvet Dunhill pouch and carefully inserted one of the cigarettes. He'd only seen cigarette holders in very old films and was fascinated by her smoking ritual. As he watched her work, he noticed for the first time that each of her delicate hands possessed just three fingers and a thumb. Fascinating. Sensing his scrutiny, she felt an explanation was called for.

'Didn't anyone ever tell you it's rude to stare? I was born with these hands and they're perfectly in proportion. What's more, I've created a lot of fine work with them I'll have you know, so I'd appreciate it if you stopped fackin staring.'

He couldn't help but oblige. Satisfied that the cigarette was seated correctly, she produced a vintage Zippo lighter from her bag. When it caught, the lighter took on the characteristics of a flamethrower, which she waved in the general direction of the cigarette and her face. After a few seconds, the face emerged, apparently unscathed, from an acrid cloud of blue smoke. While she worked her way down the cigarette, her gimlet eyes remained fixed on him but she remained silent. She may have been weighing him up, calculating whether or not to waste any more of her valuable time on him. The cigarette was soon consumed. She removed the butt from the holder and flicked it into the night, then shook some grim-looking brown drips onto the floor.

'Better there than in my ...'

She was probably going to say 'lungs' but a bout of phlegmy coughing intervened. When she'd recovered, she stared hard and long at him through the remaining tendrils of stale smoke.

'You know, you have an interesting face. Betwixt and between, neither handsome nor ugly. Lovely skin colour. Big hair. You know, interesting faces interest me and I feel a strong urge to paint you. You must sit for me in my studio. Here's my card.'

And that was it, he'd been dismissed. She turned away from him and walked back indoors, looking for Monty no doubt. She hadn't even asked for his name. On that note, he really needed to get some business cards printed. How would he describe his occupation right now? Retired? Semi-retired? Lazy bugger? Dilettante? As he headed for the exit, he could hear Pamela summoning up a fresh stream of invective aimed at a formless lump of rock masquerading as a sculpture. This time he left her to it.

*

It took a couple of weeks for his curiosity to get the better of him. The call didn't get off to the best of starts.

'Hi, there. It's Robert.'

'Robert? Robert who?'

'Smith. Robert Smith, same name as the bloke from The Cure.'

'Sorry. Never heard of you. What cure? If you're trying to scam me, there'll be hell to pay, believe me. I know people.'

He'd forgotten what had happened at the gallery. She'd shown no interest in his name when they met. Only his face, it seemed.

'We met at that dreadful exhibition. Two Temple Place. You gave me your card.'

There was a silence.

'Ah, yes. You're the mulatto. I thought you might be worth painting, didn't I? What's your name again?'

He decided to avoid taking offence at the archaic and demeaning terminology.

'It's Robert. Listen, Pam, could we ...'

'Hold on. Hold your horses, boy. Before we go even an inch further, I need to make something crystal clear to you. My name's Pamela. Don't call me Pam, I don't like it, erm, Robert. Never have.'

He was glad they'd got that sorted out. Despite the poor start to the call, they agreed to have lunch together in London. The venue would be Le Gavroche in Mayfair, one of Pamela's regular haunts. She contacted some people, called in some favours and secured a table within the week. Splendid.

*

He'd always had a problem with posh restaurants and they didn't come much posher than Le Gavroche. Although he'd attended countless business lunches across Europe in some very fine dining establishments, he'd never felt completely at ease during them. Some of it may have been due to his upbringing, which had furnished him with an inferiority complex of epic proportions and a large chip on each shoulder. Some of it could have been about the hushed, almost reverential atmosphere in these places, an atmosphere where any small faux pas could be magnified out of all proportion. Some of it might be connected with the food, the eye-watering price of which brooked no argument. If you felt the need to complain, you'd better know what you were talking about. Not to mention the suffocating attention to detail and the overbearing waiting at table. The fear of asking too many daft questions, like that time in Woburn when he'd caused consternation by asking for his venison to be served 'well done'. He had a feeling that Pamela would take all of this in her well-heeled stride while he'd make a complete prick of himself.

His dining companion was late. Un-bloody-believable, given she only lived a few streets away. He was left dangling, twiddling his thumbs, trying desperately to avoid eye contact with the other diners. After half an hour of torment, a brief commotion at the front desk and a flurry of over-apologies and air kisses alerted him – and the entire restaurant – to her arrival. She was elegantly dressed and looked 'the business'. He was a bag of nerves and actually stood up for her when, after a further delay – 'just need to powder my nose, darling' – she belatedly arrived at the table. She got up on her tip toes and kissed him gently on the cheek. This time, she remembered his name and even apologised to him for being late. Once they'd been manoeuvred back into their seats by a platoon of overly fussy waiting staff, he turned his attention to the intimidating stack of menus on the table. She'd probably clocked the desperate look on his face.

'Don't bother trawling through that lot, darling. Let's have the set lunch. It's always excellent here and you get some perfectly reasonable wine with it. And coffee.'

Brilliant. He was off the hook and finally able to relax, perhaps even loosen his tie a smidge. He could now focus his entire energy on not upsetting his companion. He needn't have worried. Pamela was in a relaxed, expansive mood and they enjoyed a leisurely and delicious lunch. When the coffee and petit-fours turned up around half three they were still chatting non-stop, mainly about art and artists.

'So, there you have it. A complete change of direction for me. I want to build an art collection and put it on display in the new house I'm having built. Trouble is, I know what I like but I'm a complete duffer as regards the finer points of building a collection. Any points, if I'm honest with you.'

'Far be it for me to interfere darling, but would you like me to help? Strictly on a business footing, of course. I've loads of knowledge and oodles of contacts in the trade.'

'That'd be great, it really would. Can we agree something next time we meet?'

'Do you have to rush away? If you've got time now, I thought we might go to my studio after coffee and I can show you around. It's not far from here. South Ken. You never know, something might catch your eye and you can add it to your collection. My pieces aren't cheap but there's no obligation to buy.'

'You're on.'

The bill turned up and he did the right thing, trying not to wince as he did so. He still hadn't got used to being seriously wealthy. Maybe he never would.

As the weather looked threatening, they hailed a black cab for the short journey to Pamela's studio. Although she'd inherited a large house in North Yorkshire from her parents, she preferred to remain in London at her 'live-in' studio. The studio was exactly that – a purpose-built artist's studio in a block of similar properties. Late Victorian or Edwardian at a pinch. There was a cavernous main room with high ceilings and enormous windows, the latter providing plenty of light even on a greyish day. It was piled high with sculptures and paintings in various stages of completion, set amid the clutter and chaos created by a working artist. At the back of the main room was a mezzanine area housing a cosy-looking double bedroom. Off the hallway, there was a well-equipped kitchen and a bathroom. After briefly showing him around her place, she fixed them some drinks. Two Gin and Its, her favourite tipple.

'You're going to have to tell me what a Gin and It is. I've led a sheltered life, I'm afraid.'

'I bet you haven't, darling. There are a few variations but my favourite is one-part sweet vermouth – that's the 'It' by the way – two parts gin, a dash of orange bitters and three cocktail cherries on a stick.'

'Three?'

'It's bad luck to have an even number of cherries. My late mum told me that – ergo, it must be true. Chin-chin.'

They laughed. They clinked glasses. They sipped their drinks. He was a tad underwhelmed by the Gin and It.

'Nice. A bit sweet, mind. I'm not sure I could drink these all night.'

'Oh, really? I could.'

After the second round of drinks, they became more relaxed. They got a bit closer, a little more tactile. He began to wonder where this was going. Not very far, apparently.

'Right, enough canoodling for now. I'm in a sketching mood. I said I'd do your portrait and I meant it. No time like the present. *Carpe diem* and all that, although there's precious little left of it.'

They untangled themselves and adjusted their clothing like they were a couple of teenagers caught at it by their parents. She plonked him down on a chair and told him to adopt a serious, neutral expression. After a fit of the giggles, he calmed down sufficiently to adopt what he thought might be a suitable pose. It was Pamela's turn to giggle then, although her giggle sounded more like a gargle.

'You look like a dusky version of one of those worthy aldermen from Victorian times. Like you've got a broom handle stuck up your arse. Never mind.'

She donned a rather splattery smock, grabbed a large pad and dashed off at least a dozen charcoal sketches in less than half an hour.

'Why can't you take a few photographs and have done with it?'

'I think you're missing the point, darling.'

At one stage, the sun made a brief appearance, flooding the studio with light. There was a look on her face, one he hadn't seen before.

'Do you know something? This light won't last for ever. I want you nude. Get some preliminary sketches done. If I can find some more charcoal.'

This came out of nowhere. He thought she might be testing him. Or mocking him.

'Are you sure about this?'

'Of course. I'm an artist, aren't I, so don't be so old-fashioned about it. I've seen plenty of male bodies, most of them fackin horrible, a couple of them dead. You can drape your clothes over the chair. When you're ready, I'll arrange you into something approaching a suitable pose.'

She would brook no argument and although it was a bit sudden, there was something rather thrilling about what she'd suggested so he complied. He'd never done this before and since childhood he'd found undressing in front of somebody acutely embarrassing, like he was about to be punished – or worse. What's more, it was seriously cold in the studio, despite the sunshine. Pamela kept her cavernous studio at a temperature slightly above freezing, protecting herself from the chill with copious layers of clothing. Having disrobed, he presented himself as a pallid, shivering life model with a bluish tinge. The less said about his rather shrivelled manhood the better, although Pamela didn't hold back.

'How the fack am I expected to draw that? It's barely visible!'

She dissolved into a gust of laughter which was quick to mutate into a paroxysmal cough. An old joke he'd once heard about Bamber Gascoigne on *University Challenge* popped into his mind – something to do with 'a starter for ten'. After wiping away the tears, blowing her nose profusely and, reluctantly it seemed, turning on one bar of the ancient, hopelessly inadequate electric fire, she got very much hands on and contorted her life model into a half decent pose, 'something she could work with'. As she did so, his blood decided it would start flowing again and embarrassingly, a passable erection imposed itself between them despite his best efforts at containment.

'Now, I absolutely can do something with that. Can you hold that? The pose I mean.'

He'd stopped shivering for now.

'Sure. Take your time.'

She went to work, dashing off another series of sketches, each one torn off the large pad when finished and thrown on the floor. She'd occasionally stop to smoke another cigarette, an amused half-smile on her face. Every time she got hands on to adjust his pose, she left a few more charcoal dabs on his flesh. After another half an hour, she stopped work. He took this as a signal to get dressed and walked across the bitterly cold, tiled floor towards his clothes.

'I'd rather you didn't, darling. Not yet, anyway. Sit down, why don't you?'

No more sketching apparently. There were no preliminaries, not even a kiss, although she did untie her hair, shaking it loose. She knelt down in front of him and proceeded to fellate him, expertly. There was nothing graceful or even gentle about it and she made no effort to pull away when he came. During the whole episode she'd remained fully smocked. When he gestured towards the bed up on the mezzanine and offered to reciprocate, she took him in hand and guided him up the stairway.

She was naked in an instant and lay back on the bed, waiting patiently for him to start exploring her small but exquisitely proportioned body. As he went about his work, each of her orgasms was accompanied by a low, cat-like growl, very primal. They finished off with a good old-fashioned shag, Pamela on top, controlling the action. Afterwards, they lay together in the fading light. When he was on the verge of falling asleep, he thought he might be about to outstay his welcome.

'I ought to leave soon. I'm booked into the Lanesborough tonight.'

'Why not stay here with me, darling. I'd like that very much.'

Without hesitation, he agreed. He could take a hit on the booking at the Lanesborough. It was now dark outside although the streetlights provided a modicum of light. Her hand got busy again, exploring the nooks and crannies of his body, eventually alighting on his penis, currently flaccid.

'Fascinating. You've been circumcised.'

'You've noticed, although I had very little choice in the matter. Do you have a problem with it?'

'On the contrary. I like it. I'm curious, that's all. I assume you're not Jewish?'

'Not to my knowledge. It was a tradition in my mother's family. All boys were to be subjected to MGM.'

'MGM?'

'Male genital mutilation. Quite a common operation when I was a baby. Free on the NHS. Barely believable.'

There was silence for a short while. Her hand remained where it was.

'Robert, darling?'

'Yes?'

'I need to tell you something important before we go much

further.'

'OK.'

'Something you need to know.'

'I'm listening.'

'I like having sex with men – and women. I've been this way inclined since school. An all-girls school to be precise. I don't think I'll change. Too old for that.'

'Oh. Sounds interesting. Hang on, didn't you say you'd been married? To a bloke, I mean.'

'I was. Reginald was significantly older than me. Put it this way, towards the end he couldn't and I wouldn't and he didn't seem to mind me going off-piste occasionally, as long as I was discreet. He was the love of my life for a short while. He died a few years ago, bless him. Heart attack. The old boy didn't leave me a brass farthing and I had to stump up for his fackin funeral.'

He carefully considered what she'd just told him.

'Well. I'm happy if you're happy. Thanks for telling me by the way. I appreciate that.'

'So, are we an item? Can we do this again?'

'We certainly are. We certainly can. Come here.'

Robert and Pamela became lovers, getting together whenever her busy schedule allowed for it. There was no shortage of passion in their relationship but it never occurred to either of them to fall in love. She valued her freedom too much and he wasn't willing to argue for something more, even if he wanted to. Falling in love wasn't going to happen.

*

After a few months together, their relationship took a more serious turn. They'd just enjoyed an exhilarating evening of sexual high jinks in the studio, aided and abetted by a couple of Pamela's girlfriends, sometime models. The girls had left and they were lying in bed exhausted, surrounded by a mess of discarded takeaway boxes and empty champagne bottles. The place looked like a grenade had hit it, but, as Pamela reasoned, there was no point in tidying up as the cleaners were coming in tomorrow.

Robert's voice emerged from the darkness. It was the voice of a man who'd been spending far too much time dwelling on what might happen should he die. His legacy, such as it was.

'Pamela?'

'Yes, darling.'

'Let's tie the knot.'

A pause. Quite a long one. Call it a silence if you like.

'You've got to be joking. What's the point? For a start, I'm too old to have kids, even if I wanted them, which I don't. Never have.'

'Look, I'm fifty now and I've never been married. I'd like to right that wrong. I'm not going to do the bended knee stuff and I don't have a ring. Marry me anyway. Please.'

'You're proposing? No bollocks?'

'I'm serious. We don't have to do anything flash or fancy. Something quiet and tasteful. Drinks with a few friends afterwards. You know.'

'It's a lovely thought, darling. Before I decide, there're a few conditions I'd like to put on the table.'

'Thought as much. What are they?'

'I don't want to change my surname. It's so old hat and "Smith" doesn't do it for me. Sorry.'

'Not a problem. Carry on.'

'We don't have to live together.'

'That's a shame. I'm building a big, beautiful house. Plenty of space for both of us when it's finished. We could live there together and not see each other for days, believe me.'

He'd shared the latest architect's plans with her recently. Despite his best efforts, she hadn't been impressed by the proposed house. Quite the opposite. She could well have deployed the words 'fackin', 'monstrosity' and 'faux', among others.

'It's a large house, I'll give you that. Sorry. I don't mind visiting you there from time to time if you want me to.'

'Of course, I want you to. OK, right. We don't have to set up home together. We can make that work, I'm sure. We've got three houses between us and there're plenty of hotels out there. We'll manage somehow. Anything else?'

'We don't have to be faithful to each other. Total honesty. Full disclosure.'

'Agreed. Full disclosure. Is that it?'

'It is. I hope we'll be very, very happy together. When we're together, that is.'

Decision made, although neither of them were anywhere near 'of sound mind' when they took it.

The wedding was arranged in quick time. The ceremony took place at the Kensington and Chelsea Registry Office and two witnesses were in attendance. Robert chose one of his mates and Pamela persuaded Monty to step up. The ceremony was followed by lunch at Le Gavroche for a select few guests, most of them invited by Pamela. After staying the night at the studio, they flew out to Spain for the honeymoon. They set up shop in a luxury hotel in Elciego, a town in the Rioja wine region, where they enjoyed beautiful weather, fine wine and fine dining. They also enjoyed some spectacular sex and lots of it. This was by far the most passionate relationship Robert had enjoyed in his entire life and he was keen to make up for lost time.

When they returned to England, they came up with a way of living, loving and working that suited both of them. They'd regularly spend time together in one or other of their houses and work on their joint project – Robert's growing collection of modern and contemporary art. Theirs was what you might call an open marriage and it worked well for both of them although he didn't feel the need to stray very far. Until one cold day in St Petersburg when he met a beautiful young Russian woman and fell in love for the first time in his life.

Chapter 3

The impromptu meeting/collision with Pamela has distracted Robert, plunging him unwillingly into the minutiae of the day. These include a tiresome detour to supervise the catering team, which he thought he'd delegated to Joanna but hadn't. As a consequence, his housekeeper has blanked him.

Around half past twelve he remembers he hasn't seen Varvara yet. It's vitally important he talks to her before the guests start arriving. He needs her by his side today but can't help worrying she'll lock herself away and fail to attend the afternoon's proceedings. The chances of this happening are high, especially after she found out Vladimir, her much-maligned brother, was on the guest list. Robert knows she dislikes him with a vengeance but, like a lot of things about her family, she hasn't offered him much of an explanation. Time is short – the guests start arriving at two and there are close to two hundred of them according to the RSVPs. They include the great, the good, the not-so-good, the fourth estate – and Vladimir.

As he approaches her workshop, he can't hear any activity from within. Like all visitors, he has to contend with the security system he designed and installed for her. After following the usual elaborate process – including fingerprint recognition – he hears a reassuring click that tells him he's been admitted to her inner sanctum. She's been watching his struggles on the CCTV and has the vestiges of a grin about her lovely face. She breaks off polishing a rather ornate, partly assembled necklace, puts it down on the bench and walks over. She throws her arms around him and delivers a long, very sexy kiss. Dressed in her grubby overalls with her long blond hair pinned back and no make-up, she has no right to look as good as she does.

'Hi, Bobby. Would you have some coffee?'

Nobody else calls him Bobby. She's allowed to call him whatever she likes.

'Oh, right. Yes please. The usual.'

As she makes the coffee, he gets to the point.

'Can I talk to you about today my love. It's a big day for me and I'd like you by my side, sharing ...'

The rest of it is drowned out by a loud, whumping noise above and around them; the first of the helicopters. She looks up anxiously.

'It is the sort of crazy thing my brother would do. That will not be him by the way because he is never knowingly early at any event. He prefers to be a centre of attention when he turns up. I am wondering who or what he has clinging to his arm this time. Something unpleasant probably.'

He's very much in love with her, but the next half hour could be hard work. It wasn't always like this.

*

During 2013, Robert had a plan to visit all of the great European art galleries, spending quality time with some of the best art the world had to offer. Most of the galleries were in major cities, enabling him to build extended stays around the visits. He hoped his close encounters with great works of art would supplement his studies and inform his decisions on what to buy for his growing collection. He was aided and abetted by his wife, who continued to guide his decision-making. His money, her nous. They made a great team.

His first visit of the year was to the Hermitage in St Petersburg, weather permitting. Pamela usually accompanied him on his travels but she'd been unable to join him this time as she was booked to do a radio broadcast for the BBC. She knew the Hermitage collection well and had given him a long, detailed list of the artworks he should get to see. It was no surprise the list didn't mention the latest incarnation of works by Jake and Dinos Chapman, *The End Of Fun*, which was due to close soon having courted plenty of controversy. She wasn't usually backward in coming forward about the Young British Artists but regarded the Chapman brothers as particularly repellent and therefore way beneath her contempt. 'Fackin gross pair of publicity-seeking charlatans', was one of the milder one-liners she reserved for people like them. Perhaps it was for the best she wasn't travelling with him, as he harboured a grudging respect for their work, especially their trademark tableaux.

He'd arranged to stay at the Grand Hotel Europe, a historic art nouveau establishment on Nevsky Prospekt, and had booked himself a suite, one of the best – opulent but not massively expensive. He'd wanted somewhere close to the Hermitage, but quiet. On arrival, he left his bags with the concierge and did what he usually did when visiting a new place – he went out to explore, making the most of the winter sunshine. He didn't have much of a plan for his stay but intended to spend the following day at the Hermitage where he'd pre-booked a couple of guided tours. The one in the morning would take him around the entire building and the other would focus on the Jake and Dinos Chapman exhibition. The following day, he'd do a self-guided tour of the city and stay another night before returning to the UK.

That evening he enjoyed dinner in splendid isolation in the superb l'Europe restaurant, an art nouveau masterpiece boasting the biggest and best stained-glass window he'd seen outside a cathedral. Great food, great wine, exemplary service. Before turning in, he called Pamela. All was well and she was looking forward to her appearance on national radio, something which didn't unduly faze her as she'd done it before. They arranged to meet up in London when he returned.

After a good night's sleep and an excellent breakfast, he fired up his laptop and familiarised himself with the enfants terrible of British art and their oeuvre. Their contrariness had pushed them to the front of a queue jostling for recognition and they'd hit the jackpot when they hitched themselves to the juggernaut being driven by the dreaded YBAs. The famous 1997 exhibition at the Royal Academy, *Sensation*, cemented their reputation as fully paid-up members of the wilfully perverse branch of art. The awkward squad in other words. Their much-vaunted publicity machine had got off to a flying start in Russia, with rumours that their exhibition had raised hackles in the government and might actually be breaking the law.

He was looking forward to his day at the Hermitage and was there as soon as they opened the doors. He arrived at the assembly point for the first tour and joined a group of rather garish Americans who, despite the temperatures being well below zero outside, were dressed as if they were going to the beach. The guide was a small, bearded, patrician type – not so much Vladimir Lenin, more Professor Calculus out of the Tintin stories. His English was excellent and his knowledge of the beautiful building was immense. Robert was content to drift along and absorb the information while trying not to cringe at the banality of some of the questions aimed at their guide. Professor Calculus took these in his stride and received a round of applause at the end which he acknowledged with a polite bow. There was an hour before his next tour so Robert enjoyed a light lunch in one of the cavernous restaurants.

When he arrived at the entrance to *The End of Fun*, there was nobody around. He loitered without very much intent for a while. He started speculating he might be in the wrong place or the tour had been cancelled or they'd closed the museum without telling him. At two o'clock precisely, a young woman dressed in a dark, sober business suit walked towards him and inspected him briefly. She was tall and slim and exceptionally beautiful. So beautiful that he didn't quite know where to put himself. She frowned at the papers on her clipboard and without looking up, addressed him in precise English.

'Name?'

'Robert Smith.'

She made a great play of putting an elaborate tick against his name on a list. Well, it wasn't technically a list as it only had one name on it.

'I am your guide for the exhibition. Please follow me. Do you know very much about the artists?'

'Only by reputation.'

The young woman just stood and looked at him. Or through him, more like. Blue eyes – hers not his. They entered the exhibition space where one or two visitors were dotted around. As they grew accustomed to the light, she started her spiel.

'*The End of Fun* is an exhibition which brings together several works by Jake and Dinos Chapman, British conceptual artists. As you apparently know them by reputation Mister Smith, I will not bore you with my painfully prepared synopsis of their career.'

'Please, call me Robert.'

'That would be unprofessional.'

'Do it for me. Please.'

'Very well. Robert. Hmm. We are in the ...'

'Do you have a name?'

'Sure, I have a name. Does not everybody? Mine is Sokolova. Miss Sokolova.'

'I meant a Christian name.'

She seemed flustered. She might even have been blushing – it would have been difficult to tell in this light.

'Very well. Call me Varvara if that makes you feel any better.'

'Varvara. I like that. Please carry on.'

She looked a bit put out by his impertinence but carried on.

'We locate ourselves in the newly restored East Wing of the General Staff Building. The first display is a new piece called *The End of Fun* and was produced on purpose for this exhibition. It consists of hundreds of miniature plastic figures set in three-dimensional collages placed in nine glass display cases. The display cases are arranged in the room to resemble a swastika if viewed from above. In each display case, a single landscape of hell unfolds in which the tiny figures ceaselessly kill one another with diabolical cruelty. Do you like it?'

He was completely thrown by the question but tried his best to recover with a garbled response.

'I'm not sure. I'm not even sure the word "like" can be applied to this stuff. How can I put it? With conceptual art, I'm usually full of admiration for the ideas but the execution of them often leaves me cold. In this case, I'm not even sure I like the ideas. Well, there's only one idea isn't there and that's been appropriated. It strikes me as banal, lacking in imagination. It could be the point they're trying to make.'

They spent an hour together, examining details within the display cases. The violent scenes depicted in the collages were relentlessly horrible but the more they homed in on the detail, the more risible the scenes became. Perhaps that was the point. At one stage, he even found himself admiring the craftmanship of the pieces, which must have taken hundreds of hours of effort.

The other exhibits served up more of the same, including a reprise of the *Disasters of War* where the brothers had put together their own gruesome take on Goya's already gruesome series of prints from the nineteenth century. As they left the exhibition space, he felt pretty much ground down by the whole experience. Despite this, he'd been captivated by his charming and attractive guide and had really warmed to her as she gradually thawed – if you see what I mean.

'Do you have any further questions for me before I leave?'

'No more questions. Would you join me for a drink? To thank you for showing me around?'

'I am sorry, Robert. I have another guided tour coming up. Another time maybe?'

She handed him a business card, smiled at him and set off at a brisk pace towards her next assignment. He wanted to follow her but decided against it, not wanting to adopt the behaviour of a stalker. Instead, he meandered around the gigantic museum, working his way through Pamela's list but failing to engage fully with some of the finest art in Europe. His thoughts were elsewhere, focused on Varvara. She was very young but he couldn't help himself – he had to see her again.

*

Back at the hotel he called Pamela who told him she'd put up a good showing on the radio that day, despite the presenter being a 'fackin dickhead of the highest order'. He lied to her about engaging fully with all the artworks on her list. He mentioned the tour with Professor Calculus but didn't dare mention the Chapman brothers. He didn't feel a pressing need to mention his encounter with the beautiful tour guide.

After half an hour or more of agonising, he picked up Varvara's card and summoned up the courage to call her. He was momentarily taken aback when it switched to an answering service in Russian but managed to leave a rather muddled message after the bleep. To his surprise, she called him back within the hour. There were a few polite exchanges during which she agreed to his carefully rehearsed request to show him around the city the following day. Her proposed fee was very reasonable and, leaving his tourist credentials aside, he was looking forward to spending a whole day in a beautiful city with a knowledgeable, attractive young woman. They arranged to meet in the hotel lobby at ten. He decided to chance his arm and asked if she'd mind joining him for dinner tomorrow at l'Europe. After a long pause which set his nerves jangling, she agreed, adding that it had long been an ambition of hers to dine there.

Later, he ordered room service and turned in early. His dreams were unusually vivid and tremendously exciting but his recollection of them disappeared when the alarm call from reception shook him awake.

*

A fifty-something bag of nerves was waiting in the lobby that morning. He'd taken the earliest breakfast possible and had spent an inordinate amount of time fretting about his appearance. To be fair, he didn't think he looked quite as old as he was. He still had all his own teeth, most of his own hair and kept himself reasonably fit. He used a Turkish barber back in England who regularly burnt off his ear and nose hair with a taper. He'd inspected all his facial orifices today to ensure it wasn't growing back. His behaviour was ludicrous. What to wear? His clothes had been chosen by the same fifty-something man. He wished he'd paid more attention when Pamela had berated him recently about his complete lack of sartorial taste. Talking of his wife, he felt a delicious frisson of guilt wash over him regarding his dalliance with Varvara, even though they had an unwritten agreement about such things and the dalliance was a mere figment of his imagination. Should he have a scotch or two to steady his nerves? Bad idea – smelling of drink at ten in the morning would not have been a great look.

She appeared at ten on the dot, looking around the lobby for him, clipboard in hand. He beckoned her across to join him and ordered a pot of coffee. She settled back in one of the venerable leather chairs, crossed her long legs and smiled at him warmly.

'Good morning, Robert, I hope you had a good night of sleep.' She placed a sheet of paper on the table. 'Here is my invoice – my banking details are on there or I have a machine for credit cards, no problem.'

'Good morning to you too. I'll pay into your account if that's OK.'

No nonsense. He liked that. Strictly business. He transferred the money using his phone.

'There is such a lot to see in our beautiful city. You and I will not be able to do everything in just a day and give it the right justice. Having this in my mind, I have picked out some highlights for you in the central area. The weather is cold but the sun is shining, so I suggest we can walk.'

The coffee arrived and he poured. She told him she enjoyed good quality coffee and took it black with sugar. She pushed a printed itinerary across the table. The tour would start with a stroll along Nevsky Prospekt, a historic thoroughfare, 'packed with high-end shops, exotic restaurants, and luxury hotels'.

'You have visited the Hermitage but I would bet you have only, as you say, scratched the service. When you come back again, we can do that.'

The last bit took him completely by surprise. He'd had no plans to return but he did now.

'I have left out the Peterhof Palace, which is a way out of the town. It needs a day on itself.'

'When I come back?'

'Sure. You will need a week at least. Or some weekends.'

He worked his way down the itinerary and having asked a few questions, said he was more than happy with what she'd proposed. They finished their coffee. He took a comfort break and to his shame he half expected his guide to have done a runner when he emerged. He didn't see her right away but relaxed when he spotted her at reception, chatting and laughing with the staff.

The tour started well and Varvara was an excellent guide. In what was left of the morning, they strolled down Nevsky Prospekt, window-shopping mostly. She provided a running commentary on the architecture and history and he focused on listening and looking. Near the end of the impressive avenue, they took a short detour and entered an enormous open space called Palace Square, one side of which was taken up by the Hermitage. He'd failed to notice the square yesterday.

'Bolshevik troops started the Revolution here in 1917 by storming the Winter Palace, where the royal family lived.'

'What happened to the Winter Palace?'

She laughed at him. In a good way.

'Oh, Robert, you are looking at it. It is now called the Hermitage.'

He ought to be paying a lot more attention to this stuff rather than ogling – discreetly, he hoped – his glamorous tour guide.

'Where to now?'

'Would you like some lunch?'

She knew a place where they could eat well on authentic food for a reasonable price. It was called Banshiki and shared a building with some steam baths. The food was both unusual and delicious – black dumplings turned up at one point – the ambience was relaxed and the staff were friendly and helpful. She knew them all rather well and was able to switch effortlessly from Russian to English to French without breaking sweat. They spent such a long time in Banshiki, they had to put a line through the last visit on the itinerary.

'We can always do Vasilyevsky Island the next time you visit.'

Those words again – 'next' and 'time'. He was getting to like the sound of them. They'd drained a bottle of Russian sauv blanc during lunch and had finished off with a few tots of home-made liqueur, on the house. They were therefore slightly the worse for wear when they headed for the first afternoon destination. She thought it advisable to hold onto his arm in case one of them stumbled and fell on the ice. They made their way slowly to St Isaac's Cathedral.

'The cathedral is named after Saint Isaac the Confessor, a Christian monk who founded an important monastery in Constantinople. Throughout the building work, it was plagued by criticism about it being "plain and not too impressive".'

It looked mightily impressive to him and he was keen to look inside.

'You might be disappointed to hear that it is no longer a place of worship. It is now a museum with some interesting pieces, nothing outstanding. I suggest that we have a quick look at the exhibits and climb to the colonnade. The views of the city from there are panoramical.'

She was absolutely right. The exhibits were worthy, no more than that. During the climb to the viewing platform, she demonstrated an alarming disparity between her level of fitness and his. When he caught up with her, he drank in the views of the city and she pointed out various places of interest, including their final destination, the ornate, multi-coloured Church of the Savior on Spilled Blood about a kilometre away, close to his hotel.

When they arrived at the church, she outlined the history of the place. Alexander III ordered its construction in 1883 on the site where his father had been assassinated. It took over twenty years for the church to be completed. It was seriously damaged during the Russian Revolution in 1917, used as a morgue during World War Two and then, ignominiously, a potato warehouse. It took almost thirty years of restoration to get the building back to its original onion-domed splendour.

'Can we go inside?'

'It is now a museum of mosaics. We can look inside another time as it is now closed for the day. So, Robert. Have you enjoyed our tour?'

'I have indeed. It's been a wonderful experience.'

'What time would you like to have me this evening?'

He'd completely forgotten about their dinner.

'I've reserved a table for us at eight. Would you join me for cocktails? Say, about seven in the lobby bar?'

'I will be there. I am looking forward to it so much. See you at seven.'

She kissed him gently on the cheek, flashed him a smile and

walked away. He continued watching her until she disappeared around the corner. He hadn't been this excited about a dinner date for a very long time.

*

At about a quarter to seven, a shaved and scrubbed Robert Smith allowed himself to be swallowed up by one of the sumptuous sofas in the Lobby Bar. He was wearing the smartest clothes he could find, freshly cleaned and spruced by the hotel staff. He'd called his wife earlier and reported back on what he called a self-guided stroll around a beautiful city. He didn't mention his exquisite young tour guide and definitely didn't mention he'd be enjoying her company at dinner that night. Right now, he was attempting to make sense of the cocktail menu, which ran to several pages. He decided against ordering the beer that he craved, deeming it inappropriate to start drinking before the arrival of his very special guest.

As an antique clock started to chime seven, Varvara arrived. He thought there was something almost military about her meticulous timekeeping. She was directed towards his corner of the room by a waiter who couldn't help standing and staring as she made her way across to him. From a distance, she looked stunning and close up she looked even better. She'd chosen to wear some serious shoes with some serious heels and when she kissed him, she had to lean down slightly. She carefully wiped the lipstick off his cheek, her gorgeous face stationed a mere couple of inches from his. He caught a waft of her perfume, a floral one. He didn't know much about perfumes but he was keen to find out more about this one.

'Good night, Robert. I am very much looking forward to this.'

She waved her arm around the room. He was so overwhelmed by the young woman sitting opposite, he was temporarily lost for words. He thought she looked like a bloody film star.

'You said that we might enjoy some cocktails before eating?'

'Ah, yes, cocktails. I was about to have a look at what's on offer but thought you might be able to advise.'

'I am not an expert but I would recommend a vodka-based cocktail. The speciality here is tasty and delicious. It is called a Mayakovsky. Can I be a little impudent and ask for some caviar blinis? Just a small plate for the two of us?'

'You can indeed.'

After they'd tucked into their cocktails and blinis and made suitable 'these are delicious' noises, he relaxed an iota or two and they carried on where they'd left off during the tour. She shared a load of information with him about the history of the hotel, far too much for him to process. It didn't matter – he could listen to her all day and he liked everything about her. He ought to stop staring at her so much though. They'd worked their way through the best part of two cocktails each before they were beckoned through to the restaurant by the maître d'. She was unable to conceal her delight when they were shown to one of the balcony tables, set into its own discrete alcove.

'These tables are historical and are demanded very much. We are very lucky to have one. Rasputin was a regular patron and preferred these tables because he could observe the behaviours of the people below without drawing attention to himself.'

'The Mad Monk?'

'Yes. A very bad Russian. Let us be kind and call him a charlatan. I think you will find he was not even a monk.'

'That stained-glass window at the far end. Spectacular, isn't it?'

'It is. But have you looked up at the roof?'

He looked up and saw a stupendous expanse of stained glass running almost the entire length of the restaurant. How did he miss this on the first night?

'I'm right out of superlatives, so let's order. How about the tasting menu?'

'Do you think I have room for it?'

'I doubt it, but you don't have to eat everything.'

Gourmet food, superb wines. The usual excellent service. What was there not to like? It took them almost three hours to do it justice and Varvara hoovered up everything put in front of her. They finished with ice cold vodka shots, each of them swallowed in one gulp. After he'd stopped choking, he enquired after the requisite protocol.

'Should I have said something like "nostrovia"?'

'Why would you want to say that? It is not even a Russian word.'

'Oh, sorry. So, there's no Russian substitute for "cheers"?'

'No. We pay tribute to the person we are drinking with or somebody close to them. Your wife for example.'

Ouch. He'd mentioned earlier that he was married. He was determined to have no secrets from her, although he'd promised Pamela much the same thing and was already coming up short. Varvara seemed to accept his status and when their shot glasses were replenished – on the house – she said:

'To my charming, generous and very handsome new friend, Robert Smith.'

She reached across the table and held his hand.

'The night is in its youth, Robert. Let us go clubbing. I know a place.'

There must have been a look of abject panic on his face.

'Excuse my silly joke. You do not look the right type to go clubbing. Beside from that, I have a tour to lead early tomorrow across town and I will need some sleep soon. Which room are you staying in?'

As he replied, he thought the evening might be about to take an unexpected turn.

'The Malevich Suite. Very interesting, lots of constructivist flourishes and reproductions of his signature works.'

'I am immediately curious. Would you show me this suite of yours?'

He had to ask himself repeatedly if this was really happening. Within minutes, he was giving her the grand tour of his suite. The ornate, sumptuous bed was very much the elephant in the room. There was no doubting he'd fallen for Varvara in a big way and wanted so much to have sex with her but didn't want to push too hard in case he ruined everything. She liked Robert a lot but was working out how to avoid having sex with him without putting him off seeing her again. Eventually, they settled for a brief hug and kiss, as far away from the bed as possible. It was the right answer.

'Good evening, Robert. Will I be seeing you again?'

She most certainly would. He respected her for not jumping into bed with him that night and for the first time in his life, he thought he might be falling in love. He got to thinking about Pamela and how he might get round to telling her about his new girlfriend. He could make this work. Couldn't he?

*

They're sitting together in the workshop, sipping coffee. Varvara has extended him the courtesy of stopping work and is listening politely to what he has to say about the launch. She knows it's a big day for him and his wife but she has only a passing interest in the art and doesn't see any point in taking part. There's also the fact her brother will be skulking around the house, turning a day of celebration into an ordeal. The last thing she wants is to bump into him.

'It's not only a celebration of my art collection, my love, it's also a turning point. I've pretty much reached the end of my conventional art collecting – unless I see something exceptional that is. Paintings and drawings and sculptures – they don't inspire me like they used to and I'm getting bored. I want to move on, explore the cutting edge of modern art. I've been meaning to share this new direction with you and I'll be announcing my plans during the speech later.'

'So, you just want me to look pretty and smile at everybody.'

As usual, she's uncomfortably close to the way he's thinking.

'It's more than that. It's about my, erm, credibility. Yes. I've been working on this event for ages and having to explain your absence to everybody who knows us will make it really difficult for me, take the shine off the day. Could even ruin it for me. I could lie I suppose.'

'Hmm. It is as much Pamela's show as your own so why cannot she be by your side today? That makes more sense, does it not? She is your wife.'

'It won't be the same. For all her qualities, Pamela can be quite abrasive at times, which isn't ideal when you're trying to welcome people into your house. Besides, she has important work to do running the tours.'

'So, you just want me to look pretty and smile at everybody?'

'OK, yes. Do this for me. Please.'

He hopes his tone is striking the right balance. Desperation wouldn't have been a good tactic, especially today. He needn't have worried. She is without doubt the most decisive woman he has ever met. It's quite scary sometimes, like she's thrown a switch.

'OK. I will get cleaned up and join you. No problem.'

'What?'

'No problem, Bobby. I will be there at two. Do not worry yourself.'

Although he'd been expecting a much harder ride, he's absolutely thrilled she's agreed to join him. She finishes her coffee and shoos him away. After tidying up her workbench, she locks up and heads for her bedroom where she quickly showers, chooses an outfit and gets dressed. It doesn't take her long to apply a few dabs of make-up and choose some pieces of jewellery, all of them handmade in her own workshop. Now, shoes. She has some superb high-heels, worn once, but she doesn't want to tower over Robert on his big day. Instead, she picks out some Louboutin court shoes with two-inch heels. These should position her at roughly the same height as him. The playback from the full-length mirror pleases her and she feels ready to meet her public. Sorry, Robert's public. Before she sets off, there's an opportunity to fire off a text to Piotr and see how he's getting on. She needs to see him soon or she'll forget what he looks like.

*

So, there you have it. The art collector, his house, his wife and his fiancée. Among others. For a while he'd tried to keep both women on board but it was a delicate balancing act, always destined to crash and burn. Despite his unwritten agreement with Pamela, who'd dutifully reported back on her occasional dalliances, he'd felt incapable of telling his wife about his young Russian girlfriend. In his defence, his relationship with Varvara was considerably more than a dalliance. He'd successfully kept it under wraps until he'd been presented with an ultimatum during one of his visits to Russia. Something like 'it is her or it is me'. The message wasn't at all well-received when he shared it with Pamela.

Chapter 4

It was a lazy, drizzly Sunday morning, drifting towards lunchtime and a planned visit to the local pub. Robert was staying at Pamela's studio for the weekend. They were in bed drinking coffee and reading separate sections of yesterday's *Times*. There was a bit of an atmosphere. She was pretending to read an article about auction prices for fine art while wondering why last night's sex was devoid of anything that could remotely be described as passion. He was pretending to do the crossword while fretting about the need to come clean about his young Russian girlfriend who was now his fiancée.

The tension finally got to him. He chucked the crossword on the floor and blurted it all out – 'projectile confessing' for want of a better phrase. Pamela didn't react immediately. When she did, she didn't even look up from the paper.

'So, let me get this straight "darling". You haven't been telling me the whole truth about your visits to St Petersburg?'

'Pretty much.'

She put the paper down, removed her reading glasses and

looked him in the eye. The look – an intimidating blend of incredulity and pent-up anger – wasn't friendly.

'We had a deal, didn't we? I'll show you mine and you show me yours. I've shown you mine and I expected you to show me the same courtesy. Instead, you fackin lied to me. Several times.'

'I know we had a deal and I'm sorry I allowed you to think she was a male art dealer in his mid-sixties. I had no idea it would get so serious so quickly.'

'All that shit about you being able to source an original Malevich, but it might be difficult? You took me for a fool. All that time, you were shagging some random oligarch's daughter. Bleeding hell, Robert, she's half your fackin age. Why?'

She had a point, although she wasn't to know her choice of the word 'shagging' was well wide of the mark.

'I love her.'

'Oh, great. You love her. Don't tell me. She loves you too.'

'I think so.'

'You think so. Fackin hell. How do you know she's not just stringing you along, you complete and utter dickhead? You might be getting on but you're a good catch, worth a bit. So, every time she snaps her fingers, you're on the next plane to sodding St Petersburg. It's embarrassing, Robert. Extremely fackin embarrassing.'

'I'm not embarrassed.'

'I'm not talking about you! I'm talking about me!'

'Matter of fact, we're engaged and I've arranged for her to join me in England. She's coming to live with me at Highfield. You know, the house you've never liked?'

If it's possible for somebody to take a step back while still sitting in bed, Pamela did just that.

'Engaged? How? You're married to me.'

'Perfectly acceptable. I've taken advice.'

It hardly ever happened, but Pamela was lost for words. Her mouth was moving but no sounds were emerging. More importantly, she'd run out of suitable swearwords and had to draw the line somewhere. The two combatants looked at each other, the looks a combustible mixture of sadness, loathing and in Robert's case, attempted contrition. And something else entirely.

'One last fuck?'

They were at each other in an instant and nothing was off the agenda, even if it hurt. It was as if all their passion had to be burned off in one final explosion of lust. When they'd finished it was all over, if you get my drift. The two ex-lovers showered – separately – and dressed.

'I meant it when I said it was the last. You can forget about hunkering down in your fackin ridiculous mansion with The Girlfriend and having me as an occasional shagbag. I suppose you'll want a divorce.'

'I'd rather we didn't. If you don't mind, that is. I'd like us to stay married.'

'Strange request, even for you. I suppose it doesn't matter one way or the other and it saves me the hassle of solicitors at dawn. OK, I think. I'll let you know for sure when I've calmed down. Give it a month. Maybe a year, you complete and utter bastard.'

There was a pause while she chewed this over. To her, the marriage part of their relationship was always a bit of an irrelevance, although there might be something about The Girlfriend's circumstances that she wasn't party to. She'd surprised herself by how upset she was getting.

It was entirely the wrong moment but Robert thought now was as good a time as any to go for broke.

‘Would you continue to help me, please? With the collection, I mean. I’ll pay you.’

‘Fackin cheek!’

He took this as a yes. She then threw him out. I’m only guessing here, and it would have been completely out of character, but she may well have cried. Quite a lot, I’d wager.

Chapter 5

Robert has about thirty minutes left before the first guests start arriving. He drops by the kitchen and chances his arm by asking Joanna to make him a sandwich. She looks shocked – by his effrontery presumably – but he remains hopeful. Desmond and Lizzie are finishing off a breakfast/brunch combo and Monty's mopping up what's left of a plate of bacon and eggs. Robert perseveres with Joanna and puts in an order for a bacon sandwich with a large dollop of ketchup, receiving a scowl in return. This is as good as it gets and might eventually result in a sandwich.

Success. Within ten minutes, he's wolfing down the sandwich and chatting with Desmond between chomps, bacon fat dribbling down his chin. Lizzie's left them to get ready but Desmond's cutting it fine. A clean tee shirt is all they can reasonably expect from him at this late stage. He's a very wealthy man but he hasn't let it change him. Thinking about it, Robert had played a small supporting role in Desmond's recent successes.

*

They'd been enjoying a drink together in The Mary Arden, the nearest he had to a 'local' back then. Not for the first time, Lizzie had thrown Desmond out – 'I deserve it, bro' – and he was staying at Robert's place while he 'got his shit together'. Robert had recently sold his business and the conversation had moved on to what he was going to do next. When Desmond floated the idea of him appearing on a TV show, he gave him short shrift even though it'd been pitched as 'nothing much, just a pilot'. He'd spent most of his fifty years comfortably beneath the radar and saw no reason to change that now. Desmond was family however, so he felt duty-bound to support his nascent career in broadcasting – something that had been nascent for a good many years. He took a gulp from a tepid beer, which had been neglected for so long it had gone flat.

'I'm not sure about this, bruv. Would you run the format by me one more time?'

Desmond sighed. His latest pint and rum chaser had been drained long since and he'd only just got back from a smoking break.

'For the millionth time bro, the show's called *The Interview.* I've pitched it to the Beeb in Birmingham and they've agreed to fund a pilot programme, half an hour. It's a simple format where a journalist takes a local worthy through his or her life, set against a backdrop of news footage from the time. The news items are there to trigger personal recollections and provide a basis for digging a bit deeper, but not too deep. It's quite gentle, non-controversial. You're a bit of a 'closed book' to most people, so any insights might just grab 'em. The BME thing's a bonus.'

'It's only a pilot?'

'Yes.'

'Will it be broadcast?'

'Yes. But only if it's any good.'

'OK, I'll do it. Do I get paid? Mate's rates, of course.'

'As long as that means "zero rates" bro, you're on. Otherwise, I'll go for my first choice.'

'Who is?'

'Lenny Henry.'

'Good luck with that, bruv.'

*

Cometh the day of the recording, cometh etc. He was at the studio being teased and tousled by a cheeky make-up lady called Tash. He was enjoying the attention and her bonkers banter was very entertaining.

Reality took a deep bite out of him as soon as he walked on set. Harsha – one of the regular newsreaders at the studio, a fierce-looking but ridiculously attractive Asian lady – had been persuaded to play the part of the interviewer. All he had to do was opine briefly on pieces of news footage from the past before being steered on to more personal aspects of his life and career as it unfolded. He took his seat across from Harsha and waited while a mike was clipped in place. After a couple of sound tests, he was about as ready as he ever would be. Just before the start he caught a brief glimpse of Desmond behind the cameras, grinning manically and giving him the thumbs up. Both thumbs. After the first clip had played and been discussed, Harsha ventured a question.

'So, Robert. What's your earliest memory?'

'Being hit.'

'What?'

'Being hit by my so-called dad, who everybody thought was a nice quiet guy, kept himself to himself, wouldn't hurt a fly etc. I was hit a lot when I was a kid, but for some reason I remember every second of this one. A huge slap around the face. Knocked me flying, banged my head on the wall. I wasn't very old. I hadn't even started school.'

He stared straight at Desmond, who knew exactly what he was talking about. Their dad hadn't stuck around with his mum long enough to cause any lasting damage.

'Why did he hit you?'

'Can't remember. Anything might have set him off. Even looking at him in a certain way. He was cruel, basically. A bully. Him and my mother were worse when they'd had a drink or three. They lashed out a lot, but he was the worst, a real nasty bastard.'

'Cut. No swearing, Mister Smith. If you don't mind.'

'Sorry. I didn't realise "bastard" was a swear word.'

'Three, two, one ...'

'I was a boy. I couldn't exactly fight back, could I?'

'How long did this go on for?'

'Until I was nine or ten. The bastard – sorry – keeled over and died. Massive stroke. Within a couple of years, my mother had joined him. In hell with a bit of luck – if you believe such things.'

'Did you learn anything from these dreadful experiences?'

'I learned how to make myself invisible. As long as I stayed that way, I wasn't drawing attention to myself and I had a quieter life.'

As the clips continued to roll and the conversation became more relaxed, he started to warm to his task. The few years he spent with his grandparents gave him renewed hope. They were kind people, hard but fair. His schoolwork improved enormously as a consequence and he was marked out as a potential high-flyer. Unfortunately, it proved to be a false dawn. Both grandparents were getting on and both of them died within a few months of each other. With nobody else to step in, he was taken into the care of the local authority. He was thirteen.

'So, you were pretty much on your own again. What was that like?'

'I didn't mind being on my own but they were wasted years to be honest with you. I was moved from one temporary home to another and never got a chance to settle and establish myself. The quality of the foster parents in that first year ran the whole gamut from bad to worse. Many of them treated it as a business rather than a calling, making sure they did just enough. It was never enough. It was no surprise to anybody when I started bunking off school.'

'I suppose not. When did your time in care finish?'

'In those days, the responsibilities of the local authority finished when you reached your sixteenth birthday.'

'You were very young. It must have been a shock when they let go of you.'

'Quite the opposite. I was delighted to escape and soon found a job of sorts with a local company who installed burglar alarms. I liked the work and the money was just about enough for me to live on. The council found a small flat for me, which kept me off the streets. I continued with my studies at night school and emerged with some pretty good qualifications. Good enough for an offer to study at Newcastle University in their computer lab.'

'Impressive. How did that work out?'

'Brilliantly. The laboratory was highly regarded at the time and I picked up a first in Computer Science. I stuck around for a year to get my masters. Set me up.'

'For what?'

'My first business. During that masters year, I got a grant and started a small business.'

'Doing what?'

'Me and a mate from the lab started putting together high-tech security solutions for customers who needed that sort of thing and were prepared to pay handsomely for it. I bought him out in the end – fair price, mind – and spent twenty-odd years keeping our solutions at the cutting edge of technology. When I sold the business, the turnover had grown to a quarter of a billion pounds or thereabouts.'

'Why did you sell out?'

'I prefer to call it selling up. Quite frankly, I'd become bored. When an offer from a big multi-national came in, I jumped at it. I stayed on for a bit in a consultancy role – two grand a day plus retainer – but nobody in the new regime saw fit to consult with me. So I left.'

'What do you plan to do now?'

'I have my charity work ...'

'Charity work?'

'Yes. I'm involved in a small charity called 'Who Cares?' They support young people who're either in care or about to leave the care system. They need all the help they can get and it's the least I can do.'

'Anything else?'

'I have an interest in art and artists. I might do something in that area.'

'Art? That's quite a departure from computers and technology.'

'I guess you're right. Before I left the business for good, I put together a few contemporary pieces to brighten up my office and enjoyed doing that. There are some beautiful things out there and it would be nice to see them, appreciate them and if I like something enough, acquire it.'

'Become an art dealer?'

'No, not dealing. Collecting. Exhibiting. When I've learned a bit more about what I might be buying.'

They'd reached the end of the pilot show. Harsha thanked her guest and expertly guided it to an orderly close. The ordeal was over and the questioning had only scratched the surface of his private life, such as it was. Harsha and Robert went for a drink afterwards and he got the opportunity to enjoy her ferocious beauty at close quarters. It didn't last long though. It never did.

The pilot show was left on the shelf but Desmond persevered with the concept. It emerged eventually on commercial television with a slightly amended format, a 'name' presenter and much more interesting guests. Lenny Henry was the guest for the first episode in the first of several successful series. It became an international hit.

Chapter 6

Robert's standing nervously in the entrance hall, meeting and greeting a steady trickle of visitors and pointing them in the direction of the booze and the buffet. He's wearing a brand new Brioni suit but beneath the posh threads, he's clammy with nervous tension. The two visitors approaching him have been ferried from the helipad in a golf buggy chauffeur-driven by Simon. Vladimir Sokolova plus one. Oh, God!

'Vladimir, my man, glad you could make it. Great to see you!'

He prepares as best he can for the inevitable Russian bearhug. Umpth! He eventually extricates himself from the hug and smoothes down his suit.

'And this must be ...'

'Luana. My girlfriend. She is from Albania.'

'Delighted.'

He'd only met Vladimir – don't call him Vlad, too many connotations – a couple of times. Once in St Petersburg and once in London. On each occasion, Varvara had made sure she was somewhere else. Despite the negative vibes and threatening appearance, he'd struck Robert as being utterly charming. He also seemed genuinely interested in him, his relationship with his sister and his growing collection of art. The Russian had been educated for the most part in England and, armed with an MBA from Henley Business School, had returned to Moscow to join the family business. When asked, he'd been vague about what the business did – commodity trading or something similar. His expensive English education had furnished him with impeccable manners, an air of superiority, condescension, a sense of entitlement and near perfect spoken English to go with his innate Russian arrogance. It had also furnished him with a predilection to having sex with men and boys. Right now, he was looking for someone.

'Is my sister here? I get the feeling she has been trying to avoid me for reasons unknown.'

'Oh, I'm sure she's not. She said she's looking forward to seeing you.'

'OK. Where is she?'

'I think she's still getting ready. Why don't you and, er, erm, tuck into the champagne and stuff. There's some caviar somewhere. Why not sign up for one of my wife's art tours – she's waiting over there. They come highly recommended, first one at three thirty.'

Before turning to greet the new batch of guests, he watches as Vladimir and his partner weave their way towards the nearest waiter. Varvara had told him recently her brother had been in and out of addiction clinics for most of his adult life, with cocaine his go-to stimulant. He and his plus one are already looking very much the worse for wear. He has no idea what to make of Luana. Varvara said her brother spent much of his time trying to hide his homosexuality from their father. He has to admit, Vladimir's girlfriend is one of the ugliest women he's ever seen. What's more ...

'Yes, I know. They are not a she, not yet anyway, although they may get there in the future if they can raise the money for treatment. My brother has access to a steady supply of Albanian transsexuals, almost probably trafficked. Luana is the latest. He thinks he is fooling his father, who knows very well his son is gay and has accepted it with some reluctance. I feel sorry for Luana and the others. They come, they get used up and they go.'

It's dead on two and Varvara has arrived at his side as promised. She looks fantastic and is wearing the dazzling smile she reserves for Robert and very special occasions. She stays with him for a while, helping him meet and greet the guests as they file in.

*

Three o'clock arrives and it's time for the big speech which he'll deliver outside on the vast terrace, currently bathed in bright sunshine. He's prepared some notes but has no idea where he's left them, so he'll deliver the speech off the cuff.

'Ladies and gentlemen.' He has a fleeting thought about Luana – too late now. 'Welcome one and all to the launch of my collection of modern and contemporary art which is displayed in this house, Highfield. Our home.'

He smiles warmly at Varvara, ignoring Pamela's famous death stare as he does so. OK so far. It's the only part of the speech he can remember from the mislaid notes. Undeterred, he describes the broad themes of the pieces in the collection and the stories behind some of them. He concludes by acknowledging the people who have helped him put it all together.

'None of this would have been possible without masses of help and advice from my wife, Pamela, who is ...' Where is she? '... somewhere around. Ah yes, there she is.'

He points to where she's waiting patiently for the first tour party. She affects a wave, the sort of wave a member of the royal family might conjure up on the balcony of Buckingham Palace – half-hearted, desultory, dismissive. The audience applauds and she bows theatrically. She might be taking the piss – difficult to tell with her.

'As you all know, Pamela is a successful sculptor and painter, a Royal Acad... Academical ... Academician, no less. She's also a well-known – and feared – art critic. She'll be leading tours of the collection throughout the afternoon and early evening. Please sign up for one and get the benefit of her copious knowledge. Just don't let her go overboard with the praise for her own work.'

It gets a laugh but Pamela finds it appropriate to show him the finger at this point. How rude is that?

'Many thanks are due to Monty Gallimore of Gallimore Fine Art, who's been instrumental in sourcing many of the works in the collection.' It would be inappropriate *in extremis* to mention his exorbitant finder's fees. 'Monty? Monty? Where are you?'

Oh, shit. He might have gone back to bed. No, there he is, acknowledging the ripple of applause. The speech meanders on for another five minutes before he spots the woman he loves, trying but failing to blend in near the back of the audience.

'Before I let you at the Lanson again, I'd like to mention Varvara, a beautiful young woman who has brought the sunshine back into my life.'

Another round of applause, although Pamela has a face like thunder and is in no mood to join in.

'And, finally folks, a very important piece of news.'

A respectful silence descends on the gathering.

'Having pieced together this wonderful collection of paintings and sculptures, I'm now keen to move on to an exciting new phase of the project. I want to explore some different aspects of the art world, moving beyond paintings and sculpture towards video pieces and the exciting new market in digital artworks. I'm hoping to bring together the disparate worlds of art and technology and I'm asking you all to follow my progress. It could get very interesting.'

He receives generous applause from everybody except Pamela, who is busy assembling the group for the first tour – mainly press – barking out instructions as she does so. She doesn't approve of her husband's new direction and when he'd first mentioned the change of emphasis to her, she'd told him in no uncertain terms.

Varvara gives him a generous hug and a long kiss for his 'wonderful oratory', which he receives graciously. As he prepares to remingle, he spots two things that cause him concern. First, Monty is in a state of collapse and is being carried towards his bedroom by two of the waiting staff. Second, Vladimir and Luana are heading towards the bathroom yet again. It's now down to him and Pamela to make a success of the day – assuming she's prepared to stick with the plan. Varvara has disappeared and is presumably on her way back to her jewellery, her PR work done and dusted for the day. The security at her workshop will provide her with an impenetrable barrier – more than enough to fend off any unwanted approaches from her brother.

Chapter 7

It's now dark outside. Despite Robert's customary forebodings, the party has been an unqualified success. Most of the guests have long since left and a small group of his friends and acquaintances are enjoying late drinks in his favourite place at Highfield, the sunroom. The drink is flowing, there's a seemingly endless supply of leftover food and the mood is relaxed. To his delight, Varvara has finished her work for the day and is draped around him on one of the sumptuous sofas, her relaxed presence a sure sign that Vladimir's no longer on the premises. The only dark cloud is being cast by the relentlessly miserable Joanna, who continues to serve up the food and drink despite labouring the point that she's working way beyond her contracted hours. For the avoidance of doubt, she keeps looking at her watch and glaring at Robert. He finally relents and dismisses her. When she leaves, Simon joins her. It's an open secret that they're lovers – hard to imagine for those who know them – and have set themselves up as a couple in the staff house. Simon's no oil painting that's for sure but nobody's worked out quite what he sees in Joanna, although she's an excellent cook.

In a miracle of biblical proportions, Monty has crawled out of his pit and is working his way through his second glass of what looks like sparkling mineral water but probably isn't. He's currently arguing with Pamela and her girlfriend about the finer points of Mannerism and championing the virtues of Parmigianino's work. Although he's never heard of Parmigianino and certainly can't pronounce his name, he suddenly remembers the name of Pamela's girlfriend and almost shouts it out in triumph. Veronica, yes. Veronica is a curvy, vivacious woman, an artist and sometime artist's model, about a decade younger than his wife. When Monty nods off, mid-sentence, Pamela and Veronica quietly head for their bedroom. As they leave, he can't help noticing Pamela's hand clamped firmly on one of her lover's Rubenesque buttocks.

It's heading towards midnight and only Desmond and Lizzie are sentient enough to keep Robert and Varvara company. He finds an unopened bottle of scotch, the last in a small batch of exquisite and ridiculously expensive rare single malt. Trying not to wake Monty, he offers them a generous glass each and then struggles to find his special stainless steel 'ice' cubes in the kitchen of many mysteries. Varvara springs into action and locates the elusive tray of cubes within a few seconds, enabling them to settle back with their drinks.

Desmond treats them to a mini-concert of gentle calypsos. He's an accomplished guitar player and has a great, warm baritone so it's a real treat for the tiny audience, one of whom sleeps through the entire performance. He's borrowed the guitar from Robert who bought it – a Martin D-45, no less – when he had a grand plan to learn an instrument. Despite what he might refer to as his best efforts, he didn't have the staying power and the plan was quietly abandoned. The superb guitar has been gathering dust in his music room ever since. For the record, mint D-45s cost upwards of ten grand each and this one's lack of use riles Desmond so much, he regards it as a tragedy.

First Varvara and then Desmond and Lizzie finish their drinks and, unlike the cubes, they melt away. After replenishing his glass, Robert is left on his own save for the supine, snoring Monty. His thoughts drift towards the proposed new direction for the art collection. Despite the hype and hyperbole, there's precious little digital art being produced out there. In fact, for all his excitement, the market hardly seems to have got off the ground. He'll park that aspect for the time being and focus instead on video art, starting with a trip to Spain.

Chapter 8

Make no mistake, Robert is a huge fan of Bill Viola, a world-famous American video artist. When he found out about a retrospective of Viola's career being held at the Guggenheim in Bilbao, he got very excited and jumped at the chance to visit. He'd tried his best to persuade Varvara to join him but she'd declined. Despite his many reassurances, she's persuaded herself that leaving the country is not a great idea for the time being. She fears the UK Border Force might be disinclined to let her back in. As a fallback option, Pamela had stepped in but insisted on her own terms. 'Lovely city, darling, but you're on your lonesome as regards the video art.'

She called him a couple of days ago to tell him she'd have to cancel. It wasn't good news.

'I absolutely adore Bilbao and would have loved to join you, darling, but the truth is I'm not very well.'

'You don't sound great. What's up?'

'It's fackin cancer, worse luck. I got the diagnosis in June and started treatment the day after your party. The treatment's laid me lower than a snake's belly, I don't mind telling you.'

Given her prolific smoking, he would have laid odds it was in her lungs. He would have lost the bet.

'I felt some lumps in my neck and thought I'd get them checked out. I had some tests and they came back positive for thyroid cancer. It's the papillary type fortunately, which has the better outcome.'

'Enough said. Why didn't you tell me?'

'I didn't want to spoil the party. What would you have done anyway? Tea and fackin sympathy knowing you, and precious little else.'

He didn't rise to the bait.

'What sort of treatment are you having? The best there is, I hope.'

'The best there is, yes. The NHS. The private sector isn't interested in the complex, life-threatening stuff.'

'How's it going?'

'I'm still a bit sore from the initial surgery and I'm having radiotherapy as a precaution.'

'What's the outlook?'

'Surprisingly good although it looks like I'll be on hormone replacement tablets for life.'

'You'll keep me up to date with progress, won't you?'

'You'll be one of the first to know, darling. I might even invite you to my remission party if you're lucky. Bring The Girlfriend, why don't you?'

*

It's early September, towards the end of Viola's triumphant run at the Guggenheim. Robert's staying in Bilbao for a couple of nights and has booked a suite in a hotel called the Barceló Bilbao Nervión. The exhibition is close by, just a short walk along the river on the opposite bank. He starts the evening in the hotel bar, which is a curiously frigid, unwelcoming place, furnished throughout with elegant chrome and leather seating. He can't get comfortable on the seats, so remains at the bar. He doesn't stay long – just long enough to sink a glass of beer. He spends the rest of the evening roaming the charming streets of the Casco Viejo – the old town. He stops off for supper in the main square, choosing an outside table at one of the many cafés. It's a warm night and he's more than content to sip his Rioja, munch his pintxos and watch the groups of people wander back and forth. Around eleven, he calls it a night and makes his way back to the hotel.

His walk takes him across a major road in the town centre near the city hall and when he reaches it, there's a fair amount of traffic whizzing around. The embankment is lit up so he takes a short detour to admire the view and take a few pictures. He pockets the phone and heads back to the road. As he steps off the kerb, his mind's elsewhere. If you're English and you're in a country where they drive on the wrong side of the road, there's a tendency to look right when you should be looking left. In Robert's case, there's a car hurtling towards him at speed on the correct side of the road. One question begs an immediate answer – is the driver paying enough attention to notice the English idiot who's stepped out in front of him? The idiot isn't prepared to wait for an answer and despite all the red wine swilling around inside him, his sense of self-preservation kicks in and he bursts into a run. The car misses him by a hair's breadth and doesn't stop. Doesn't even slow down.

The incident leaves him shaken and not entirely unscathed. When he pushed off on his life-saving sprint, he heard something pop followed by an immense stab of pain in his lower left leg. It's all he can do to stagger to the other side of the road where he collapses in an undignified heap. There's soon a small crowd of concerned people around him, all of them thinking the car had hit him. He eventually feels well enough to get to his feet and waves all the well-wishers away. He limps the remaining short distance back to the hotel, where he sinks a succession of single malts in the unwelcoming bar, now packed with punters. Wisely, he uses the lift on the way back to his room.

When he gets comfortable, he fires up his laptop and searches out a diagnosis for his injury. It's a torn calf muscle according to the NHS website. Ice for the swelling, tablets for the pain and plenty of rest. Physio to follow – see diagrams. About twelve weeks to make a full recovery. Twelve weeks! He tries his best to ignore the ancillary information on the site about the risk of blood clots but can't help noticing some additional spiel on the risk of dying from such complications. He calls Varvara – it's after midnight but she's still in her workshop – and decides not to mention his near-death experience. No point in worrying her. After the call, he necks a double dose of painkillers and a sleeping tablet before turning in.

*

On waking, he's mightily relieved to discover he's still alive although his leg continues to give him serious grief. The day ahead threatens to be challenging despite a barely legal stockpile of double-strength ibuprofen. Walking is problematic and he has to book a taxi for the short hop to the Guggenheim. Doubting his ability to stay the course, he focuses all his efforts on the Viola Retrospective, which occupies an entire floor of the museum. He homes in on the dramatic later works, one of which is called *The Dreamers*. He reads the catalogue entry.

In The Dreamers from 2013, we experience seven flat panel displays. Each panel depicts an individual lying under water, seemingly resting on a pebbly river bed. They all remain still apart from tiny agitations caused by the flow of water, and their eyes are closed. They seem at peace with themselves and at ease with the world gently washing around them. The sound of the water envelops the onlooker, providing a womblike, contemplative calm.

As he tunes into the work, he's drawn inexorably towards the panel showing a young girl who bears an uncanny resemblance to Tina, a friend from his teenage years. She drowned in a tragic accident that he has never been able to forget. The girl on the screen appears to be at peace, comfortable with her predicament. She wears a scarlet, ruched, sleeveless top and dark trousers, her long auburn hair streaming out and around her head and shoulders, caressed by the gentle current. He closes his eyes and becomes as one with the dreamers.

'Senor. Senor. Ondo zaude?'

A concerned attendant gives him a gentle shake. Turns out he's lost over an hour to *The Dreamers.* He needs a break, giving him time to rest his aching leg, take some more painkillers and plan on where to go next. Among the remaining Viola installations, *Going Forth By Day* looks the most promising. He reads the blurb.

Inspired by medieval frescoes such as those by Giotto in Padua's Scrovegni Chapel, Going Forth By Day interprets biblical and mythological themes in the spirit of our times. Five simultaneous videos play out on the walls in a long dark gallery, each of them exploring themes of human existence – individuality, society, death, rebirth. As they play, they draw the viewer into a series of evolving narratives.

He's initially overwhelmed by the competing sights and sounds but gradually tunes in to the stories, finding each of them utterly engrossing and deeply moving. He spends a couple of hours immersed in the experience and is only forced to leave when the nagging pain in his leg becomes too much to bear. One thing's for sure – if he's going to get a video installation for his collection, this will surely be the one.

Chapter 9

David's mobile pings. It's a text message from his mum who's in another part of the house, asking him if he'd like a drink. He prods the touchpad on his wheelchair, choosing number four on the 'drinks' menu – a Dr Pepper, full sugar. He prefers Irn Bru – full sugar – but he's had one of those today and his catheter will soon be brimming at this rate. He turns his attention back to one of the screens on his desk and continues preparing for the upcoming Zoom call. It's with a guy called Robert Smith, a potential new client.

Ten minutes later his mum and carer, Martha, enters the room. As the door opens, it triggers a switch that swaps out the active screens on his desk, replacing them with benign stuff like random websites and computer games. This achieves a couple of things. Given that he wears headphones a lot of the time, it alerts him that his mum is in the vicinity. It also protects her from accidental exposure to some of the more worrying stuff he might be working on. The sort of stuff he might run up against during his regular visits to the dark web.

'Here you go, love. One Dr Pepper, as ordered.'

'Thanks, mum, you're a saint.'

'How's it going?'

'Can't complain. I've got a call coming up soon. Could be some work in it for me – paid work. Help you with the rent.'

'I've told you before young man. You don't have to give me money. I can manage and there's plenty in reserve.'

'I want to pay my way, mum, best I can.'

'I know you do, love. Can I help you with anything?'

'Could you just wibble me about a bit in the seat please? I don't want to get any sores again, even if I can't feel 'em.'

It's disheartening to watch. All those full fat fizzy drinks are slowly transforming a once-promising teenage athlete into a shapeless blob. It's quite a struggle these days for Martha to manoeuvre him by herself without lifts and hoists, although she wouldn't dream of mentioning this to her son.

'Anything else, love?'

'No, thanks. I'll drop you a text if I need changing or emptying. As per usual.'

'Alright. I'll leave you to it. I'm going out later down the shops. Let me know if you need anything.'

'Will do.'

*

Martha Jones's relationship with her son had changed irrevocably on Saturday, 29th October 2005. David was taking part in a Colts rugby union match and was propping in a scrum. The ground was muddy and the scrum collapsed, leaving the usual tangle of bodies and muttered recriminations. When it all got sorted out, a fifteen-year-old boy was lying prone in the mud, unable to move. After two weeks in intensive care and many months of physio and psychotherapy, David had returned home to a life of sorts.

His father had long since moved away. His mother's boyfriend at the time was never particularly reliable and had proved to be a waste of space when David got injured, running for the hills at the first opportunity. For more than a decade she'd been coping alone with just a couple of short daily visits from a care assistant – a different one every day, it seemed – to help her out with the heavy work. Bathing and bedding, for example. The insurance payout had been significant and had funded an array of adaptations to their modest semi-detached house, helping David cope with the narrow confines of his new life as a quadriplegic – going on tetraplegic – ex-sportsman. After several operations and years of grinding physio he'd regained some movement in both his arms although they remained weak. Surgical interventions to restore more movement in his wrists, hands and fingers had been less successful.

Several doors had slammed shut on him when he got injured but he'd forced one open far enough to usher in a new career as a freelance software developer known to the outside world by his moniker, Link_03. He's become bloody good at it and has all the waking hours he needs to get even better. His business has three main offerings – web developer, ethical hacker and games tester. He does the web stuff for commercial organisations, delivering design, development and hosting engagements like the one he has with Varvara Sokolova.

The hacking stuff is strictly not for profit. He's a member of an underground association of maverick techies called The Chain Gang, where what they do is governed by collective responsibility amid military-style security. Right now, they're busy disrupting the activities of some rather unpleasant South-East Asian crime syndicates who make their millions from betting scams. By the time they've figured out what's happening to them, The Chain Gang will have moved on without leaving a trace. Running rings around them, basically. David's adventures in hacking have given him unparalleled expertise in emerging technologies. One of these is something called blockchain – the 'beating heart' of cryptocurrencies.

His post-accident career had started with the computer games testing and he still enjoys it immensely even though it doesn't pay brilliantly well. It's the only part of his work he's prepared to share with his mum and he channels everything he earns from it into his mother's housekeeping account, whether she needs it or not. He invests the rest of his earnings in stuff that takes his fancy. Collecting CryptoPunks for example.

Varvara had got in touch with him following a recommendation from a friend in the jewellery trade. After the first call, she had no idea who she was dealing with but had heard and seen enough to convince her to sign up for a website makeover. Despite all the bonkers secrecy and subterfuge, the relationship works well and between them they've created an impressive online showroom and shop for her jewellery. She's taken full advantage of his wide-ranging technical skills and is now on first name terms with him, if you can call 'Link' a first name. He's also advised her on secure messaging, ensuring she's been able to communicate with Piotr without alerting anybody who might not wish them well. They'd briefly alighted on cryptocurrency as a potential payment option for some of her higher-end pieces but she'd wanted nothing to do with it. Far too risky. When Robert had mentioned going into digital art however, she'd recommended Link without hesitation and had offered to set up a meeting.

Chapter 10

It's been almost a year since the launch of Robert's collection and the quarterly guided tours he runs are regularly oversubscribed. He's found it difficult, however, to get any traction on the digital art and has lost momentum. He hates to admit it but he's been bewildered by the technology surrounding the whole scene and what he needs most is expert help.

Right now, he's enjoying a coffee with Varvara in her workshop. She's been demoing her latest website to him and he's been mightily impressed with its quality and performance. She's arranged a Zoom call for him with Link where they can discuss the emerging market in digital art and how he might break into it. She's warned him about Link's rather bizarre approach to online security.

'Do you need me on the call today, Bobby? I would like to continue working on the necklace. It is an important commission and I do not want it to be a late delivery.'

'Yeah, no problem. If you could set up the call and introduce me at the start?'

'Sure.'

'It's a while until it starts. Could I watch you while you work?'

'Yes, surely. Bring over your chair.'

She uses expensive materials in her jewellery range. Twenty-two carat gold and top-drawer, semi-precious stones, exquisitely worked. Time-consuming stuff. These days, people with money and taste are prepared to pay handsomely for one-off commissions and the person who's commissioned this necklace and matching earrings will be paying just shy of twenty grand when they're finished. Like many of her clients, this one is from the Russian Federation. There are twenty-four links in the necklace, each link set with a fine Australian opal. It takes her four or five hours to make each link meaning that he's watching one tiny part of the process. She talks him through what she's doing as she expertly works the gold in the mount, ready to receive the highly polished stone. Painstaking work.

'When do you glue the stone in place?'

'Bobby, please. We do not use glue. Glue is for cheats. The reason I am taking such a long time over this is that the mount will hold the stone in place without the need for glue.'

'How so?'

'See. I cut a small strip of gold and form it until it is the size and shape of the opal stone, but slightly taller. It is called a bezel. I carefully solder the bezel on to the necklace link. I insert the stone into the bezel and make small adjustments until I have a perfect fit. To finish, I fold the gold back over the stone to hold it in play. Here is a piece I worked on earlier.'

The finished piece looks perfect. He continues to observe the process until he can't wait any longer to ask his big question. It has nothing to do with jewellery.

'Varvara?'

'Yes?'

'How are you getting on with the counselling, my love?'

It's immediately obvious he's mistimed the question, which isn't welcome and cools the atmosphere between them.

'I would rather we did not talk about it very much. We have made progress in a few areas but we are too early in the process for any breaking through. Please, do not worry yourself – you will be first to find out when I have better news.'

He backs off, although he'd like to know a whole lot more. The truth is, he's fallen deeply in love with a beautiful young woman who cannot bring herself to have sex with him. Or anybody for that matter. When they first met, they'd tried to enjoy the physical side but each attempt had ended in tears and recriminations. He thought the situation might have improved when she joined him in England but it didn't. On the few occasions she's opened up to him, she's hinted at something deeply traumatic in her past. Something unspeakable, it seems. He'd pleaded with her to seek professional help and she eventually relented.

She returns to her work. Another piece of the necklace, another link in the chain. At one minute to four, she fires up Zoom and logs into the call. She puts Robert and Link together and returns to her workbench.

*

On screen, he's looking at a cartoon-like avatar, a crude head and shoulders view of a slightly dodgy character. It's so crude, you can make out the individual pixels. At the other end, David Jones is looking at a fifty-ish, biracial man wearing Varvara's pink, rhinestone-encrusted Beats headphones. The man has a slightly worried look on his face, although he's not to know it's his normal look. David takes a quick swig from his latest Irn Bru and starts the conversation.

'GOOD AFTERNOON, ROBERT. WHAT CAN I DO YOU FOR THIS AFTERNOON?'

Let me explain. Given some of the work he does, it's essential that David protects his identity – hence the moniker and the avatar. Another aspect of his security setup is a voice changing app that disguises his voice in real time. As a consequence, he sounds a bit like Stephen Hawking but with a northern-English accent. For the listener, it takes some getting used to.

David's done his research on Robert and feels like he knows him as well as he can, given the paucity of reliable information about him out there. There's zilch about him on the dark web unlike the Sokolovas who have a rather large footprint down there.

Robert has conjured up a mental picture of Link – male, chubby, bad complexion, greasy hair, in dire need of a bath. Faded, threadbare Iron Maiden tee shirt. It explains why he's initially wrong-footed by the robotic drawl, stripped of emotion and nuance. He recovers well.

'Good afternoon to you and thanks for agreeing to meet with me. I've seen your handiwork on Varvara's website and I'm very impressed. Great stuff.'

'YOU'RE WELCOME. FLATTERY WILL GET YOU EVERYWHERE.'

'I don't know if she mentioned why I'd like to talk to you. Briefly, I'm looking for some technical perspectives on digital art if that's alright. So far, I've put together a half-decent collection of conventional art and I'd like to augment it with video art and pieces of digital art. I'll be honest with you though – I don't know where to start.'

It isn't entirely the truth. He's been prowling around this stuff for some time without making anything that could reasonably be described as progress.

'OK. I'D SUGGEST STARTING AT THE BEGINNING.'

The robotic voice makes a weird attempt at laughter, providing him with a clue that a real – rather than synthesised – voice is being deployed beneath the disguise.

'SORRY ABOUT THAT. HAVE A LOOK AT MY AVATAR. WHAT DO YOU SEE?'

He sees a small cartoon-like head. Closer scrutiny reveals a crude, two-dimensional character assembled using a small number of coloured pixels. It's the sort of thing an IT techie might deploy to represent him (or her) on social media and messaging apps. SpongeBob SquarePants or Jabba the Hutt also seem popular. It looks vintage, like something he might have produced at university using a box full of punched cards – but not in colour.

'DESCRIBE IT TO ME PLEASE.'

'I'll try. So, I'm looking at a dude with a light brown complexion and wearing what might be called muttonchop sideburns, like Gaz Coombs out of Supergrass. He's wearing some cool purple shades and a Peaky Blinders-style flat cap.'

Silence from the other end. He stares a little harder.

'Oh yes, he's got a gold stud earring in his right ear. One yellow pixel by the look of it.'

'VERY GOOD. LET ME EXPLAIN. YOU'RE LOOKING AT A CRYPTOPUNK. IT'S A RANDOMISED, COMPUTER-GENERATED IMAGE AVAILABLE TO ANYBODY TO DOWNLOAD AT NO COST. IT'S IN A ONE-OFF EDITION OF TEN THOUSAND DIFFERENT FACES GENERATED BY A COMPUTER PROGRAM. A PIECE OF DIGITAL ART, NO LESS.'

'There must be something more to it. I was doing similar things at university back in the mainframe days. Punched cards, paper tape etc.'

'WHEN DINOSAURS ROAMED THE EARTH?'

Another burst of unsettling, metallic laughter.

'APOLOGIES. YOU'VE NO DOUBT CONCLUDED THAT THIS CARTOON HEAD HAS NO ARTISTIC MERIT AND THEREFORE NO INTRINSIC VALUE. YOU'D BE WRONG. THIS PARTICULAR ONE IS UNIQUE AND IT'S BEEN MINTED.'

'Hold on. What do you mean, minted?'

'IT HAS A BULLETPROOF CERTIFICATE OF AUTHENTICITY SET UP AND STORED ON A NEW TECHNOLOGY CALLED BLOCKCHAIN. IN THIS CASE, IT'S THE ETHEREUM BLOCKCHAIN AND IT POWERS A CRYPTOCURRENCY CALLED ETHER. THE ETHEREUM PLATFORM HAS THE EDGE OVER OTHER CRYPTOCURRENCIES BECAUSE IT OFFERS SMART CONTRACT FUNCTIONALITY. WHICH BRINGS ME RATHER NEATLY ONTO NFTS.'

'Could you go a bit more slowly, please. I'm struggling to keep up.'

'SORRY.'

'OK. Carry on.'

'THE COMBINATION OF AN ORIGINAL ARTWORK — OR AN ORIGINAL ANYTHING — AND THE CERTIFICATE IS CALLED A NON-FUNGIBLE TOKEN OR NFT. THIS MAKES IT TRULY UNIQUE, JUST LIKE A CONVENTIONAL PIECE OF ART AND ITS ASSOCIATED PROVENANCE. DESPITE THE ARTWORK BEING SIMPLISTIC AND ENDLESSLY REPRODUCIBLE, THE NFT HAS BOTH VALUE AND DESIRABILITY. ARE YOU WITH ME?'

'I am now, thanks. Who owns this particular piece?'

'I DO. I HAVE SIX OF THEM IN MY CRYPTO WALLET. I KNOW A FEW PEOPLE WHO ARE INTO THIS STUFF AND THEY PRACTICALLY

GAVE THEM TO ME. WE'RE ALREADY SEEING THE FIRST SIGNS OF A MARKET DEVELOPING. COULD MAKE US A LOT OF MONEY, NOBODY KNOWS. THE IMPORTANT THING IS I CAN AFFORD TO LOSE THE 1.5 ETH IT COST ME TO INVEST.'

'Sorry, what's an ETH?'

'SHORT FOR ETHER. ETHER'S LIKE BITCOIN BUT UNDER THE RADAR SO FAR.'

'How much is 1.5 ETH in real money?'

'HANG ON A MO. LET'S HAVE A LOOK.'

[09/07/2018: 1 ETH = 355.51 GBP (Source AOEx)]

'ABOUT FIVE HUNDRED QUID, GIVE OR TAKE. DEPENDS WHAT DAY IT IS. OR HOUR OR MINUTE OR SECOND OR MILLISECOND. CRYPTO IS A BIT VOLATILE TO SAY THE LEAST. NONE OF THIS IS REAL, TO BE FAIR.'

There's quite a lot for him to digest. For the rest of the allotted hour, they discuss the ways and means of seeking out, acquiring and securing digital art. One aspect becomes crystal clear. To be a serious player in the digital art market, you need a capability in cryptocurrency and its underlying technology called blockchain. He badly needs somebody like Link_03 who can move and shake the technology on his behalf. By the end of the call, he's agreed to retain him/her/it/them to carry out technical services for him while he gets his digital collection off the ground. It's the Wild West out there and he doesn't want to get shafted unnecessarily.

While undoubtedly interesting and potentially lucrative – who knows at this early stage? – he regards CryptoPunks and the like as a passing fad, collectibles at most. He's much keener to invest in what he would call genuine, talented artists who're producing pukka works of art in the digital space. He's determined to show the work he acquires rather than keeping it hidden away in a virtual vault or whatever they call them.

After the call, he writes up his notes and walks across to where Varvara's standing at her workbench, finessing one of the links in the necklace. He stands behind her and puts his arms around her. She's comfortable with this, which he interprets as a small, early sign of progress in her treatment.

'Did you find what you were looking for, Bobby?'

'I did indeed. Thank you so much.'

He can smell her hair, her body. What he wouldn't give to make love to this woman right now. He reluctantly pulls away from the embrace. It's the right and proper thing to do.

Chapter 11

'Could I use the big car today please, Bobby?'

By the big car, she means the Porsche 911S Turbo. It may be one of Robert's few indulgences but it continues to scare seven shades of shit out of him every time he ventures out in it.

'Sure. Where're you going?'

He feels a whole lot better whenever Varvara leaves the house. It happens all too rarely and he worries about her becoming a recluse.

'Oxford. Would you like to come with me this time?'

Although she asks the question, she knows the answer. He's already booked out and won't be able to join her.

'I'd like to my love but I can't this time. I'm expecting a chap round this morning to talk about plasma screens.'

The Porsche is parked on the driveway. Close by lurks the creepy Simon who's attending to something or other near the ornamental fountain – a stray weed perhaps. She hurries towards the car, head down, trying to avoid his 'all seeing eye'. Unfortunately, he spots her and ambles over, eager to chat. He positions himself in front of the car.

'Morning, Miss. How are we today? Going out, I see.'

He's fishing for information. Standard behaviour. He inspects the bonnet and uses a dirty hand to wipe an imaginary speck of dust off it.

'I am good. Yes. I am seeking out supplies for my work.'

'Oxford?'

'Maybe.'

'You will be careful with the Porsche, won't you? I don't want you coming to any harm. It can be a bit of a beast in the wrong hands.'

She has a feeling he might be referring to her hands. She strokes the front wing.

'Do not worry with yourself, Simon. It is a pussycat but be assured I will drive it with the utmost care and attention.'

She very much wishes she'd worn one of her trouser suits today. Simon's sidling round, seeking a ringside seat for her attempt to get into the Porsche without displaying her knickers. She's had to endure this sort of unwarranted male attention since her teenage years in Moscow and doesn't welcome it. 'Asking for it', in the parlance of her father and his despicable drinking buddies. She puts her hands on her hips and gives Simon both barrels.

'Why are you standing around? What are you waiting for? Do you not have lawns to cut, light bulbs to exchange?'

He provides no answers. A grimace is all he's prepared to offer but he does turn away and return to his work – with some reluctance, I might add. She eases herself into the car. She's red in the face and takes a few moments to calm down. She's complained about the 'handyman' many times but Robert's known him for years and seems to have a blind spot regarding him, which is difficult to comprehend.

She fires up the car, revs the engine and roars off down the drive, fishtailing as she goes, spreading dust and pea grit everywhere. Not to worry – Simon will clean up after her.

*

She's going to Oxford to meet Piotr. She'd been trying to track him down for more than ten years when she found out through an attaché at the Russian embassy in London – an old army colleague – that he was in England. Her attempts to find him were continually frustrated by a combination of the UK immigration service at one end and the barely concealed interference of her father and his associates at the other. She'd begun to despair of ever seeing him until her chance meeting with Robert in St Petersburg. Their growing relationship provided a powerful argument for her to move to England and she joined him in the UK in 2013. Their hastily arranged engagement clinched the deal. Since then, it'd had taken her some time to track Piotr down and at least another year to pluck up the courage to meet him.

As usual she drives to the park and ride at Water Eaton, parks the car and buys a ticket. While waiting for the bus, she notices that part of the car park has been taken over by numerous cars – Mercs mostly – and caravans. She guesses a travelling funfair has arrived in town but there's no sign of any of the rides and sideshows yet.

The 500 shuttle bus rolls up and she climbs on board, securing one of the seats at the front on the upstairs deck. She loves riding on the English double-decker buses and settles back to enjoy what she usually does up here – using her elevated position to look into the houses lined up along the route. A series of tiny glimpses into other people's lives.

She gets off the bus at Summertown shops. From there it's a short walk to a diner called Joe's Bar and Grill, where she's agreed to meet with Piotr during his lunch break. On arrival, she looks around the café and spots him at a table near the back. He's looking intently at his phone, oblivious to the bustle around him. He looks up, spots her, smiles and waves. He immediately pockets his phone. They embrace and kiss.

He's wearing school uniform. This particular uniform is ubiquitous around here, as is the small tribe of Russian kids who wear it. St Clare's is a popular school for those who can afford their immense fees, and there are plenty of Russians in the world who can. How so?

A good many of them were in the right place at the right time during the breakup of the old Soviet Union. Some of them cleaned up big time, one of whom happened to be Varvara's father, Igor. Within a few years, he'd gone from being a middle-ranking civil servant with his finger in a few minor pies to a major player with a thriving business, a small proportion of which is legal and above board. He has all the trappings of a wealthy businessman but he's an oligarch with a small 'o', constantly jostling for position, always watching his back, destined never to reach the Premier League where top predators like Abramovich and his ilk bask. They'd had the brass neck to target the billions rather than the millions, all of it effectively stolen from the Russian people while they were distracted by other things. Like trying not to freeze and/or starve to death. At the top, in a league of his own, the apex predator. Putin.

The story goes that Piotr is the result of one of Igor's many extra-marital relationships, mother unnamed and unknown. The man himself is deliberately evasive about this story and prefers to position himself as a kindly godfather. Since his birth, Piotr's been brought up by foster parents and bankrolled by Igor, who's investing in him as a hedge, a viable alternative to the rather inadequate and needy Vladimir. The young pretender was delighted when a half-sister appeared out of nowhere about a year ago. They've since struck up a warm friendship that has endured despite them only being able to meet occasionally.

She stands back from him and looks him up and down.

'Look at you. I swear you have grown much taller since we last met.'

They don't want to draw undue attention to themselves so they speak in English. They take their seats and look at the menus.

'Would you prefer something healthy today, dahling? For a change?'

'No thanks. Can I have the usual please?'

For him, 'the usual' in here is Joe's full English with a mug of strong, excessively sugared tea. She orders this and selects the smashed avocado and poached eggs for herself. A glass of sparkling water completes the order and is scribbled down by the waiter who lingers at their table just long enough to become tiresome. She dismisses him with a wave of her hand.

'So, how are your studies going?'

'Very well for the most part.'

'What are you meaning, for the most part?'

'I'm enduring a few struggles with business management and economics. Fucking boring, basically. Naturally, I'll persevere and get the points I need. As you know, our father will settle for nothing less.'

Piotr is studying for an IB Diploma, where the IB stands for International Baccalaureate, an alternative to A levels and welcomed throughout the world as a pre-university qualification. He'd like to attend a British university if he can. The last thing he wants is to go back to Russia where there's nothing waiting for him apart from a year's national service. Igor continues to pay the piper it seems but is yet to call the tune.

'How are things with you, Varvara?'

'Good, very good. The jewellery is selling like hot drinks and I have a whole waiting room of commissions.'

'Good news I'm sure but I was not meaning your business matters. I was meaning you and Robert. You know.'

'We are very happy and very together.'

'You're taking your time with him. You'll get married soon and have children?'

'Soon.'

To tell the truth, she's seriously worried about her future with Robert. Marriage and children seem a long way away right now. Their brunches arrive and Piotr wades into his large platter as if he hasn't eaten for a week. She picks delicately at her more modest meal, taking time to observe the young man opposite.

'When I finish the exams can I come and see you and Robert?'

This is delivered with a mouth full of partly chewed bacon, egg and sausage. It seems table manners don't feature all that much on the IB curriculum.

'That would be good. I will discuss it with him and you can come and see us, stay for a while. We live in a big, beautiful house in the countryside. You will adore it.'

She hasn't yet found a way of telling Robert about Piotr and is finding it difficult to broach the subject for a number of reasons. One in particular.

'I have some news for you. I've met a girl.'

This comes as a complete surprise to her although it shouldn't have. The boy of a year ago has developed into a handsome young man. His voice has broken, he has the beginnings of a beard and he's an inch or two taller than her.

'How lovely for you, dahling. I am intrigued already. Is it one of your school friends?'

'No. Emily is a student studying at Magdalen. She works part-time in the Bodleian Library, which is where I met her during a school visit.'

'Is it serious?'

'Do you mean are we sleeping together?'

'Well, yes.'

'We are. She has a flat near mine in Jericho and we spend our time there when we aren't studying. The school has rules about this sort of thing so I keep them unaware.'

It's a lot for her to process. Piotr's only seventeen but in a way, she's mightily relieved he isn't following in the squalid footsteps of her brother. At the same time, she's wary of any new people in his life and always suspects the dead hand of her father's paranoiac need to control everybody and everything. It doesn't seem likely in this case.

'Tell me more.'

'She's twenty. Studying math. She's from Canada and intends to go home when she gets her masters. I think she's beautiful, I like her a lot and she's fun. Here, this is her.'

She studies the photo on his phone. She sees a smiling, attractive young woman with long blue hair, shaved on one side. Assorted piercings and punk/goth stylings complete the look. It's unnerving but Emily looks a lot like she did when she was a teenager and into the Russian punk scene in a big way. The happier days before Igor's heavy hand intervened and knocked all traces of defiance out of her. She feels sorry for Emily and hopes she doesn't get too entangled with her family.

'She looks great. You are a very lucky boy. I wish you well, both of you.'

The boy sitting across the table from her and the girl in the picture are young and a long way from home. She's confident his relationship with Emily will run its course and they'll go their separate ways before long. Piotr's on his own a lot of the time and deserves to have a soulmate – as long as it doesn't impact on his studies. Talking of which, he tells her he doesn't want to be late for his afternoon class. At the bus stop, they share a hug and she gives him a sisterly kiss.

'Thanks, Varvara.'

'For what?'

'For being my friend, that's all.'

They go their separate ways. Tears. There are always tears when she leaves him but she takes care to keep them well hidden until he's out of sight. At some stage, she'll have to take him on one side and tell him the truth.

*

When she gets back to the Porsche, some lowlife has been busy with a screwdriver, leaving a deep, unsightly gouge along the entire driver's side. She clenches her fists and lets out an almighty scream.

'BASTAAAARDS!!'

She doesn't care who hears her, although there aren't many people around. She glances across at the clump of caravans and Mercs and sees a bunch of scruffy youngsters who can only be described as 'taking the piss'. She secures the car and strolls towards them. They obviously don't see her as a threat, so ramp up their show of defiance. When she's close to them, she breaks into a run and they scatter. This sets off their pack of mange-ridden dogs and they start snarling and howling, straining at their leads. In the ensuing chaos, she grabs one of the teenagers and forces his arm up his back.

'Where do you live, you little shit? Tell me.'

If he could have spoken English he would have said, 'You're hurting me'.

He points to an expensive-looking, highly polished caravan, overburdened with chrome. She forces him, crying in pain, across to it.

'You in there. I want a word with you. Now.'

The caravan lurches around crazily and she hears shouting inside. The door bursts open. An unkempt, unfit-looking man moves towards her with intent, armed with what looks like a baseball bat, metal-tipped. A woman with a pock-marked face stands in the doorway, arms folded, waiting for the fun to start. Varvara lets go of the whimpering teenager, who runs away, cradling his arm.

It doesn't last long. Within a couple of seconds, her assailant is rolling around on the tarmac. A well-timed headbutt has splashed his nose across his face, blood everywhere. The woman meanwhile has ducked back inside the caravan and locked the door. Varvara is on a roll now and isn't quite finished. She picks up the bat and caves in the windscreen and headlamps of the nearest Merc. She returns the bat to its owner and leans in closer to offer him some advice.

'You should call the police. Believe me, they will be more than pleased to help you out.'

Chapter 12

For a careful, conservative chap like Robert, dipping his toe into the brave new world of digital art had been quite a leap. The first task had been to establish a foothold in the murky world of cryptocurrencies, an area that Link didn't regard as murky at all. Another brief Zoom call was all it took. The robotic voice guided him through the basics.

'FIRST, YOU NEED A WALLET TO MANAGE YOUR CURRENCY AND EVENTUALLY YOUR NFTS.'

'A wallet, yes. I presume it's not made of leather. How do I go about getting one?'

'I'M SENDING YOU A LINK TO A WEBSITE. IT BELONGS TO A BROKER SPECIALISING IN CRYPTO.'

'Right. I have it.'

'OK. CLICK ON THE LINK. YOU'LL BE STEPPED THROUGH A PROCESS. THERE ARE SEVERAL TYPES OF WALLET AVAILABLE. I SUGGEST YOU USE A HARDWARE WALLET.'

'What's that exactly?'

'It's a small electronic device which costs less than a hundred quid. You drive it using an app that runs on your laptop or smartphone or both. It's much more secure than the other options, I can assure you.'

'Why's it more secure?'

'Because your tokens aren't stored on the device. It just holds your private key, which it uses to prove you're the owner of a certain address on the blockchain. You never expose your key to the network so it's almost impossible to steal it. Here endeth the first lesson.'

Within a week and with only a few minor interventions from Link, he's successfully negotiated his first brief foray into cryptocurrency. The end result is a secure wallet able to access an Ethereum account holding the princely sum of 5 ETH. A quick look at the exchange rate is called for, noting that 'GBP' is the ISO standard code for pounds sterling. Not bad. Not bad at all.

[23/07/2018: 1 ETH = 349.11 GBP (Source AOEx). Fund value £1,746]

There was one more important thing to take on board. Another Zoom session was required.

'When you first set up your wallet, it provided you with a randomly generated, twelve-word phrase. This is your recovery seed and I hope you noted it down and stored it safely as instructed. Robert?'

'Yes, definitely.'

'Don't ever forget or mislay your recovery seed.

WITHOUT IT, YOU'LL BE UNABLE TO RECOVER YOUR ACCOUNT IF YOU LOSE ACCESS TO IT. THE CRYPTOCURRENCY WILL BE BEYOND REACH. FOREVER.'

This is a big worry. He doesn't trust himself to consign it to memory. Twelve words is about eleven too many for his brain and its old-fashioned wiring loom.

'How do I make sure I don't lose it? Is there another electronic gizmo for that?"

'SADLY, THERE ISN'T. THE LAST THING YOU SHOULD DO IS STORE IT DIGITALLY. EASILY HACKED, BELIEVE ME.'

'So, what do I do about it?'

'THE ADVICE IS TO WRITE IT DOWN ON A PIECE OF PAPER AND PUT THE PIECE OF PAPER IN A SAFE PLACE. LIKE YOU'VE JUST DONE. A FIREPROOF SAFE WOULD BE USEFUL.'

'You're having a laugh, aren't you? With all that hyper-advanced cryptology beavering away in the blockchain it all seems a bit low tech, don't you think?'

'I AGREE WITH YOU. IRONIC REALLY. THERE'S A VARIATION ON THE THEME IF YOU'RE INTERESTED?'

'I'm all ears.'

'THERE'S A DEVICE CALLED A CRYPTOTAG THAT ENABLES YOU TO STORE YOUR RECOVERY SEED. YOU ENGRAVE A REPRESENTATION OF THE TWELVE WORDS ONTO A TITANIUM SHEET USING A PUNCH. IT'S CAVEMAN TECH BUT IT'S PRETTY MUCH BULLETPROOF AND DEFINITELY FIREPROOF.'

'I'll need one of those. Stop me worrying.'

'ANOTHER LINK IS WENDING ITS WAY TO YOU. HAPPY HUNTING, CAVEMAN.'

*

The first transaction had been a test involving one of Link's CryptoPunks, the pixel guy with the earring. After a bit of good-natured haggling, he'd agreed to buy the NFT for 3 ETH. It's now safely stashed in his account and it's his first piece of digital art although he's in no hurry to put it on show any time soon. He's set up and ready to go. He needs to top up the account and now is as good a time as any. He buys three hundred ETH, which brings his investment in crypto up to a GBP equivalent of about a hundred grand. More than enough for the time being given the state of the NFT market.

He sits back and takes stock. He's learned a hell of a lot about the digital art market in a short space of time. He considers Link's CryptoPunks for a moment. They're examples of generative art, which is art generated using computer algorithms, and he questions whether this is art at all. He'd much rather focus on what's called non-generative art, which is original art created by sentient beings using digital technology. He'll have to be patient as it seems there's only a small group of digital artists working in the crypto space. A modicum of help is at hand though in the shape of the first online marketplaces for digital art NFTs, offering technical services to artists and helping them to create and sell NFTs minted from their original artwork. One to watch is a new company called SuperRare and he's joined a handful of early subscribers to the service. With a little assistance from Link, he's used this rather scratchy new platform to purchase work from a few gifted artists whose work he admires.

Up until now he's ventured roughly half of his fund on these acquisitions and has started displaying some of them in the house on his new fleet of networked plasma screens. He has no idea whether his initial investment will bear fruit over time and there are two aspects to this. First, the stability of the Ether cryptocurrency. As of now, it seems reasonably stable but who knows what might happen. Second, the future resilience of the artwork. There's no precedent for establishing the durability and longevity of the artists, all of whom are relative unknowns. In the context of such things, a hundred grand is a relatively small amount and he can afford to write it off if it all goes 'Pete Tong'.

*

Out of nowhere, he gets a call from Vladimir. This never happens and he's immediately on his guard. He's not even sure where he got the number from.

'Hey, Robert. How is it hanging my friend?'

'Very well, thank you. Where are you?'

'Back in England for a working holiday, staying in London. I am checking out a few of my father's property investments.'

Igor is rumoured to have several valuable pieces of real estate dotted around the capital. The UK government continue to roll out the red carpet for people like him, encouraging them to invest their dubious millions in British property and businesses. They're known as golden visas and hundreds of Russians have taken advantage of them. Not many searching questions are asked prior to them being waved through. Once ensconced in one of our leafy suburbs, they're free to come and go as they please.

'I am here until the end of next week. Come and meet me, make a day of it. I have a small proposition to discuss with you. Strictly business.'

He thought the chances of this proposition being above board were less than negligible but thought he'd ask.

'It's not dodgy, is it?'

'Of course not. I would not dream of such a thing.'

‘Will Luana be with you?’

No harm in asking. He didn’t want to meet them any time soon.

‘No, Luana is no more.’

What? Surely not.

‘No more?’

‘She had to go back to Albania. Family problems.’

‘Oh, right, OK. What’s the plan?’

He hasn’t been to London for a while, so he’s up for a day in the smoke. He’ll tell Varvara he’s visiting an art dealer – it wouldn’t be wise to admit he’s meeting her brother. He agrees to join him at the National Gallery in the morning, do a quick tour and have lunch at the Portrait Restaurant next door – great views down Whitehall apparently – followed by drinks at Igor’s place. The small business proposition is about a joint investment, the detail to be revealed when they meet. Fair enough. He’d hear what he has to say but has no intention of engaging. He doubts whether Varvara would approve anyway.

Chapter 13

The tour of the National Gallery hadn't gone entirely to plan as they'd barely made any progress beyond the medieval art. He'd no idea Vladimir was into this stuff. Leaving aside the glittering altar pieces and exquisitely worked devotional pieces, the Russian was particularly taken with the *Wilton Diptych,* a small hinged panel painting from the late fourteenth century, closely associated with King Richard II. It was all he could do to drag him away from it to have some lunch. During the meal they chat about the art they'd seen that morning.

'Consider the *Wilton Diptych* for a moment, Robert. Such a beautiful piece. If I was to consider buying it, how much would I have to pay?'

'Are you joking?'

'Do I look like I am joking?'

He doesn't and to be fair, he never does. He hasn't given up quite yet.

'Papa has a valuable collection of Byzantine icons that is on display in a secure room in his dacha. You must come to Moscow and see them sometime. So, I have it in mind to buy the Wilton piece for his collection and I am prepared to go as high as one million of your pounds.'

Not for the first time, he begins to wonder what sort of planet these people inhabit.

'I don't know what to say. The diptych is unique and very precious. Like almost everything in the National Gallery, it belongs to the nation and it's not for sale. If it was for sale, the tag would have "priceless" written on it.'

'I prostrate myself before your better judgement Mr Smith and formerly withdraw my offer of a million.' He wags a finger at him. 'Do not forget though, my friend – everything has a price.'

Following lunch, they hail a cab that whisks them to Embassy Gardens, a new development near the US Embassy. It includes at least one of Igor's London apartments, which is where Vladimir's staying during this visit. The lift delivers them to the umpty-umpteenth floor and they enter the apartment. It's pretty special.

'Nice place. Must have cost a fair bit.'

'About a million pounds excluding fees. Papa has three apartments in this block. The other owners are from the Middle East and China mostly. A few Russians. Less than half of the apartments are actually lived in.'

'Do you rent them out?'

'No, they remain empty. Tenants would only complicate things, especially if we have to sell at short notice. Why are you looking at me like that? Like you are hurting.'

'I'm not thinking about the loss of income as I know you don't need the money. It's just the thought of all these des reses lying empty while there's a housing crisis everywhere.'

'Do not worry yourself. None of your common people would be able to afford the rent on this place.'

It's pointless to continue. Vladimir leans back on one of the sofas and makes a sweeping gesture.

'I like this one because it has plenty of space and the balcony overlooks the sky pool.'

'Sky pool? What's a sky pool?'

'Come with me and have a look.'

They walk out onto the balcony and look down. Beneath them is a spectacular rooftop terrace arranged around a transparent swimming pool spanning the gap between two low rise towers. Nothing between the pool and the ground. Fantastic views. Stunning in a crazy way.

'Impressed?'

'Very much. Shame it's in London though. I've never really warmed to our esteemed capital city.'

'You are a small-town boy are you not? Made it good, of course.'

'If you say so.'

'Hey, it is a warm, sunny day. Let us hit the terrace, get some champagne and try out the sky pool.'

'I don't have any ...'

'Have no concerns. I have some swimming trousers you can use.'

*

The sky pool is quite something, although people prone to vertigo should steer well clear. The water is warm and not very deep, perfect for wibbling around which happens to be Robert's excuse for actual swimming. The champagne is Pol Roger and is hitting the spot. After leaving the pool, they find a table in a corner of the near-empty Orangery restaurant and get down to business.

'So, my friend, how is the collecting going?'

'Quite slowly I'm sorry to say. I've stopped buying conventional art unless I really like it and I've shelved my grand plan to get my own video installation. As for digital art, its early days and it's still finding its feet. Most of the development seems to be targeting the youth market. Banal, simplistic stuff produced by clever algorithms rather than talented people. There are a few genuine digital artists trying to get some traction but it's mainly small stuff.'

'Are you disappointed?'

He shrugs his shoulders.

'Frustrated more than anything else. It's an interesting area technically and I've had to engage a big brain to help me navigate the crypto-blockchain-type stuff. I'm scraping together a small collection of what they call NFTs that may or may not be a good investment. My techie reckons the market is about to take off and I should hang in there.'

'Ah, the much-vaunted NFTs. I have taken a look at these. My friends who work in IT inform me it is going to be the next big thing, big enough to blow the conventional art market out of the water. My accountant instructs me to avoid it at all costs. Head or heart, Robert?'

'A bit of both, I would suggest.'

Their mixed platters arrive and they tuck in. With their hunger assuaged, the conversation continues.

'Which cryptocurrency are you using?'

'Ether. Bitcoin is so last year, and I'm told that Bitcoin validation is so resource-intensive it's bad news for the planet.'

'Did you know Ethereum was set up by a Russian?'

'I did indeed. Anyway, enough of this. I thought you said you'd got a business proposition?'

'Yes. Here is what I propose. A joint investment fund to spend on

NFTs. Me and you, equal shares. Let us say an investment together for a total of one million pounds to start with. I am content for you to bid for the digital art that you can find out there and put it in safekeeping for us. We can have a reckoning from time to time and see how it goes.

'Hmmm. It's interesting but I'm not sure we'd be able to spend anywhere near a million in the current market. I should warn you that given the fluctuations in cryptocurrencies right now, you should be ready to lose your stake or a substantial part of it. I'm not joking.'

'I take your point of view. How about we halve our stake. A quarter of a million pounds each. I would be prepared to take a hit at that level. Would you?'

'That sounds a bit more doable. I'll run it past my legal eagles and have them draw something up for us.'

Vladimir pulls a grotesque face.

'Thanks, but no thanks. Please, no legalities. A simple handshake will be good enough for me. I know you won't fuck me around.'

Although he probably means it to be vaguely reassuring, the last bit sounds more like a threat.

They are now a team, unlikely as that seems. They're about to become players in a market where the risks are high and the rewards are, let's face it, unpredictable. They celebrate the deal with another bottle of Pol, a seafood supper and a drunken dip in the ridiculous sky pool, now lit up like a cheap disco. After hitting the vodka, Robert ends up rather ratted although he has the presence of mind to avoid the dreaded white powder, which happens to be in plentiful supply. He stays the night in one of the spare rooms. Before passing out, he cobbles together a garbled text for Varvara, letting her know he's crashed at a hotel and won't be home that night. He has just enough about him to ensure he doesn’t burden her with the details. Any of them.

Chapter 14

Robert's progress on building his digital art collection has been painfully slow and is now pretty much stalled. His purchases have barely scratched the surface of the funds now available. The biggest hit on their investment has been a huge blip in the exchange rate which at one point halved the fund's value before starting a slow recovery. Even so, their crypto account has suffered some big losses. As he'd said to Vladimir on their last call:

'Mate, it's best not to look at the exchange rate on a daily basis. It would be very bad for your health and wellbeing.'

[10/09/2018: 1 ETH = 151.96 GBP (Source AOEx): Fund value £304,680]

The Russian has experienced nothing but declining returns since he came on board but it doesn't seem to have spooked him. At least he's been dissuaded from upping his stake for the time being.

It's proving difficult to find any good quality digital art worth investing in. He'd discussed these problems recently with Monty over a fish and chip supper and a few beers in Cheltenham. Before getting to the 'nodding off' stage, he'd given Robert the contact details of a specialist dealer he'd bumped into, Marissa Sanchez, a Spaniard. She'd recently penned an excellent article about the emerging digital art market in *Arts and Collections* magazine and could well be the person to reinvigorate his search for suitable pieces.

After reading the article, he'd got in touch with Doctor Sanchez and found her to be charming, genuine and knowledgeable. During the call they'd agreed to meet in her home town, San Sebastian, to discuss possibilities and explore options. He'd missed out on visiting the well-heeled seaside town on his last visit to the Basque Country and was keen to make good on that. He'd built a long weekend around the meeting and would be travelling alone. Varvara was still nervous about leaving the country so was reluctant to take the risk. He didn't bother asking Pamela as he'd assumed she wouldn't be interested. He's booked a suite in an impressive-looking place called the Hotel Maria Cristina, a Belle Epoque era hotel. The website promises 'understated luxury and complete discretion', whatever that means.

He picks up a rental car at the airport in Bilbao and drives across to San Sebastian, arriving mid-afternoon. He drops the car at the rentals office and after checking in, dumps his stuff and carries out a cursory inspection of the town. He takes a blustery walk along the sweeping crescent of the beach and back and returns to the hotel in good time for his meeting with Doctor Sanchez, which will take place in the hotel's Café Saigon restaurant. When he'd mentioned where he was staying, she'd recommended this eatery and had talked enthusiastically about their superb range of Asian food. Before getting ready, he strips off and takes full advantage of the room's spa bath. After spending far too long being bubbled, he gets out and readies himself for dinner.

*

They'd agreed to meet for drinks in the Dry Bar and he's turned up early to try a cocktail or two. He starts with a Gin and It, a kind of tribute to Pamela, although he doesn't enjoy it very much. He's about to order his second cocktail when a very smart, good-looking woman with a long mane of jet-black hair eases herself onto a bar stool and flashes him a big smile.

'Robert Smith, I presume.'

They shake hands.

'The very same. You must be Doctor Sanchez?'

'Call me Marissa. I would prefer it.'

'Marissa it is. A bit rude of me to start without you. I was about to er ...'

'Please, go ahead.'

'Would you join me?'

'Yes please. They do a superb range of Riojas in here. I will take a large glass of the local Reserva – they are all excellent.'

'Is that so? I'll join you if I may.'

They exchange pleasantries over their wine, feeling each other out, starting to relax. Before very long, the barman informs them their table is ready and they go through to the restaurant.

During the meal, he finds out a fair bit about Marissa, including the fact she's a widow. Her husband was a policeman who was killed in an explosion, one of the last victims of an ETA atrocity, this one a car bomb. The tragedy happened eight or nine years ago, but he can tell she hasn't yet come to terms with her loss. Since her husband's death, she's buried herself in her work and there hasn't been a place for a significant other in her life. After the meal, they order coffee and pacharans and finally get to talk about the emerging digital art market. The conversation goes well enough and leaves him hopeful that she can help him track down some genuine new talent. They're enjoying each other's company and decide to continue the evening in the bar. They settle down with their drinks, then this:

'Do you mind if we talk about something else? The real reason I wanted to meet with you and talk.'

He's momentarily taken aback but allows his curiosity to get the better of him.

'I'm listening.'

'First of all, I am not a real art expert, sorry. Sometimes, I wish I was.'

It might be a combination of the booze, the late hour and the pleasant company of an attractive woman, but he remains surprisingly sanguine about this.

'You had me fooled, that's for sure. It sounds intriguing though. What do you do?'

'I'm in law enforcement. Currently, I'm seconded to Europol as an agent and I specialise in financial crimes.'

'Very interesting but why the cloak and dagger stuff?'

'Would you have travelled all the way to San Sebastian to talk to a policewoman?'

'Probably not. You've gone to a lot of trouble to get me out here. Why is it so important that you talk to me?'

'Let me tell you what we are doing. After hearing it, you can decide whether or not to help us.'

'Go ahead.'

'OK. I will start with a question. How much do you know about the Sokolovas and what they do?'

Not nearly enough, as it turns out. During the following thirty minutes, Marissa paints a sobering picture of the rise of the Russian oligarchs, triggering the growth of a network of organised crime stretching across the world. A significant player in all of this is Igor Sokolova, who presides over a sprawling hydra of businesses. Some of them are above board, most of them aren't.

'Igor runs his business empire with an iron fist and has surrounded himself with a group of rather unpleasant characters.'

'I've never met Igor, although Varvara gets upset at the mere mention of his name. What about the son, Vladimir? He told me he worked in his father's business.'

'Igor has given Vladimir a small piece of the business to run. He doesn't trust him enough to do very much else. We do know the son organises regular cocaine shipments into Western Europe.'

'Let's say he's just gone down even further in my estimation.'

'As you are probably aware, the son has developed a taste for the merchandise, which does not play well with Igor. His patience will run out at some stage and he will find a way to sideline his troublesome son. When I say sideline, well ...'

'Spare me the details. I get the gist. Sorry, please carry on.'

'There is of course your fiancée, the rather enigmatic Varvara.'

She delivers this with a smile.

'Hang on. Wait a minute. Is she involved in some way?'

'It is a possibility.'

The look on his face warns her she needs to back off a little. She doesn't want to risk losing him.

'But we do not think so. You know better than me what she thinks of her father and her brother.

'I do indeed.'

'We don't have much detail on her past, but we do know she spent a few years in and around the Russian armed forces. Difficult to tell what she got up to, as so much of the detail is classified.'

'She's never mentioned the army to me. I wonder why?'

The question is left hanging, although it might explain one thing – her obsession with her fitness regime.

Marissa resumes. 'In law enforcement, we have to tread carefully with Russian businessmen, especially those with connections to organised crime, which is most of them. We are powerless to prevent their money-making activities – they are what they are. If the local jurisdictions are unable – or unwilling – to rein them in, we are reluctant to interfere. Actually, we cannot interfere.'

'Why is Europol so interested in what the Sokolovas are doing?'

'There are activities that we can interfere with, like importing narcotics into Western Europe. Our best bet is to keep them – and people like them – in line by looking for opportunities to disrupt them. Keep them guessing. My organisation works tirelessly to build cases against people such as these and when we get it right, they get hit really hard, although we seldom take them down entirely.'

'How do you make them pay?'

'We look to exploit a serious weakness at the heart of their business model. Money laundering. As I said, since the collapse of the Soviet Union and the subsequent economic reforms, a few people have become very rich indeed. Igor got into oil and gas. Like a few other people, he was in the right place at the right time. He could buy oil at the old Soviet-subsidised rates and sell it to Northern European countries at up to forty times the price.'

'So far, so predictable. That's what happens when you let capitalism rip.'

'It does. However, as soon as you start making lots of cash, you become a target. If you are a target, you need to protect yourself. The protection racketeers formed a symbiotic relationship with the oligarchs and it was not long before they became partners in crime. With lots of cashflow, people like Igor saw the attraction of moving into illegal businesses such as drugs.'

'Where are you going with this?'

'Patience please – it's complicated. The oligarchs and their protectors were sitting on huge piles of cash. Dirty money. Money that wasn't safe in Russia. It needed to be removed from the country and transformed into clean money, before trickling back. Globalisation and financial deregulation created exactly the right conditions for money laundering on an industrial scale. So, when tens of billions of dollars and roubles need to be laundered, a Russian problem becomes everybody's problem.'

'And people like the Sokolovas would invest in London property for example.'

'Yes. Igor has quite an empire in London, as you are probably aware. Bad for the UK but not illegal. Positively encouraged by the UK government, it seems.'

'Can we get to the point please?"

'Of course, sorry. Cryptocurrency. An almost perfect vehicle for laundering large quantities of dirty money. If you join crypto and art together via NFTs, you get the next big target for criminal gangs – the digital art market.'

Marissa spelt it out in some detail. To sum it up, cryptocurrency is largely unregulated and can be used as a straightforward in/out laundromat. A massive downside for all investors in crypto is the volatility. NFTs could prove to be a much safer bet in that they promise to be an investment where the only way is up. Like fine art or rare scotch whisky. The other big deal with NFTs is that they are difficult – but not impossible – for the authorities to seize in cases where sanctions are in force. Marissa continues.

'NFTs are new and it's only a theory at the moment. I understand that you and Vladimir are working together now. Early days of course.'

'How did you ...'

'We just know, Robert.'

It starts to dawn on him that he's being played. The relatively innocent joint venture with Vladimir could be the first step in a bid to provide his business with a useful new way of laundering their money, helping him curry favour with his dad. He would be the person providing a veneer of respectability. A dupe, basically.

'What can I do to help?'

'Play along with him and his family. The current market in NFTs is slow but we're expecting it to pick up within a year or two, with many more pieces of digital art coming to market. A second market will develop and there will be an upsurge in the desirability of unique works and an increase in the value of the more sought-after pieces. The more the Russians invest, the more they stand to lose when we move in and seize their assets. I would ask you to be patient because it takes time and effort to construct a case against these people.'

'Will I be in any danger?'

'I will not lie to you. If the market develops as expected, the Sokolovas will not be able to help themselves and will start to invest serious money. It would make your current investment fund look like chicken feed. That's when the danger starts to ramp up, although we will do everything in our power to protect you and those close to you. But no guarantees.'

He let the 'no guarantees' bit sink in.

'How do I keep you up to speed on all this without certain people finding out what we're up to?'

'I will set up a secure way for you to keep us informed.'

'Can I have time to think this through?'

'Sure. Sleep on it. How about we meet tomorrow and I can give you the grand tour of my home town. Oh, and Robert?'

'Yes.'

'Whether or not you agree to help us, please do not tell anybody about this. Not even your fiancée. Especially not her.'

*

For most of the next day, money laundering is pushed into the background while Marissa and Robert focus on enjoying themselves. In the morning they take the funicular railway to the rickety funfair at the top of Monte Igueldo and sample some of the underwhelming rides – just for the hell of it. They then enjoy a windswept walk along the coastal path, stopping often to admire the spectacular views across the bay. Back in town they take lunch at a tiny place called the Antonio Bar, where Marissa knows all the staff and the food is simple but delicious. After lunch, she suggests a walk on the headland of Monte Urgull. By now, the wind is asserting itself and the surfers have long since run for cover. They have the headland to themselves. It's exhilarating stuff – howling wind and crashing waves – but they're eventually persuaded by some concerned policemen to head back to town for their own safety. Marissa stays close to him as they walk back to the hotel, holding on tightly as they battle against the wind.

'Have you made up your mind about working with us?'

He'd spent a sleepless night and most of the day weighing up the odds. It hadn't been an easy decision but he deeply resented being played by the Russians.

'Yes. I'm in. It's time I did something vaguely useful for a change.'

'Thank you, Robert. Very much. I will make the necessary arrangements.'

There's an awkward moment as they briefly consider kissing. They shake hands instead and turn away.

'Robert?'

'Marissa?'

'Would you like to join me this evening? At my apartment? I can prepare food for us and we can discuss the details of our partnership.'

'Why not? I'll bring a bottle or two of that Reserva.'

'Save your money. I have plenty of wine.'

They drink and talk long into the night. In the morning she drives him to the airport in Bilbao. It's the least she can do.

Chapter 15

'Baba Yaga understood that there was no help and started to follow the children herself. In her great hurry she forgot to look for the towel and the comb, but jumped astride a broom and was off. The children heard her coming and threw the towel behind them. At once a river, wide and blue, appeared and watered the field. Baba Yaga hopped along the shore until she finally found a shallow place and crossed it.

Again the children heard her hurry after them and so they threw down the comb. This time a forest appeared, a dark and dusky forest in which the roots were interwoven, the branches matted together, and the tree-tops touching each other. The witch tried very hard to pass through, but in vain, and so, very, very angry, she returned home.

The orphans rushed to their father, told him all about their great distress, and thus concluded their pitiful story:

"Ah, father dear, why dost thou love us less than our brothers and sisters?"

The father was touched and became angry. He sent the wicked stepmother away and lived a new life with his good children. From that time he watched over their happiness and never neglected them anymore.

How do I know this story is true? Why, one was there who told me about it.'

Igor closed the well-worn story book and returned it to his daughter's bedside table. He sat close to her on the tiny bed.

'It is a stupid story. Baba Yaga had a broomstick so she could have flown over the water and the forest.'

'Clever girl. It is only an old story my darling – have no worries.'

He could still smell the shampoo and soap suds from the bath she had earlier.

'Would you read me another story, papa? One that is not so stupid?'

'No. It is school for you tomorrow. You need your beauty sleep, princess.'

His wife was preparing his supper in their cramped kitchen. His teenage son was helping her out. Everything was cramped in their apartment. Cramped and cold. How he yearned for a bigger, better place, even a small garden. One day.

He stroked his daughter's long fair hair, tucked her under the covers and kissed her tenderly. Varvara – the apple of her father's eye. He switched off the light but made no effort to leave. He always found it difficult to leave her alone.

*

All Russian citizens aspire to own a modest dacha or second home and plenty of them do. Wealthy Russians own large, impressive dachas, more than one in some cases. Some very wealthy Russians own a 'dacha' in or near Moscow. Igor's main dacha is in

Peredelkino, a former artist's colony – home to such worthies as Boris Pasternak – which is now an exclusive suburb of Moscow. It's only five kilometres from the centre of everything that's anything in the Russian Federation. If he'd been fit enough, the ailing oligarch would've been able to walk there in less than an hour. As he's grown richer, he's grown fat and increasingly sclerotic. The extent of his exercise these days is restricted to the occasional potter around his extensive gardens, Don Corleone style. For travel anywhere else, it's a chauffeur-driven limo, a Mercedes-Maybach S600 Pullman. Bulletproof, just in case.

Like many Russian men of his vintage – Igor's in his mid-sixties – he's a war veteran and has the scars to prove it. In his case, he drove a T62 tank into Afghanistan and, eight years later, drove it out after an inglorious campaign that achieved precisely nothing apart from over a million civilian deaths. Thousands of his comrades died there. His only souvenir from the conflict is a sprinkling of American shrapnel about his upper arm and shoulder, courtesy of the Mujahideen. If ten years of futile war in the 1980s had taught him anything, it was the need to seize any opportunity to make life better for him and his family. The collapse of the Soviet Union a few years later provided him with just such an opportunity and he never looked back.

He turned his good fortune into a successful business, but maintaining his position has exacted a heavy price. His efforts to keep a step or two ahead of the competition and protect his empire has transformed him into an unprincipled monster and, far from protecting and nurturing them, those closest to him have become collateral damage. Dysfunctional doesn't really do them justice. As we speak, he presides over a wife, Svetlana, who has left him and only communicates with him through advocates; a son who almost certainly hates him but doesn't dare admit it and a daughter who definitely hates him – with good reason – and wouldn't hesitate to destroy him given half a chance. Igor of course would deny he's been anything other than a loyal husband and father who has tried his best to provide for his family, receiving no thanks for it. There is nobody left in his inner circle prepared to disagree with him.

Every month, Igor hosts a board meeting at his dacha. The meeting has a standard agenda and lasts a couple of hours, followed by a leisurely lunch. The day plays out with a lazy afternoon in the basement health spa. In truth, the Sokolova family business is like an iceberg – about an eighth of its activity is above the waterline and legal and the remainder isn't. The morning board meeting with its agenda and reports and minutes and filings and taxation issues deals with the visible part of the business. The remaining seven-eighths of the business is dealt with during the afternoon. Maximum security. No electronic devices. Nothing written down.

The official meeting takes place around the table in Igor's vast kitchen. There's a thin covering of snow outside and it's well below zero but in here it's warm and snug. Strong coffee and pastries are on offer throughout, served by uniformed staff. In attendance are Managing Director Igor Sokolova, Finance Director Valery Medvedev, Security Director Apti Yamadayev, Special Projects Director Vladimir Sokolova and Company Secretary Yulia Yuzhny. The usual apologies for absence have been received from the Director without Portfolio Svetlana Sokolova. The meeting follows a standard agenda and is expertly shepherded by Igor, completing its business well within the allocated couple of hours. The main item had been to sign off the annual accounts and reappoint GAF as the independent auditor. GAF is one of Valery's arm's-length companies so there's no problem in waving it through. Yulia leaves before lunch, her services no longer required. The remaining board members repair to one of the sitting rooms for cigars while the staff prepare their food. After lunch, they file down to the spa area.

*

Four naked men are ensconced in the rather cramped sauna. It's not a pretty sight. Two fat, hairy men with post-lunch flatulence, Igor and Valery. One tall, hulking man, Vladimir. One small, wiry man, Apti. Valery needn't detain us and you know more than enough about Igor and Vladimir. Apti's an interesting character. He's a Chechen with a fearsome reputation gained during the Second Chechen War when he fought on the side of the Russians. He's the wrong side of forty but still looks like a teenager. He wears his hair long and sports one of those soft, straggly chin beards favoured by Chechen men. He's a quiet man who takes his security responsibilities seriously and is rewarded well for his efforts. Both protector and enforcer, he's on duty all the time and never seems to sleep. The two older men have known each other since their army days and are totally relaxed. Vladimir isn't part of this inner circle and never will be. He's only tolerated because he's family.

Despite the laughter and bonhomie within the group, there's a big problem looming for the large portion of the business below the waterline. Some big deals are coming to fruition soon and they'll be bringing in vast quantities of cash, roubles mainly. Most of it will need to be dispersed and cleaned. After all, there are only so many Mercs you can buy, houses you can own, religious icons you can acquire. They know the authorities in Europe are on full alert for any unexplained movements of money and are even waking up to cryptocurrencies. It's not getting any easier. As Apti ladles more water onto the coals, Vladimir spots an opportunity to contribute.

'I met up with Robert Smith recently. In England.'

The name is new to Apti and he's immediately suspicious. He stops ladling. He needs to know more.

'Who is this please?'

Igor steps in to explain.

'This is the man who my daughter has chosen to live with in England. He is an art collector like me. A wealthy man with a low profile.'

'Yes, papa, thank you. I met with him in London, and I can tell you he has grown tired of collecting conventional art and is looking to invest in the digital art market. This type of art is still small scale as it has not yet dealt with a fundamental problem. When a piece of digital art is created, there is nothing to prevent it being reproduced millions of times. The original therefore loses both its uniqueness and its value.'

'Go on.'

'I do not fully understand it, but the cryptocurrency people have found a way to certify the original version of each piece of digital art. They link a digital certificate to the original artwork and store it as an encrypted token on the blockchain.'

'You have lost me, son. Valery?'

'Sounds vaguely interesting. We have done some small-scale work with cryptocurrencies. They have the advantage for us of being unregulated but they are very unstable, making them unreliable as an investment. This sounds like something else. Same technology, same lack of regulation, more certainty regarding payback. Worth having a look, but where is the catch Vladimir?'

'I am not sure there is one. The encrypted token is called an NFT. It is unique, it has a value and it can be traded like any other artwork. As you said, playing the cryptocurrency exchanges can be a wild ride but in theory, the value of a desirable NFT will only increase over time.'

Now he has an audience. Even Apti is listening.

'If the market in NFTs is going where everybody expects it to go, there will be some very desirable pieces coming to market soon. It would provide a safe haven for some of our cash. Unregulated. What is there not to like?'

'OK, son. You must put a detailed proposal together. Make a case for us and if Valery likes it, we will try it.'

For the first time in a long time, Vladimir's received a fair hearing. Earlier, he'd taken a quick look at the exchange rate on his phone to see how his investment was doing. Going up again by the look of it.

[01/10/2018: 1 ETH = 178.30 GBP (Source AOEx)]

There are one or two more topics on Igor's unwritten agenda.

'Apti?'

'Yes, boss.'

'Could we have a word? In private.'

Vladimir and Valery take the hint and move next door to the steam room, leaving Igor and Apti to have their private word.

'First, we have a problem.'

This is how most of their conversations start. The great thing about Apti is that he makes problems go away. Permanently. This time it's a small-time operator in Georgia who's muscling in on part of their smuggling empire. Although Igor admires the entrepreneurial spirit of such people, he has to snuff it out before it becomes a bigger problem. The target doesn't just need to be taken out – he needs to be taken out in a very public way. Made an example of, in other words. It calls for Apti's special skill set and a name is all it requires to set the ball rolling.

'One more thing, my friend.'

'Yes, boss.'

'I'd like you to get back to England and see how my investment is shaping up. Make sure he is OK and getting everything that he requires. Run your ruler over anybody who might be getting too close to him. I am thinking seriously about bringing him back here after his finals. Get him started.'

'Yes, boss. And Vladimir?'

'Leave him to me. He is in the proverbial last chance saloon but let us see if he can redeem himself.'

'Yes, boss.'

*

On the short drive back to central Moscow, Vladimir thinks he has every right to feel pleased with himself. For the first time ever, one of his schemes has received a qualified nod from the board. He's arranged to visit his mama this evening and will call in there first to share some supper with her and see how she's coping with life. When he gets back to his apartment, his first priority will be to score a couple of lines. His next will be to call up a male prostitute. A young one preferably.

Chapter 16

After his first meeting with Marissa, Robert had received a couple of confidential briefings, both of which had stressed the need for absolute secrecy in any dealings he might have with her and Europol. He had to admit, he was getting quite a buzz from his involvement with the 'powers that be', tempered by a realisation he was placing himself and those close to him in potential danger. It's taken him no more than a couple of weeks to determine some precautionary measures of his own, starting with an upgrade on the security at Highfield. He's sought out some of the contractors he's worked with in the past on such things and has some preliminary plans and outline budgets in place. The project is at the start line, waiting for the nod.

First, he has to talk to Varvara about what he has in mind. The only drawback is that he won't be able to give her the full picture, especially the Europol aspects. There's also the staff to think about. He needs to keep Simon onside for the usual reasons but doesn't want him or Joanna hanging around the place while the work's being done. He needs to persuade them to move out for the duration of the work and to soften the blow he'll keep them on the payroll. He'll even pay for some temporary accommodation in the area and will leave the option open for them to return when the work is completed.

Every Friday, Robert and Varvara spend a quiet evening together, talk about what they've been doing during the week and share details of what they plan to do the following week. Joanna is given the night off and Varvara prepares the supper, which they eat off trays in the sunroom. It's washed down with some vintage sparkling wine, usually English. This particular evening they're enjoying smoked salmon salad paired with a Nyetimber Blanc de Blancs Brut 2014. After clearing their plates and recharging their glasses, Robert starts to fret about how he might broach the subject of the security upgrade. First up, there's some news. Revelatory news.

'I need to tell you something, Bobby. Something that I have been keeping by myself for a while. I am sorry for that.'

To his shame, he braces himself for news of a secret relationship. How could she do this to him?

'You know I have been visiting Oxford on a regular basis. I do have a jewellery supplier in the city, but I have also been visiting somebody who I have become very close to.'

Despite his feelings for her, he senses his hackles – whatever they are – quivering into life. Do hackles quiver? Never mind. She can sense the unease in him.

'Try not to be angered, please.'

He's trying desperately to be non-judgemental but is finding it difficult. He asks her to continue.

'Before I came to England with you, I knew of a boy who had been fathered by Igor. He had him adopted, maintained an interest and arranged for him to be schooled in England, like Vladimir. I tracked him down. His name is Piotr and I am sure he is my half-brother. I cannot be fully certain, but I think my father is grooming him to join the family business with a view to him taking it over one day. Not the best news for Vladimir although he is probably unaware of the threat.'

Given what had been happening to his hackles, Robert's mightily relieved at the news.

'Why didn't you tell me?'

'I did not think you would be pleased. With the deception, I mean to say.'

'On the contrary, I'm very pleased for you and him. I think it's wonderful news, my love. I'd like to meet him – soon as. How old is he?'

'He is seventeen. He is most of the way through a baccalaureate. When he passes his exams, as he surely must, I am concerned that Igor will want to take him back to Russia to complete his education. He may not want to go quietly but it will not save him. My father can be very persuasive.'

'Then he must come and stay with us as soon as he finishes his exams. I insist.'

'Oh, Bobby, that would be wonderful. We might have to bring in his girlfriend as well.'

'Are they, erm ...'

'Yes, they are.'

'Bring it on. We've plenty of rooms here.'

'There is another more serious aspect to this situation. It is not good news.'

They agreed to open another bottle. Robert obliged and topped up their flutes.

'Right. You were saying?'

She tells him about her last visit to Oxford. She'd met with Piotr and Emily and they'd spent a pleasant couple of hours wandering around the Ashmolean Museum, enjoying the treasures. After treating them to cream tea at the rooftop restaurant, she got them a fresh pot and left them holding hands and gazing into each other's eyes. In the museum's lobby on the way out, she'd spotted an unmistakeable and most unwelcome figure among the sea of visitors. Apti Yamadayev, Igor's enforcer. He was probably there at his boss's behest to keep a malign eye on Piotr. She'd quickly dodged behind one of the pillars to regain her composure. When she emerged, he'd disappeared. She'd checked in with Piotr later to ensure he was still safe and well. Not wanting to scare him unduly, she hadn't mentioned the encounter with Apti.

'He is an evil little bastard. I am certain he did not see me in the lobby but he may well have seen us in the restaurant.'

'In that case, my love, decision made. I suggest we move on to the next thing I'd like to talk about. It might help to set your mind at rest regarding our safety.'

The recent unwelcome appearance of Apti has provided him with an ideal opportunity to explain his proposals for security upgrades at Highfield. First, however, she has a proposal of her own to discuss.

'Are you still going to invest in the video art installation?'

'No, sadly. It's all proved to be rather difficult. I'd love to have one but I've decided not to invest for the time being.'

'What a shame. You had your heart set on it and I was looking forward to seeing it perform.'

'Yes, it's a shame. Everything's much easier to arrange if you're a big gallery with big sponsors. The Bill Viola studio was very good about it.'

She sips her wine and considers this for a moment.

'Does this mean there will be space available in the garage block?'

'I suppose it does. Yes. I'm not likely to add to our extensive collection of two cars any time soon. Two cars that hardly ever get garaged.'

'Very well. In that case, I would like to propose an extension to my workshop. I will pay for the alterations out of my own business account. I have had some plans drawn up.'

'You have? Well, I'm sure they'll be fine. Actually, I have some alterations in mind for the house, so we could add your workshop extension to the list.'

'Alterations to the house? What else could we possibly need? This house is a palace.'

'I want to talk more about security, my love. Our security. We need better protection, especially now with dodgy characters like Apti floating around. In England of all places. Don't they watch the airports these days?'

'Is it because of the valuable items in your art collection?'

'It's not about our possessions. They're well protected and there's plenty of insurance in place. It's about people. You and me. And now I know about him, Piotr. And his girlfriend, I suppose.'

'Emily.'

'Yes. We're all potential targets and I sense we're more vulnerable than we were. Take kidnapping for instance. Your father's no saint and Apti sounds like a dangerous character to me.'

'You're starting to frighten me, Bobby.'

'I only mentioned it as an example, that's all.'

'What has changed?'

'What do you mean?'

'What has fucking changed? I am not blind or stupid. You had people round last month, measuring things and taking notes. People I have not seen before.'

'Ah, them. Nothing to worry about. They were helping me look at a few ideas.'

'Tell me the truth. Stop beefing about the bush.'

'OK, OK. I'm doing some business with Vladimir. A joint investment. An informal arrangement. Nothing much to talk about.'

'You are an idiot sometimes, Bobby. I have told you how dangerous my family can be. I do everything I can to avoid them. Now you are getting in bed with my deranged, drug-damaged brother. Shame on you!'

'It seemed like a good idea at the time.'

After a bottle or two of fine champagne, anything would have seemed like a good idea to him. Even an exceptionally bad one.

'Can you get out of it?'

He was acutely aware of the arrangement with Marissa, which relied entirely on him and Vladimir continuing their business arrangement.

'I suppose I can. It was only a handshake, after all.'

'A handshake! I bet he backed away from having anything in writing. Am I correct?'

'He did. Yes. I'm not used to doing business like that. I'd had a few drinks, I must confess.'

'The whole handshake thing. It is the way it works when the business is "off the books". Deniable. It is still a deal. How much?'

'Half a million quid. Between us. To be spent on digital art, nothing else.'

'How could you be such an idiot! Expect trouble and plenty of it. Whatever you do, make sure it stays at half a million. I know exactly what they are capable of – even if you do not.'

'I knew you wouldn't be pleased when I told you. I'm sorry, my love.'

'Is there anything else you have not told me? While I am in the mood?'

'No. That's about it.'

'OK. I have had my say. I will now show you my plans if you show me yours. Deal?'

'Deal.'

Her plans are quite straightforward. They involve an increase in the workshop space, the addition of an extra workbench, a separate office and a small showroom. His alterations and improvements are more ambitious and anything but straightforward. They will take at least six months to complete.

'I am impressed. There will be a lot of noise and disruption. Will I be able to work through it?'

'For the most part. Your extension work should only take a couple of weeks to complete at a guess. Month tops.'

'What about your very own undynamic twosome?'

'Simon and Joanna will have to go. I don't want them around until the work has been completed. I'll ask them to leave.'

'This gets better and better.'

Now is not the time for him to reveal the duo might be coming back later. He thinks back a decade or so, when Simon was a union rep at his company. After a 'beer and sandwiches' staff meeting, he and Simon had carried on drinking and talking down the Giddy Aunt pub. At some stage during that ale-drenched session – and to his lasting regret – he must have let slip more than he intended about an incident during his teenage years in care. He couldn't recall exactly what he'd said about it but Simon left him in no doubt that he'd use it against him if he needed to, forcing him to keep him close – and on the payroll.

Varvara gives him a big kiss on the lips and risks a tentative incursion with her tongue. The barriers might just be starting to come down. Slowly and gently. The kissing stops eventually and she goes to her bedroom, leaving him with a stupid grin on his face. A grin that acknowledges he doesn't deserve her.

Within a week, an advance guard of builders are on site and working on the first phase of the project, which includes the extension to the jewellery workshop. After a couple of weeks, Simon and Joanna move out of Highfield and into local rented accommodation.

Chapter 17

After almost six months of carefully coordinated din and disruption, the building work at Highfield is nearing completion. During that time, Robert has been surviving on scraps from a digital art market that continues flattering to deceive. Varvara's working life is pretty much back to normal and she's continued attending the counselling sessions in London. She's making significant progress according to her psychiatrist. She visits Piotr in Oxford whenever she can and she's very much looking forward to him coming to stay at Highfield soon. When the shit hits the fan – as surely it must – she has an iron determination to protect Piotr from whatever's coming their way.

She has another appointment in London today. As usual, Robert drops her off at the railway station – Warwick Parkway. It's a no-frills commuter station that does a job, nothing more, although it's newer and bigger than most. Within five minutes, the intercity train to London Marylebone pulls in and she locates her booked seat in a sparsely populated first class carriage. The journey takes about two hours on a good day. It's then a short walk to Harley Street from the station.

When Robert had first suggested getting help, she'd been unconvinced to say the least but feared he might walk away if she didn't at least try something. They'd talked a lot about what was out there and had agreed on a course of psychosexual counselling. They found a clinic in Harley Street and she'd been attending sessions every two weeks for nearly a year.

In recent visits, she'd been reliving her wild time as a young teenager in Moscow and talking about her deteriorating relationship with her parents, especially her father. Despite once being close to her – too close by all accounts – Igor had become a cruel, unfeeling man who lavished everything on his daughter except love and kindness. Back in 2000, she'd spend whatever time she could with a bunch of semi-feral youngsters who were into the punk scene in Russia, such as it was. She was only fifteen and there were inevitable clashes with her horrified parents. They'd sought all sorts of increasingly desperate solutions, including Russian-style psychiatric 'assistance'. It was a downward spiral that ended badly for her one night. In previous sessions they'd stopped short of reliving that night but the time would come. Maybe today.

Her therapist, Leonid Fedorov, is an experienced and highly qualified psychiatrist who just happens to be Russian by birth. They've established a good rapport and they both feel she's made significant progress in her efforts to reclaim her sexuality. She's terrified at the prospect of what she must go through but accepts that it will have to be done. Leonid will make the decision for her. If not now, soon.

'Miss Sokolova?'

'Correct.'

'Doctor Fedorov will be with you shortly. Would you like some tea or coffee?'

'No thank you. A glass of chilled, sparkling water will be perfect. No ice. No fruit slices.'

'Right away. Take a seat.'

She doesn't have long to wait.

'Varvara. It's good to see you again. How are you?'

'I am well. Very well in point of fact.'

'Please. Come through.'

*

Leonid's consulting room could be described as a comfortable sitting room. Nothing scientific or clinical in look or feel. They sit opposite each other in armchairs, slightly offset to downplay any hint of confrontation. Everything is carefully calibrated to make the client feel completely at ease.

'You're looking much better today. Are you feeling better?'

'I am. Better all around.'

'What about sleep and sleep patterns?'

'I am sleeping more easily these days. Since my service in the military, I have learned to manage with five or six hours at night. As you know, I sleep alone.'

'The night terrors?'

'They still happen but on a lower frequency. I have learned to reach in and force myself awake when they get too bad. I find myself in the "dark room" from time to time.'

Leonid consults his notes, although he doesn't need to. The 'dark room' is a recurring theme not unrelated to her father's questionable behaviour when she was very young.

'How is Robert?'

'He is well, if a little bit stressed. The building work at home is very disruptive but it is now close to completion, thank God.'

'And how are you two getting along?'

'Good. We are still very much together in spite of everything. My feelings for him are as strong as ever and we are growing closer for sure. He has been very patient with me.'

'When you say "closer", what do you mean exactly?'

'Innocent stuff mainly. Kissing, cuddling, caressing, feeling our way. Kissing is getting better. It would be nice to explore further, but ...'

'I totally understand. We're making significant progress, believe me. We've had some difficult conversations in past consultations about your father's behaviour and what happened to you as a child. The last time I saw you, we continued our conversation about your teenage years in Moscow. If you will allow, let me describe you as the wild child of the punk scene in Moscow back then. Drink, drugs, sex, violence. You were only fifteen.'

'Yes, I know. Wild times but happy times. While they lasted.'

He glances down at his notes.

'You became extremely upset last time we met and I thought it best to finish the session early. We'd got as far as the big punk rock festival in Moscow in 2000. Could we start again from there?'

'Yes. Hmm, it has been in the front part of my mind lately. It was the Beat Bitva festival at the old Central Stadium where Moscow Dynamo used to play. Saturday, March 18th. Tarakany! were one of the bands performing there and we were all big fans. I had a teenage crush on their singer, Yuri Lenin. I do not think his name was real, do you?'

'It sounds very unlikely.'

'I went with my boyfriend, Dmitro. A Ukrainian boy, a little bit older than me. Very handsome.'

'You've mentioned Dmitro before. Remind me – were you in a

relationship with him?'

'Yes. I was no longer a virgin if that is what you mean. None of my friends were, it seemed. We tried our best to be careful.'

'Did you have the permission of your parents to go?'

'No. They locked me in my bedroom. I escaped out of the window and Dmitro whisked me away on his Tula. Very exciting but I knew I'd be punished.'

'Do you remember much about the event?'

'My memory is a bit, how to put it, fuzzy. We drank a lot, smoked a little, dropped a tablet or two. We were pretty tight. Tarakany! were great – I do remember that. They played all the favourites. Then it all kind of kicked off, as they say. Neo Nazis, skinheads. They were suddenly everywhere and there was a big fight. I lost Dmitro in the confusion. Many people were injured.'

'Did you get hurt?'

'A few bruises and scratches. I was too wasted to fight it seemed. Dmitro told me later that I was unconscious when he found me. He got to me before the riot police and I am forever grateful for that. He must have scooped me up and taken me home on his scooter. He left me in the porch by the front door.'

'Why did he do that? You could have died.'

'He knew what my father was capable of and did not want to stick around. No blame should attach itself to him.'

'What happened when they found you?'

They're inching their way into difficult territory. She's barely able to speak. Leonid gives her some water and waits patiently for her to rally. She's shaking visibly and some of the water spills. If she hadn't been a client, he'd have reached out to hold her hand.

'Take your time.'

'My, my father. He was holding a business meeting with some

important clients that night. My mother was staying away which was not unusual at that time. I think I had been sick and must have looked a real mess when they found me. It was probably embarrassing for him in front of his colleagues but it did not excuse what happened.'

She takes some deep breaths and wipes away the tears. She's still trembling.

'Do you feel able to continue? Take all the time you need.'

Leonid has to stay calm and measured for her sake. After all the hard work, he's sensing a breakthrough in what has been a difficult and harrowing case. She nods.

'I remember waking up in a dark room. No windows, pitch-black. I could not see a thing, as if I had a blindfold attached to me. I felt like shit. I had been stripped naked and was lying on a bed on my stomach. My arms and legs had been tightly secured to the four corners of the bedstead. I had been gagged. I was not going to escape this time.'

Leonid connects this memory with the 'dark room'. In his experience, all night terrors have some grounding in reality.

'It sounds like you were being punished.'

'Some punishment, do you not think? Lying there in the dark, hardly able to breathe? I thought I was going to die.'

Her anger's rising amid the tears. He's on the brink of calling a halt but believes they're approaching a big moment. It might be their only opportunity for a while and it's too important to miss. She takes a deep breath and soldiers on.

'My instinct to survive took me over. I struggled for a long time to try and loosen the bindings but they got tighter instead. It felt like my wrists and ankles had started bleeding. I must have lost my consciousness. When I came around, I sensed there was somebody in the room with me. I could hear him breathing, laboured breathing.

I could tell he was not a young man.'

She takes another gulp of water. It isn't easy but she's determined to see it through and finish the story. Confront the nightmare.

'Take your time, Varvara. You can stop whenever you like. There's no pressure.'

'Whoever it was, he climbed on top of me and started fucking me. He was a heavy man, a big man and it hurt so much, it felt like I was splitting apart. There was nothing I could do. When he came inside me and immediately pulled out, I felt revulsion but relief that it was over. It was not.'

Leonid was unable to help her now. Tears were streaming down her face. He offered her the box of tissues.

'The same thing happened again and again. Different men, same result. None of them were too fussy what they did and how they did it. None of them wore protection. All of them were drunk, a couple of them incapable. There was blood everywhere, I could feel it. So, this was my punishment.'

There's a brief silence while she wipes her eyes and face.

'Are you able to carry on?'

'Yes, I must. There is one last aspect of this.'

'Which is?'

'I am certain that one of the attackers was related to me.'

'Your brother?'

'No, he was away at school in England. I am sure it was my father, pissed out of his head and very angry, helping to teach me a lesson I would never forget. He really hated me it seemed for not loving him any more.'

Up until now Leonid had suspected there was something deeply traumatic in Varvara's past. He'd no idea quite how traumatic.

'Do you want to stop there?'

'No, not yet. If you can bear to listen some more, there is another chapter. After my "punishment", I was confined to the house, locked in my bedroom. There were bars on the window and I was held against my will, a prisoner. My father then had me committed to an institute for a while, where I spent most of the time sedated, barely conscious. They must have thought I had lost my mind. While I was there, they examined me and found out I was pregnant. Can you imagine that?'

'I cannot. Nowhere near it. Did they allow you to go to full term?'

'I was whisked away to the countryside. I thought they might try to make me get rid of it, destroy the evidence. Instead, I gave birth three months after my sixteenth birthday. They took my baby from me and gave it away. It was a boy, that is all I knew.'

'And then?'

'As soon as I felt well enough, I ran away. I spent a couple of years in the wilderness, moving around, ducking and diving. As soon as I was old enough, I joined the army. It saved my life.'

'Do you ever wonder what happened to the boy?'

'Every day. Ever since he was taken from me but not any more. I tracked him down and found him. In England.'

'My God! Does he know the truth about you and him?'

'No, not yet. It is complicated, do you not think? I know I am his mother – the science does not lie – and it is beyond doubt as well that my father is his father. Why else would he be taking such an interest in him, paying for his schooling and living expenses? Grooming him. How do I explain that to him? He is aware that Igor is his father as well as his benefactor. Up until now, I have only told him that I am his half-sister, which is the truth – but not the whole truth.'

Having made the long-awaited breakthrough, Leonid thinks it's unwise to continue. She looks utterly spent.

'I'm calling a halt now. You know that everything you have told me stays within this room between you and me. I hope it has helped you to talk to somebody about these terrible events.'

'It must have been hard to listen to what I have had to say today. Thank you from the base of my heart.'

'It's what I'm paid to do. I think we've achieved a huge breakthrough in the context of your treatment and I have every confidence that your future with Robert looks good. Let me tell you what I have in mind for the next stage of your rehabilitation.'

*

On the train home, Varvara seeks solace in a glass or two of champagne and reflects on the day. She feels completely drained but in a good way – as if sharing the trauma has lifted a great weight from her. At one point, her thoughts alight on Dmitro and what might have happened to him. When she last saw him, it was only to say goodbye as he was running for his life. She'd never seen him again but hoped against hope he'd found his way back to the Ukraine and relative safety – not that the Ukraine was particularly safe anymore.

When he picks her up at the station, Robert immediately senses a change in her. During the short drive home, she reaches lazily across and rests her hand on his thigh. It stays there until they arrive home. They remain in the car for a while like a couple on a first date. Feeling each other out.

Chapter 18

Robert has been dipping into his cryptocurrency wallet every other day, keeping an eye on the account. Not much has changed lately which is how he likes it. Today, however, he gets the shock of his life and has to double check the numbers.

[11/07/2019: 1 ETH = 230.01 GBP (Source AOEx): Fund value: £138 million]

He needs to talk to Link about this urgently and get a second opinion. It takes several attempts to get through but on the fourth attempt, the latest CryptoPunk avatar pops up on his phone and the familiar, metallic monotone kicks in.

'HOWDY ROBERT. IT'S A BIT LATE FOR YOU, ISN'T IT? WHAT CAN I DO YOU FOR?'

'Fasten your seatbelt, mate. It's quite a story. As you're aware, me and Vladimir have been pootling along with the 2,000 ETH or thereabouts in the account and we've built up a small portfolio of art NFTs. So far, so reasonable, although we've taken a few big hits from the usual exchange rate wobbles. When I took a look today, the balance was around 602,000 ETH, following two recent acquisitions of 300,000 ETH. The account now has the equivalent of £140 million in it or thereabouts. The acquisitions were paid for in roubles – lots of them. Vladimir isn't returning my calls but I have a good idea what he's up to and it's not pretty, believe me.'

Link didn't sound particularly fazed by this although it was difficult to tell with a voice stripped of all emotion. When they'd set up the account, he'd allowed full access to Link for support and maintenance purposes. As a respected ethical hacker, he trusted him implicitly.

'LET'S HAVE A LOOK. HOLD ON A TICK. DO YOU HAVE THE SAME CREDENTIALS?'

He does for the time being. While he's waiting, he polishes off the rest of his drink. He's hitting the single malt to calm his nerves.

'SHITE! OH WAIT. HOW MUCH DID YOU SAY?'

'Just over 600 thou.'

'LET ME SEE. AH, RIGHT.'

[11/07/2019: 1 ETH = 230.01 GBP (Source AOEx): Fund value: £207 million]

'THERE'S BEEN ANOTHER TRANSACTION. ANOTHER 300,000 ETH, BRINGING THE VALUE TO WELL OVER 200 MILLION GBP. I WON'T INCLUDE THE NFTS AS THEY DON'T MAKE MUCH DIFFERENCE. NOTHING FURTHER IN THE PIPELINE THAT I CAN SEE.'

'Shit almighty. Silly question but are there many high value NFTs coming up for auction any time soon?'

'Nothing that would soak up that amount of money. There might be one or two next year and I'm told Beeple's up to something big. The mega-ticket items right now are collectibles like CryptoKitties and dare I mention it, CryptoPunks. Not exactly your bag and no big bucks yet.'

'You know, I don't think he was listening to a word I said about the market. He seems to have convinced the family business to invest in cryptocurrency and NFTs big time but the NFT market's not ready for this scale of investment. Nowhere fucking near it.'

The biggest thing he regrets right now is cloning the wallet and giving it to Vladimir. What was he thinking? Was he thinking?

'Dare I ask how Ether's doing against the other currencies?'

'I've got the graph up. Hovering around 230 GBP. Quite stable, surprisingly. His crazy investment is safe for now it seems.'

'Although we both know it could tank in the blink of an eye.'

'We do. I don't want to worry you even more but some of my colleagues think Ether's well overvalued and may have peaked. Your Russian friend might be about to take a bath on his new investments.'

There's a brief silence while they both mull this over.

'What do you want to do?'

'Ideally, I can persuade him to back out the big bucks. If I don't succeed, I need to cut him off at the knees – stop him making any more ill-judged investments. Let me run something past you, see what you make of it.'

'Go ahead.'

'You know the conversations we've had in the past about the security around crypto accounts. Well, it might be time to make a few adjustments. What if we were to ...'

After much discussion and debate, they reach an understanding about what they're going to do. At one point, Link refers to it as 'stupidly stupid', given the type of people they're dealing with. They agree they won't pull the trigger until they hear from Vladimir and give him a chance to back out.

*

He eventually responds to Robert's calls and at least half a dozen increasingly fraught voicemail messages.

'Hey, Robert. All those crazy chase messages. What is the big deal all of a sudden?'

Vladimir didn't sound particularly focused, even for him. Nose candy, no doubt about it.

'Listen up. I've had a look at the investment account. What the fuck is going on? Have you gone mad? Half a million quid we agreed. Just to dip our toes in the NFT market while it gets ramped up.'

'My father asked me to write a proposal about investing some cash in NFTs. I may have bigged-up some of the aspects, smoothing the wheels you know? I did not expect very much but we have a lot of cash washing around the business right now and he went for it big time. I had no idea how much he had in mind until he told me. The rest, as they say, is history.'

'OK, let me spell this out for you. We have around £200 million worth of Ether in our crypto account. The gross value of the entire global market of NFTs is much less than that so we have enough tokens to buy every available NFT out there and still have change. We were only ever looking at a tiny slice of that. Have you gone crazy? This is so fucking big, the authorities will be all over it like a rash anytime now. Splitting it into three chunks won't fool anybody.'

'I am sorry. I did not realise what would happen. I cannot back out now. Papa thinks I am a fuckwit. This is my last chance to prove him wrong. Help me, please.'

Robert also thinks he's a fuckwit, as does Varvara. No wonder Igor has a backup plan in Piotr, waiting unwittingly in the wings.

'I'll try. Listen, all you need to do is admit you've made a mistake. You overestimated the NFT market – blame me if you like.'

He has the live feed from the currency exchange on his laptop and is getting the exchange rates in real time.

[12/07/2019: 1 ETH = 213.95 GBP (Source AOEx): Fund value: £193 million]

Ether has lost a few percentage points since yesterday and is trending downwards compared with the major currencies. Vladimir could cash in now and escape with most of the money, after commission. Knowing the vagaries of cryptocurrency though, he needed to act fast.

'Robert?'

'Yes, sorry, I was working it through. If you're quick, you can escape with nearly all the money you invested, although you've already lost a few million pounds worth. You should back out and take US dollars as they seem to be holding up better – as usual. Do you understand?'

'It will mean losing face. I do not want to lose face. I cannot.'

'Back the money out, Vladimir. We might be able to find a few million pounds worth of NFTs to buy now but that's all and they're not the NFTs I'm interested in. You need to act quickly because you could get shafted at any moment. You must understand that.'

'But ...'

'But nothing. Just fucking do it. Talk to your dad. You've got two days to cut your losses.'

He cuts the call. He's convinced Vladimir won't back out and wouldn't bet against him increasing the investment so as not to lose face. He needs to talk to Marissa as soon as possible and get a way forward agreed with her. After a difficult phone conversation, she persuades him to come and see her and talk face to face. Within half an hour, he's arranged his flights, booked a hotel in San Sebastian and sorted out a rental car. He feeds Varvara the usual story.

Chapter 19

When he gets to San Sebastian, Robert heads for the Hotel Maria Cristina. This time, he's taken one of the Garden Suites. It's been a while since he first met Marissa for what he assumed would be a conversation about his small but growing collection of digital art. Much has changed in the meantime, none of it for the better, and he fervently wishes he'd never got embroiled in the whole sorry mess. It's not so much about the art, it's more the buying and selling of it, which he's never properly got his head around. If he had, he's sure he wouldn't have ended up here.

He'd spoken to Marissa earlier in the day and during another long, windswept walk around the headland, updated her on the latest developments including the reckless and disproportionate interventions from Russia. He didn't tell her the amounts involved, referring to them instead as 'substantial'. The irrational behaviour came as no surprise to her as Europol has a bulging file on Vladimir. She assured him it strengthened their ability to disrupt the Sokolova empire and urged him to stay with the arrangement while they formulated their plan of attack.

He had a lot of time for Marissa and respected what she and her colleagues were trying to do, but he believed time was running out. He'd left her with the impression that he'd stick with it for 'a few more weeks' as she'd put it, although he'd no intention of doing so. Who knows what might happen in the next few weeks with so many loose cannons around? He's had enough. Correction, both he and Varvara have had enough. Always have a Plan B, somebody important once said. They have such a thing; it's ready to roll and it's high time they set it in motion.

Having made the big decision, he's able to relax a little bit. He treats himself to a mega supper in the hotel's Dry Bar, during which he works his way through a selection of his favourite pintxos, washed down with the best part of a bottle of 2010 Viña Bosconia Reserva. Tomorrow is lining up to be a new beginning for him and Varvara, the first day of the rest of their lives, a cause for celebration. Right now, however, he needs to find his way back to his suite and steel himself for a couple of important calls. During their earlier meeting, Marissa had provided him with the latest in a series of disposable phones, so he'll use that. Just in case.

Back in his suite, he comes face to face with a man he barely recognises. The man is staring out at him from the bathroom mirror. He looks tired and a bit ragged around the edges, which is hardly surprising given the strain he's been under. He splashes cold water on his face in an attempt to ward off the effects of the booze. He calls Varvara first.

'It's me.'

'Bobby. How is the trip working out? I did not recognise the number.'

'I'm using a phone that can't be traced. We have to be careful my love, what with your horrible father and your equally horrible brother breathing down our necks and upping the ante.'

'Breathing on our necks?'

'Never mind.'

'Are you OK? You do not sound great. Have you been drinking?'

'A couple of glasses of wine, that's all.'

'How did it go with Doctor Sanchez? Did she have any tempting deals for you this time?'

'Not this time. Nothing much worth going for.'

'I am doubtful she is such a great art dealer. You have never purchased anything from her to my knowing.'

His cover story for the meetings with Marissa is becoming increasingly threadbare, it seems.

'That's because she's an art consultant rather than a dealer. She's very knowledgeable and I value her input.'

There's an awkward silence which doesn't last as long as it ought to. She can't wait any longer to share her wonderful news with him.

'It was my final counselling session with Leonid today.'

'Oh, no. It seemed to be going so well. What happened?'

'But it is good news – great news in actual fact. We have laid to rest the trauma, confronted the symptoms and have overpowered the problem causing my condition. Leonid has given me a coping strategy and I am really happy with it. I am sure you and I can become lovers at last. If you still want to.

'I am truly speechless. Of course I want to – very much. It's fantastic news and I'm so happy for you. For us.'

'Oh, Bobby, I cannot wait for you to return. When you get back, I want to make up for all our lost time.'

It's the best news ever but they're unable to enjoy it properly or dwell on it for long. There are some pressing matters to deal with triggered by his recent meeting with Marissa. Matters of life and death, it would seem.

'Listen carefully, my love. You know the stuff we've been discussing over the past few weeks? It's time. As soon as I get home, we'll do it. Is everything prepared?'

'Everything is prepared and ready, as agreed. All the boxes are ticked. No issues.'

'Excellent. Anything else?'

'I got a call from my brother today. I have no clue about where he got my number from. It was upsetting. He seems agitated about the cryptocurrency and I have no idea why. I am very concerned.'

'Don't be. It'll be alright, you'll see.'

'OK. I will keep telling myself that.'

'Great. I fly back tomorrow. The plane gets in at twelve and I have a car sorted to bring me home.'

'I could meet you at the airport?'

'Better not. We need to treat it like any other day. I have another call to make now. See you tomorrow. And Varvara?'

'Bobby?'

'Whatever happens, I love you very, very much. Please remember that.'

*

The call has pressed too many wrong buttons for her, despite his attempts at reassurance. All the good karma about the success of her treatment had drained away by the end. What did he mean by 'whatever happens'? Why was her brother so interested in the art investments all of a sudden? How did he find her? Why did he call her? It wasn't so much the plan – the plan was good and the plan will work. They'd discussed it in detail and it would buy them as much time as they needed, whether that's weeks, months or years. There was something deeply worrying about his attitude during the call, as if he regarded their plan as the last desperate throw of the dice rather than a new beginning. There's also the usual suspicion that she's not getting the whole story from him.

She too has a call to make but she'll use a different phone for that. She needs to talk to Piotr right now while she still can. She gets through first time and they conduct the call in English.

'Piotr?'

He sounds drowsy to her. An early night?

'Hi there. It's a little bit late. How are you?'

'I am as well as you might be expecting. How are the examinations going?'

'I sat the last one today. Piece of piss, as they say.'

'Have you passed them, do you think?'

'Of course. Why would you expect anything else?'

He seems a little touchy. She guesses something isn't quite right.

'Is something wrong, dahling? You can tell me.'

She hears a long sigh.

'Emily's left me. She's fucked off back to Canada. Said her money had run out and she was not able to continue with the course. I pleaded with her to stay but "no can do". I am missing her very much.'

She gets the sinking feeling that Emily's been targeted and 'persuaded' to leave. Her relationship with Piotr would have been seen as an obstacle to getting him back to Russia. Igor seems about to act so she'll have to move even quicker now.

'I am sorry to hear that. Although I only met her once, I liked her a lot. What a terrible shame.'

'Yes. A shame.'

'As your examinations are finished, how about you come and join us right away for the holidays. Like we discussed, only starting earlier. To cheer you up. Robert is looking forward to meeting and greeting you.'

'Why the rush all of a sudden? I need at least a week to close down everything here and say goodbye to my friends.'

A hell of a lot could happen in a week. How much should she tell him? She couldn't help raising her voice.

'What are you meaning, why the rush? Do you not see? Igor is clearing the way for your return to Russia. I have already spotted one of his people in Oxford, a nasty little brick shithouse. He's keeping you under observation, believe me.'

'What? Why didn't you tell me? Fuck's sake.'

'I didn't want to scare you, dahling. Sorry.'

'You're scaring me now. Big time.'

'Igor will want you to attend university in Moscow, where he can keep his eye on you. It is only a matter of time, believe me. I know his workings.'

'You are sure about this?'

'Pack your things tonight. All of them. I will call for you tomorrow morning at nine and bring you back. You will be safe with us. Very safe.'

'OK, I will do this. See you at nine.'

Just like Varvara, Piotr could be decisive when he wanted to.

'Do not worry yourself too much. I will explain more on the drive home.'

She has one hell of a lot of explaining to do.

*

One call down, one to go. He grabs a couple of miniatures and a mixer from the minibar and splashes together a whisky and soda of sorts. He's ridiculously pleased about the prospect of him and Varvara getting it together at last and has no doubt they're about to embark on an exciting new chapter. Dare he mention children? Hold on, one step at a time – they should just enjoy being let off the leash at last. As for the plan. He takes a large gulp and reflects on what they're about to do. As he does so, a song he knows called 'How to Disappear Completely' pops into his head and stays there on repeat. What could possibly go wrong? Quite a lot as a matter of fact but it's too late to back out now.

He punches in another number and calls his wife. He won't share too much of the plan with her as the less people in the know, the better. He does, however, need to check a few things with her before tomorrow. She takes for ever to pick up.

'Yes? Who's this?'

'It's me.'

'Robert, darling, how lovely to hear from you. It's been ages.'

'It has indeed. You took a while to pick up.'

'I didn't recognise the number and thought it was a scam. I'm getting a lot of those again. Where are you?'

'San Sebastian – again. I'm getting a bit of business done with an art dealer who lives here.'

'Don't tell me. More of that digital shit?'

'Yes, I know, the same digital shit you wanted nothing to do with. What are you up to?'

'Hang on a minute. I'm going outside.'

He waits patiently. It takes quite a while. He guesses she's getting her vaping paraphernalia together. Vaping's a recent development, not unrelated he thinks to her recent brush with cancer.

'That's better. Where were we? Oh yes, I'm here with Viv on one of our road trips. We're staying down the road from you in Elciego. It's a gourmet and wine tasting holiday and it's the bee's bollocks, I can tell you. We're having a hoot. Pop down if you can.'

'Elciego. Sounds familiar for some reason.'

'It fackin well should sound familiar! We spent our honeymoon here! We're staying in the same hotel, the Marques de Riscal. There was lots of eating, drinking and shagging – don't you remember?'

'Oh, yes, of course, the shagging, lots of it. Listen, I need to talk to you about a few things. Before I do, I'm going to take a risk and enquire after your health. How's it going?'

'Very well as it happens, thanks for asking – eventually. Robust even, by my standards. I got the all-clear last week although you're never really "all-clear" are you? Remission, more like.'

'Great news. Good for you.'

'Is that it?'

'No, it's not. I'd like to share my recent experiences of cryptocurrencies and the digital art market with you.'

'What? You've got me out of a warm bed to talk about something for which I haven't the slightest interest? Fack it. If that's the best you can do, I'm going back to bed. It's cold out here.'

She stays on the call but doesn't sound particularly enthused by the prospect. He ploughs on, regardless.

'As you're probably aware, despite your loathing for such things, the market in digital art is just finding its feet. I've scraped together a small collection of genuine pieces and I'm pleased with them, got some of them on display in the house. A few months ago, Vladimir ...'

'Vladimir? You're joking aren't you. What were you thinking?'

'I don't think I was thinking. Not straight, anyway.'

'Sorry. Carry on. If you must.'

'He came on board and offered to double my rather tentative budget. He seemed genuinely interested in what I was doing. I was a bit naïve if I'm honest, as I'm pretty sure the intention was to use me.

'What do you mean?'

'Well, put it this way. Vladimir's managed to convince his family that NFTs are the way to go, providing a more reliable ROI than cryptocurrency speculation.'

'You've completely lost me. Sorry.'

'No need to apologise – I barely understand this stuff myself. An NFT is a way of certifying digital art as genuine, giving it both uniqueness and value, where the value is what people are prepared to pay for it. They use the same complex technology as cryptocurrencies. Varvara's family are into a lot of dodgy stuff from what I've learned and as a consequence, money laundering's a big part of their business model.

'What's ROI when it's at home?'

'Return on investment. An accounting term.'

'Not sure I'm any the wiser. Pray continue.'

'Vladimir's gone and loaded our joint investment account with a whole bunch of ill-gotten funds. Roubles.'

'How much are we talking about? A million? A couple of million?'

'A lot. Several million. Pounds.'

It wasn't a lie, although 'many, many, many millions' would have been more accurate.

'Fackin hell.'

'Quite. I've tried talking to him about it. I told him to back the money out while he still can. He's a weak man and he's terrified of letting his father down, so I doubt he'll ever do it. Mafia behaviour, basically. Something arcane about losing face.'

'Go on. If you feel you must.'

'The upshot is that some rather unsavoury characters are about to take a professional interest in the investment and they could call in their stake at any moment. Suffice to say, me and Varvara are not in a great place right now. Well, it'd be more accurate to say we're in real trouble, danger even. I've also done something that may yet prove to be the dumbest thing I've ever done. When those bastards find out about it there'll be hell to pay, believe me.'

'What the fack have you done, Robert?'

'It's best you don't know the detail. Put it this way, me and Varvara will be dropping out of the picture for a while and when we do, I'll need you to help me in ways that will soon become apparent.'

'I'm not liking any of this. You're not making any sense. You sound to me like you've had a few.'

'Fuck's sake, Pamela. Will you help me or not?'

It's the first time she can remember him swearing so it must be serious.

'Of course, although I'm nowhere near happy about it. How's The Girlfriend dealing with this?'

'I wish you'd stop calling her that. Coping. She's tough, I'll give her that.'

He couldn't help thinking she'd be coping a lot less if he'd told her the whole truth about Vladimir's crazy behaviour.

'Send her my love, darling. I mean that.'

'One more thing. If something untoward should happen ...'

'Hang on a minute ...'

'As I said, if something should happen to me, I'm relying on you to pick up the pieces. You're my wife, after all.'

Yes, she's his wife and is well aware of her responsibilities should anything happen. Alarm bells are now ringing loud and clear. He resumes.

'You still have the key?'

'Yes, I do and the letter of introduction, don't worry. I don't expect to be using them any time soon, whatever you say. I'll look forward to hearing from you when you're ready. But enough of this talk, it's depressing me. It's fackin freezing out here and I have a nice warm bed and a nice warm woman waiting for me. I'll talk to you some more tomorrow. Good night, sleep tight, don't ...'

Cut off in her prime. She pulls her gown closer around her and remains a while on the balcony, mulling over what she's just heard, trying to figure out how much trouble he's in. 'Plenty' sums it up pretty much. For her part, she's had nothing but contempt for his dalliance with the new-fangled digital art, knock-off stuff that has no artistic merit in her view. He's consistently ignored what he calls her 'old-fashioned negativity' and has blundered on regardless.

She takes a good long pull on her vape pen. Yes, vaping. She has a top of the range, silver-plated vape pen for normal use and a similar gold-plated one for Rosin, a delicious substance sourced and supplied by her new best friend at the local vape shop. For the next ten minutes it's just her, clouds of sweet-smelling steam and the darkness. When she starts to shiver, she calls time and tiptoes inside. She slips off her gown and snuggles back into bed. Despite her best efforts to keep quiet, Viv is wide awake.

'I wondered where you'd got to, lover. Who was it?'

'Robert.'

'What did he want?'

'He was offloading again. Sorry I woke you.'

'It's very late. Is he OK?'

'I'm not entirely sure. There's sod all I can do about it tonight.'

When Viv moves closer for a cuddle and starts to gently stroke the tiny hairs on her tummy, Pamela realises sleep is the last thing on her lover's mind. As Viv's hand moves lower towards familiar territory, she willingly surrenders herself to the experience. Right here in this moment, it feels so good to be alive.

*

Following the call with Pamela, he crushes the SIM underfoot, throws the debris in the bathroom bin and pockets the phone. He'll dispose of it later, probably in the river. It's now time to put the finishing touches to the scheme Link described as being 'stupidly stupid'.

When Vladimir bought in to his digital art fund, he'd set up a wallet for him, cloned from his own. The cloning process ensured that both wallets shared the same security, including the same twelve-word phrase for the recovery seed. Vladimir was able to use this wallet with the app to keep track of their cryptocurrency investments. He was also able to carry out his own transactions, including three consecutive cash purchases of vast quantities of Ether. Other than that, it's still only a handshake that underpins the arrangement.

Earlier in the day, he and Link had been on a FaceTime call. During the call, they'd set up a brand-new crypto wallet. He'd noticed in passing that the fund had taken a huge dip during the past week or so, losing about a fifth of its value. The fuckwit should have listened to him when he told him to back out.

[15/07/2019: 1 ETH = 179.01 GBP (Source AOEx): Fund value £161 million]

He was guided every step of the way by Link. It all went according to plan, although there was a slightly worrying twenty minutes while the blockchain churned through the necessary calculations. When he'd finished, the new crypto wallet was up and running, accessible via a new PIN. The old crypto wallet and, more importantly, Vladimir's clone had both been rendered useless. After some thorough testing, he'd thanked Link and arranged a substantial payment for his services. He binned the old wallet. The next time he wants to check how his investment's doing, Vladimir will find out he's unable to access what's left of the £200 million worth of cryptocurrency he's wasted the family money on. If Igor decides to spare his son – not necessarily a given – he's going to come looking for a way back in and he'll be both desperate and angry. As for Marissa, he doesn't think they'll be best buddies when she finds out what he's done. Too bad. He places the new wallet in the hotel safe and secures it.

When he set it up, the new wallet had generated a new recovery seed. The phrase this time is comprised of twenty-four words rather than twelve. He's made a careful handwritten note of the new phrase on a piece of hotel stationery. There's one more task to complete. It involves the new phrase, a simple mechanical punch, two titanium plates and a couple of sticky notes. When he finishes, he attaches an identical note to each plate. He puts one plate in a padded envelope addressed to Pamela and the other in an envelope addressed to Varvara. He drops off the two envelopes at concierge, asking them to sort out the deliveries and charge any expenses to his account. Finally, he puts the handwritten note through the hotel's office shredding machine – just in case.

It's just gone midnight. The room seems a long way away so he gently subsides on a nearby sofa in the hotel lobby. His body's tired but his mind's still racing. It's a clear, cool night out there and a walk round town might help him clear his head and unjangle his nerves. He knows his way around San Sebastian and is more than au fait with the centre of town. He leaves the hotel and takes a route he's walked before, heading out to the mouth of the Rio Urumea where it flows into the Golfe de Gascogne. He pauses for a while on the deserted Puente de Zurriola, grasping the rail tightly. He narrows his eyes and looks out to sea, searching for glimmers of light amid the blackness. There are none to be found. He reaches into his jacket and pulls out the phone. He pitches it into the river below.

He crosses the bridge and turns right, heading towards the train and bus stations. He walks back across the river on the ornate Puente de Maria Cristina. He strolls around the Area Romantica near the cathedral, lost in his thoughts. He sits alone on a bench for a while, enjoying the quiet stillness of the night. There are no tourists around at this hour. Across the square, a local is walking his dog. Somebody else who can't sleep.

He runs through the plan one more time, stress testing it, seeking out any remaining flaws. The plan is good to go. It could be described as audacious, brave even. Foolhardy? Whatever the merits of the plan, there was now no choice but to go through with it. He's effectively put a large part of the Sokolova millions beyond their reach and they're bound to come looking for him – and Varvara – when they find out what he's done. He doesn't think he's given Pamela enough of the story to put her in danger, convincing himself she won't be a target for the Russians.

It's grown cold – much too cold to remain where he is. He rises stiffly to his feet and makes his way back to the hotel, hands thrust deep in his pockets, warming himself up with the thought of Varvara waiting patiently for him in England. Strange as it seems, he's never seen her naked – in the flesh as it were – but he has a good imagination. Making up for lost time, he thought she'd said. He couldn't wait.

His walk takes him across the one major road in the town centre. As he steps off the kerb, his mind's elsewhere, struggling to deal with a feeling it'd never had to deal with before. Call it euphoria for want of a better word.

The car appears out of nowhere and hits him at speed, sending him flying through the air. It's a violent impact and Robert Smith is dead before he hits the ground.

The car doesn't stop.

Chapter 20

It's ten past seven in the morning. For the third time in as many minutes, Pamela's mobile starts to buzz and vibrate on the bedside table. Viv isn't best pleased with her. She can tell.

'Jesus, Pamela, answer the frigging phone. It's driving me nuts.'

She takes the call. The caller has one of those deep, rumbling voices that sounds like an old diesel engine on tickover. He's Spanish – why wouldn't he be? – but he speaks to her in passable English. He introduces himself as Inspector Leandro Morales, an officer with the Policia Municipal in San Sebastian.

'Am I speaking to Pamela Smith?'

She's a bit bleary and has to ponder for a second or two.

'Speaking. By the way, my name is – oh, it doesn't matter.'

'I am sorry to disturb you at this early time. We obtained this number from Mister Robert Smith's cell phone. It was listed as an emergency number, so I persisted with it. Can I ask please, what relationship do you have with Robert Smith?'

'I'm his wife. Has something happened to him?'

'He has been in an accident.'

'An accident? How is he?'

'He is dead.'

Silence. He immediately thinks he could have handled that better. It's too late now, so he carries on.

'I am very sorry.'

Ah, yes of course, she thought. I haven't woken up yet and I'm still in one of those multilayered dreams. What was the name of that film? *Inception*, that's it. She remembers liking it but needing to sit through it three times before she understood what was going on.

'Mrs Smith?'

She decides to stay with the dream until she wakes up.

'Dead? I was only speaking to him last night. Are you sure?'

'I am certain. He had his passport with him. There can be no mistake.'

'Oh, God help us. How?'

'It was a vehicle accident. He was hit while crossing the road, sometime between midnight and two a.m. The car did not stop at the scene, but we are looking for it – and the driver of course.'

Turns out it's not a dream and she's wide awake now. She has a bet with herself. He hadn't been paying attention or had looked the wrong way. Or both. It's not as if it hasn't happened before.

'What would you like me to do, Inspector?'

'Where are you at this time?'

'Elciego.'

'Perfect. Can you travel to San Sebastian today please? It is a formality but I will need to speak with you. I will also require you to identify the body.'

'Yes, I can do that. Is it, er, you know?'

'In one piece? More or less.'

She breathed a sigh of relief. It was going to be difficult enough for her without having to wade through Robert's bits and pieces.

'You will need to talk to people about the funeral arrangements. I can put you in touch with some funeral homes.'

'Thank you. Yes.'

She jots down a few details and arranges a time to meet Morales at the police station. She'll need to inform The Girlfriend about what's happened but can't face talking to her right now. It would be a difficult conversation for sure. She sends her a text instead, hoping that texting will help drain some of the emotion out of the news:

> I have some important news for you. It's about Robert. Will call you later. P

She'll have to cut short her holiday with Viv. It's a shame as she'd been enjoying their time together. Listening to this, you might regard Pamela as uncaring, callous even, but her relationship with Robert had always been a delicate balancing act. When he'd blurted out his undying love for Varvara, the whole thing had crashed and burned. From there, it was strictly business although they'd retained a friendship of sorts and had remained married somehow. Call it a marriage of convenience. It didn't seem to matter while he was still alive but now it looks like her life's about to change and not necessarily in a good way. Sensing her unease, Viv fixes her a strong coffee and they discuss the bad news. Viv always makes the coffee when they're away as Pamela has never got to grips with those machines that use capsules. She struggles to articulate what she thinks, eventually settling for 'What a fackin mess!'

They agree she should travel to San Sebastian as soon as possible, but not before they've enjoyed breakfast together. Viv's booked a session with the beautician this morning and she'll probably stick around for another night. She teases Pamela gently by saying one of the waitresses has caught her eye, so there's no need for her to rush back. She might not be serious but you're never quite sure with Viv.

*

Varvara is up and about early. She uses her own car to collect Piotr from Oxford, believing a Ford Focus might draw less attention than a big, fat Porsche. She drives around the block a couple of times before pulling up just down the road from a large nineteenth-century detached house in Jericho. Like all the big houses in this area, it's divided into a number of apartments and one of them is Piotr's, rent paid up front by Igor. She keeps the engine running. Her phone pings. It's a text from Pamela, saying she has news about Robert. There's no time to deal with it now as Piotr is walking briskly towards the car, carrying two bulging holdalls. As they'd agreed, he's wearing his school uniform. She's wearing a brown wig and has dressed down deliberately. Anyone observing them would assume she's somebody's mum and he's getting a lift to a school event – a football match or similar. He flings the holdalls in the back, closes the boot and gets in.

The Oxford traffic is behaving itself for once and they're soon on the M40 motorway, heading north. It's raining hard and she's very much focused on her driving. She's plenty of explaining to do this morning and is psyching herself up for an ordeal.

'I spoke to Robert last night. He is in Spain doing some business. Something to do with his art collection allegedly. He is travelling back this morning and will be with us this afternoon.'

'I'm looking forward to meeting him. Sounds like a nice guy.'

'He is a very nice guy and you will like him a lot. He was not answering his phone this morning so I left a message saying you would be staying with us for a short while from today. He will pick it up soon but I am sure he will not mind.'

The wipers are on maximum but are struggling to clear the water. The visibility is poor. It's as if somebody is playing a powerful hosepipe on the windscreen. Summer in England.

'We will call at the house first and wait for Robert to return. We then plan to move on.'

'Sounds exciting. What do you have in mind? An exotic holiday perhaps?'

'Sadly no. For a number of reasons, we all need to keep a much lower profile. Disappear for a while.'

'Is this because of me?'

'Not in its entirety, no. It is more to do with some investments that Robert has made with my brother. When I heard about them, I shouted at him for being an idiot but the amounts he mentioned were not really worth getting up in the sky about. He has not given me the whole story yet but he may be in some sort of trouble. Russian trouble. Danger, in other words.'

'What sort of danger?'

'The sort of danger that Igor excels in. Deadly danger.'

'I understand. We're going into hiding. Where are we going?'

'I will tell you later. Robert is like the British government – he takes our safety and security very seriously. The difference is that he means it and there is a detailed plan in place. When we stop at the service station, I will tell you some more.'

Unlike many stops on the British motorway network, Warwick Services is relatively new and clean and shiny. The toilets are also new but aren't particularly clean and shiny, especially the gents. When they get to the 'restaurant', she succeeds in steering Piotr away from the congealed fry-up ingredients. Instead, they play it healthy by ordering a breakfast of coffee, fruit juice and croissants. She remains alert, constantly looking around, half-expecting Apti to hove into view, AK-47 cocked and ready.

She remembers the text from Pamela and responds to it, asking for more details. This texting is getting on her nerves and she wonders why she doesn't just call, especially if it's important. They continue their journey and arrive at Highfield around eleven. Simon's dilapidated truck isn't there, which suits her just fine. The lazy bastard's probably down the pub, knocking on the door. She fixes them some coffee and biscuits and they take them through to the sunroom.

*

By around half-nine, Pamela's on her way to San Sebastian. She has an appointment with Inspector Morales at two, giving her time to squeeze in lunch at a place called Kata 4. When she arrives in town, she drops the car off and walks to the restaurant. She orders a beer and a selection of pintxos and tucks in. After a few mouthfuls, she checks her phone. There's a reply from The Girlfriend.

> Please tell me the
> news. What has
> happened? V

She doesn't need this right now but feels she can't ignore it.

> He's been involved
> in an accident. I will
> call you later. P

In many ways her late husband had been a meticulous man, infuriatingly so at times. Shortly after she'd married him, he provided her with the location of a safe deposit box, a key and a letter of introduction. He reminded her on several occasions that she was the sole beneficiary of his estate and the contents of the box would make everything a little easier. When he first mentioned this, she chided him for being so morbid. They were both in their early fifties and in good health as far as either of them was aware. What's more, she'd always been more than comfortably off and had no need of his money. He could give it all to charity for all she cared. Her flippancy seemed to upset him so she agreed to hang on to the key – to keep the peace as much as anything. As of today, she's a widow and with widowhood comes responsibilities. The safe deposit box would have to wait for the time being as it's located at a London bank. He's never mentioned a will but, knowing him, she's sure there'll be one somewhere.

The delicious food has detained her longer than expected and a hastily arranged taxi is required to get her across town to the police station. Inspector Morales is a dapper, good-looking man in his forties with impeccable manners. He ushers her into a slightly dishevelled interview room and offers her some coffee from the machine. He smiles sheepishly when she politely declines – she never drinks anything out of a machine, especially one that looks like it's never been cleaned. He waits an age while the dilapidated device gurgles, splutters and dribbles something vaguely hot and liquid into a chipped mug that is well overdue a wash. When they're both sorted and seated, he shuffles a couple of papers, gives the top one a cursory glance and starts the interview.

'I am truly sorry about your loss, Mrs Smith. Most unfortunate.'

'Thank you, Inspector. Please call me Pamela. I just need to clarify something. Although I'm married to Robert, we've been living separate lives for several years now. We never got divorced, that's all. We are – sorry, were – good friends.'

'Excellent, thank you for that. I will start by saying there has been a development in our investigation. We found a saloon car, abandoned and burned out, a few miles out of town. We have not been able to identify which type it is but we will. You must believe me, this is something that happens very rarely in this area so it could be connected to the accident in some way. It might be local hoodlums out for a joyride. The vehicle has been taken to the lab for forensic examination. We might get lucky.'

He didn't sound particularly hopeful. She had no idea why the police were so interested in his death.

'Didn't you say it was an accident?'

'I did, but we have to be sure. Can you think of any reason why he might have been a target?'

'Well, we did have a pretty fackin – sorry – weird talk on the phone last night. Said he might be involved in something way over his head. Thought he and The Girlfriend were in some kind of danger. He'd never spoken like this before.'

'Girlfriend?'

'Sorry, yes, The Girlfriend. I've always called her that. Do you understand the term "sour grapes"?'

He smiles and nods.

'Varvara, a beautiful young Russian woman. Robert fell for her big time. Half his age. I ask you. Blew our marriage out of the water. They got engaged and she moved to England but marriage never happened despite my generous offer to step aside. He lived with her in a big house near Birmingham in England. I've been in touch with her but haven't yet given her the really bad news.'

The inspector jots down a few notes and starts chewing the already-chewed-up end of his pencil stub.

'Does this, er, Varvara have a family name?'

'Hmm, yes. Sokolova, I think. Yes, Varvara Sokolova. She may have a middle name as well but I'm not party to that.'

He tries his very best to hide it, but there's a flicker of recognition when she mentions the name. He carries on writing and moves on to a second page. She thought she might try her luck.

'Do you know her, Inspector? Or know of her?'

'No, I do not think so. I will follow it up.'

She's not entirely comfortable with the response but decides to move on. They discuss the practicalities of Robert's funeral including when his body might be released for cremation. He gives her some contacts for the funeral arrangements, adding that she should ask whoever she appoints to register the death as soon as possible. He says he'll stay in touch with her and let her know if there are any new developments in the case. She decides to stick around in San Sebastian until the funeral and sets about booking a hotel for at least a week. She arranges this on her phone, settling for a room at the Hotel de Londres y de Inglaterra, a big old place on the seafront that she's used before. Sea views, of course. No point in slumming it.

She takes up Morales' kind offer of a lift to the mortuary. During the ride, he informs her that an autopsy will have to be performed as it's a legal necessity for violent deaths such as this. She'd been dreading having to do the identification but needn't have worried. As the attendant draws back the cover, Robert's face is revealed, seemingly asleep. There are a few cuts and bruises but no significant damage. She half expects him to wake up and smile at her – the lazy smile that would appear whenever they'd finished making love. She's not sure if it's allowed, but she leans over and kisses him on his cold forehead, adding a quick, whispered 'you daft bugger' as she does so.

'It's him.'

*

Piotr has worked his way steadily down the pack of biscuits. Since moving to England, he's discovered the joys of biscuit dunking. Varvara tops up their coffees. She hasn't touched the biscuits.

'It will be a while before Robert gets back. There is something I must tell you now, so prepare yourself. It is something important about you and me that I have kept back from you ever since I found it out.'

'I am intrigued. What's the big deal?'

'Very well. You know that I am your half-sister.'

'I do. That's a good thing, isn't it?'

'Yes, of course. But you are also my son, Piotr, and that's an even better thing for you and me.'

'You're saying you're my mother? That would mean Igor ...'

'Fathered you and me. He raped me when I was fifteen and you were the result. I thought I would never see you again and it took me sixteen years to find you.'

The look on Piotr's face would be difficult to describe and do it justice. He's temporarily lost for words.

'I know you are shocked – who would not be? Our family is cursed and I want to save you from them.'

'How do you ...'

'DNA. It cannot lie. Fully verified. I have all the papers. You are my son, whether you like it or not. I very much like it.'

'It's a lot for me to process. I'll need some time to understand what happened to you and why. Let me start by giving you a big hug.'

Mother and son embrace for what seems a long time. There are tears all round, plenty of them.

'Can I call you mama?'

'Oh, Piotr. You can call me whatever you like.'

'Does Robert know?'

'Not yet but I intend to tell him today. He should be back soon.'

'You must hate him very much. Igor, I mean.'

'Hate does not come close to what I feel about him. I know he is our father but he is a disgusting man. I would do anything to destroy him but he is very rich and powerful. I know I will have to be patient.'

There's another text on her phone, sent over an hour ago when it was on mute. It's another one from Pamela. It says that Robert has been involved in an accident but there are no details. Last time she checked, his plane had been on schedule and would have touched down about half an hour ago. The situation in Spain sounds serious and she needs to investigate right away. On her own.

'I have a couple of calls to make, dahling. Have a look around the house and I will come and find you later. Robert should be with us soon although there might be a delay.'

The latest text from Pamela has spooked her. First, she checks out the airport website. His flight landed on time and people are now collecting their baggage. He usually carries hand luggage for short trips and should be on his way home by now. She calls the airline and enquires about the passengers on the inbound flight from Bilbao. After being passed from pillar to post, she's told they're not allowed to tell her – data protection rules. What sort of accident? She immediately sends a text to Pamela, a rather panicky one. There's an immediate response.

*

When Morales drops Pamela at her hotel, he says he'll let her know when Robert's body is ready for collection. After checking in, she asks the concierge to deal with her bags and heads straight for the bar, where she orders a large Gin and It with three cherries. It's a weekday afternoon and the bar has only a light sprinkling of people – most of the guests are still at the beach. She chooses a table near a large window overlooking the street. When the drink arrives, she signs the chit, takes a sip – not bad – and sits back to take stock. A minute later, her phone pings. Her heart sinks as it's another text from The Girlfriend. She thinks it might be time to stop calling her that. Too disparaging given the circumstances. Petty, even. She reads the text.

> Robert has not arrived. Have checked with airport. Waste of time. Data protection. Tell me what has happened. Please. V

She decides it's time to bite the bullet.

> I am so, so sorry. Robert is no longer with us. Car accident in San Sebastian. Hit and run. Police are investigating. P

The response arrives quickly.

> This cannot be. I do not believe you. Must be somebody else. Tell me it is a mistake. V

She still can't bring herself to call her, convincing herself she doesn't know her well enough, persuading herself she's not ready or able to deal with the fallout. She taps out another text.

> I am in Spain now. definitely Robert. No mistake. Identified him myself. Today. Call you later, I

promise. P

*

Robert dead? Surely there must be a mistake? She texts again. There is no mistake. Pamela confirms she has formally identified the body. He was killed in a car accident. An accident? Her thoughts immediately turn to her family and whether they're involved in some way. It's shocking news for sure but if she allows it to overwhelm her now, she'll place herself and her son in even more danger. She bites back the tears, then takes a few moments to collect herself. There'll be time to grieve properly for him later and seek out some perspective on what's been snatched away from her. For Piotr's sake she needs to stay strong. She thinks hard about how best to deal with the situation and it doesn't take her long to decide. She will continue with the plan. Everything is in place for them to disappear completely and only reappear at a time of their choosing. She sends a final text to Pamela and sets off to find her son. Her beautiful son.

She finds him on his own in the billiards room, enjoying a game of pool on the smaller table. She tries very hard to stay calm but can't help herself. She bursts into tears. Piotr leaves the game and puts his arms around his mother. She recovers some of her composure and tells her son the terrible news. She pulls herself together long enough to brief him on the rest of the plan.

*

There's been a significant gap since the last text, during which Pamela has finished her drink and ordered another.

I am going away for
some time. Please
do not try to contact
me. V

She wasn't expecting this, especially with the funeral and everything. Surely, she's going to come to his funeral? On reflection however, her behaviour might make sense. She'd been engaged to him for a few years but hadn't married him. Robert's death might have an impact on her ability to stay in England. Leaving the country would not be a wise move in the circumstances and it would make perfect sense for her to keep a low profile.

Pamela sends another text – no response. She belatedly tries phoning her – no answer and no way of leaving a message. Wait a minute – what did Robert say about being in trouble and needing to 'drop out of the picture' for a while? Varvara had been part of that plan and may just have decided to go it alone.

It's been a fraught day and she suddenly feels very weary. She orders a room service supper and goes to bed early. She thinks about calling Viv but decides not to. Even now, she might be working on the waitress. She's a pretty little thing, so she doesn't blame her. Much. Despite her tiredness, she finds sleep difficult to come by. A restless night is the last thing she wants but it's exactly what she gets.

*

By nightfall, mother and son are safely installed in their new accommodation. It's a small, self-contained apartment comprising a kitchen/diner, living room, two ensuite bedrooms and plenty of storage space for provisions. There's a small workout area and Varvara has enough room in her bedroom for a mini-workbench and a subset of her jewellery-making equipment. The rest of the stock and equipment had recently been removed from her workshop and placed in secure storage. Both of them have laptops with access to a custom security app, allowing them to see everything that is going on around them via CCTV. They'll be able to venture out when they get more confident but it's probably best to stay put for now.

'It's been a long day, mama. An unhappy day. I'm so sorry about what has happened. Will you be OK?'

'I will have to be. Listen to me, dahling. Both of us will need to stay strong and alert to get through this. I have no idea what is going to happen next.'

'Understood. I'll go to bed now. Sweet dreams, mama. I love you.'

He plants a tender kiss on her brow.

'Good night, dahling. I love you too.'

Thrilled as she is about being with her son, she finally allows herself a little time and space to start grieving and contemplate a new version of the future without Robert. It doesn't take long for the grief to turn to anger and her thoughts alight on the circumstances of his death. Given her family's record, the odds would be in favour of a cold-blooded assassination. But why murder him? She's missing something important. Although It's getting late, she has to talk to Link. She's convinced the joint venture with Vladimir is somehow to blame for what's happened.

Chapter 21

'MISS SOKOLOVA. IT'S ALWAYS A PLEASURE TO HEAR FROM YOU. I'D BEEN EXPECTING A CALL TO BE HONEST WITH YOU, GIVEN WHAT'S BEEN GOING ON.'

'What do you mean by "going on"?'

'HOW MUCH DO YOU KNOW?'

'Not enough, that much is clear as daylight to me. But first I have some terrible news for you.'

'HOW TERRIBLE?'

'Very terrible. For me especially. Robert is dead. He was killed last night in Spain. A road accident.'

'OH, GOD. I AM SO SORRY FOR YOUR LOSS. ME AND HIM WERE TALKING ABOUT STUFF ONLY YESTERDAY.'

'What sort of stuff. Come on, Link, tell me. What the fuck is going on?'

'HE ASKED ME TO HELP HIM WITH A FEW THINGS. THINGS THAT WE BOTH AGREED WERE PRETTY STUPID GIVEN WHO WE WERE

DEALING WITH.'

'So, tell me. What was so stupid?'

'BASICALLY, HE WANTED TO CHANGE ALL OF THE SECURITY WE'D SET UP AROUND THE CRYPTO ACCOUNT BY CHANGING THE WALLET. PIN, SEEDS – THE WHOLE KIT AND CABOODLE. ALL THE STUFF HE'D SHARED WITH VLADIMIR WHEN HE CAME ON BOARD. HE HAD NO INTENTION OF SHARING ANY OF THESE CHANGES WITH YOUR BROTHER. HE WANTED TO LOCK HIM OUT PERMANENTLY.'

'Yes, but why is that so stupid? The amounts were not big bucks – less than half a million pounds when I spoke to him about it. I did chew at him for getting involved with Vladimir and warned him to keep it under control. He obviously did not hear me – or chose not to.'

'HE PROBABLY DID HEAR YOU. YOUR BROTHER HAD OTHER IDEAS HOWEVER, AND MADE SOME RIDICULOUS ROUBLE-BASED INVESTMENTS IN ETHER THROUGH THE FUND. SEEMS HE WANTED TO CLEAN UP A WHOLE WODGE OF YOUR FAMILY'S MONEY BY INVESTING IN NFTS. TROUBLE IS, HE'S JUMPING THE GUN. THE MARKET IN NFTS IS NOWHERE NEAR BIG ENOUGH. YET.'

'How much are we talking about?'

'AROUND 160 MILLION AS WE SPEAK. IT'S LOST A LOT OF VALUE RECENTLY. IT WAS ABOVE 200 MILLION AT ONE POINT.'

'Roubles?'

'GBP, I'M SORRY TO SAY. POUNDS.'

'What?'

'I KNOW.'

There's some dead air while she tries to process what she's just been told. She plays it back to him to make sure she's understood it.

'Let me get this straight. My father has trusted his crazy son with 200 million pounds worth of roubles, expecting it to be invested in digital art. It is currently sitting in their cryptocurrency account at the mercy of the market.'

'YES.'

'However, Robert's last act on earth was to put all of it beyond the reach of Vladimir by changing the wallet and the secure key for the account.'

'YES.'

'The next time he tries to log in, he will not be able to access any of it. Am I right?'

'YES.'

'Does anybody else have access to the account?'

'ONLY ME, NOT THAT I'M PARTICULARLY ECSTATIC ABOUT IT.'

'Good. I suggest we keep it that way for now. The trouble is, they will not believe the crypto account died when he was killed. They will take the double-cross personally and will come looking for the funds. When they do, it might not end well for anybody.'

They agree to keep in touch on a regular basis. Link's security arrangements are comprehensive and rock solid and Varvara's bolthole is equipped with the latest in encryption and shielding devices. Their communications are as safe as they possibly can be. Varvara doesn't know what to think or feel. She's certain now that Robert's death was a pure accident, a fatal moment of inattention. Wrong place, wrong time. Typical of the man she loved. If anybody's been behaving stupidly, it's her brother and its landed him in trouble – big trouble. Igor won't rest until he has his money back. If he doesn't get it back, he will face some big questions from his backers, all of whom are disinclined to take prisoners. Now, there's a thought.

The most important thing right now is that she and her son are in a place of safety. The more she thinks about how this might unfold, the more opportunities she sees to bring her family's empire crashing down. Revenge, pure and simple, although she will need to be patient and it won't be easy.

'Bring it on,' she says to no one in particular.

Chapter 22

After breakfast, Pamela wipes away the crumbs and clears a space on the table. She studies a scribbled list of people she needs to contact about the funeral. There are only a few names on it. She calls Viv first and tells her she won't be able to join her for the rest of the holiday. Her friend sounds less than disappointed – she may even have hooked up with the young waitress, who knows? The first number on the list is the funeral home. Morales had left her a message saying that the autopsy would take place tomorrow morning and the body would be released the same day if there were no problems. She's aware funerals in Spain are always arranged to a tight timetable and agrees a date with the funeral people. She'd briefly toyed with the idea of a repatriation and holding the funeral in England, but hadn't got very far before abandoning it. Too difficult. She takes the slightly easier option of arranging a cremation rather than a burial. He'd never expressed a preference and let's face it, he's way past caring now.

During the morning, she contacts a few acquaintances in

England who she thinks might be interested in travelling to pay their respects. By the end of the day, she has firm commitments from a handful of people. A poor showing overall but completely understandable. He'd never been much good at making and keeping friends and there are no surviving close relatives as far as she knows. She runs her finger down the list of definites:

- Desmond and his missus (can't remember her name);
- Simon Vickers plus his latest aberration (Joanne?);
- Monty Gallimore;
- Dave and Dave, a couple of his old work colleagues;
- Inspector Morales (as a courtesy);
- Herself.

She hasn't included Varvara, assuming she'll be unwilling to break cover even for the funeral. She's sent her an invitation, just in case she's misjudged her intentions. She doesn't invite Vladimir, no way.

When she gave Desmond the bad news, he'd got quite cut up about it. She likes him a lot and is looking forward to seeing him again. He's one of the nice guys, a real character, and they'd enjoyed plenty of entertaining chats over a shared spliff or two in the past. His wife – she still can't remember her name – is likeable but a bit of a luvvy. His kids are delightful if you like that sort of thing although she hopes they don't come to the funeral.

Simon has worked for Robert for as long as she's known him and she's never worked out why. Although he's been trusted to run the house, she's always found him rude, crude and obnoxious and has gone out of her way to avoid him. He'd lived in the staff annex at Highfield with his put-upon wife until she'd seen sense and walked out on him about a year ago. He's recently shacked up with a grim-looking woman, Joanna, who does the cooking and runs her own cleaning company. Pamela has invited both of them but fervently hopes neither of them turn up.

After selling his business, Robert had cut most of his ties with work. A couple of his ex-colleagues had stayed in touch and both were called Dave – Danks and Challoner. She'd extracted a 'yes' from both of them. That was about it. A pathetic turnout. She'd thought of recruiting some of her friends to boost the numbers but realised it would be grossly unfair to impose on them. She'd even considered Viv who at least had the advantage of being in the vicinity. Nah, she'll be on a plane back to the States by the time the funeral takes place.

Monty's agreed to attend. He admitted he was taken aback when he heard the news, although wasn't entirely surprised. He said he'd found him a wee bit troubled the last time they met for a drink (or three). He's more than willing to come over to Spain and also deliver the eulogy. Pamela said she'd send him a few notes on what she knows about Robert so he can work them into his speech. She thought it would be good to see the old rascal again as it'd been a while.

That evening, she starts piecing together highlights from his life story for Monty's speech. It's not easy, as he'd always been reluctant to open up about his past, especially his early years. What little he'd told her was almost certainly heavily redacted. Scraps really, like a preliminary sketch for a portrait – enough to get the gist of the man, nothing more. She puts together an email, feeding Monty a few morsels. He's a born raconteur and she's sure he'll find a way to join the dots.

Hi Monty,

I said I'd write with a few details about Robert's backstory. As far as I know, my husband was born the same year as me, 1960. His early years were troubled to say the least. Abusive parents, loving but short-lived grandparents, a few years in the care of the local authority.

Cast adrift by the care system at sixteen, he was left to fend for himself. Had to find work, did so, studied hard and gained a Computer Science degree, a masters. Set up his own business and developed it into a large multinational. Sold the business when he got bored.

Met me, married me. Traded me in for a younger, more exotic model, not that I'm bitter. Did charity work. Became an art collector - you know all about that. Ignored my advice and got into digital art and cryptocurrency. Got mixed up with some Russians. Killed in a car accident, aged fifty-eight.

She scans through the email and lingers a while on the last two sentences, turning them over in her mind. Cause and effect? Surely not.

Chapter 23

Robert's funeral. The service is being held at a local funeral home, the one recommended by Inspector Morales. It's an eleven o'clock start for the short service, followed by a simple cremation. It's Spain, so there'll be none of the smoke and mirrors you get with British cremations, with all that theatre and music and slowly closing curtains. After the service, his body will be whisked away and incinerated unceremoniously.

Her late husband had never showed any enthusiasm for religion and its trappings, so she's hired a celebrant, Mandy de'Ath, to organise and run a humanist service for the mourners. Pamela gets there early and finds time for a brief chat with Mandy, who turns out to be a charming English ex-pat, sixtyish or a bit older. She steps through the order of service and assures her she shouldn't worry about anything. The obvious question about her unfortunate surname remains unasked.

Monty, who has already raided the hotel minibar by the smell of him, is hastily scribbling unreadable comments on his barely legible speech notes. She leaves him to it as she needs to meet and greet some early arrivals, Simon and Joanna, worse luck. As she welcomes them, they lose no time in badgering her about what might happen to them and their jobs now Robert's gone. The line of questioning and the timing is hopelessly inappropriate but she agrees – reluctantly – to give them an update after the ceremony. Despite not having met them before, she exchanges a few words with Dave and Dave, thanking them both for making the effort. She welcomes Desmond and Lizzie – well remembered – who tell her they've 'dropped everything' to pay their respects and that it's 'the least they could do'. Their kids have been farmed out to Lizzie's parents. Desmond's a bit of a mess and seems to be welling up already.

She'd invited Morales to the funeral as a courtesy. He's not turned up and she can only assume Robert's death is still being treated as accidental. She's quite relieved.

A few minutes before the start, a smartly-dressed, attractive woman with a long mane of jet-black hair makes a late entrance and takes a seat near the back. Pamela hasn't seen her before. Across the aisle from her, a tall, Slavic-looking man and a rather dubious-looking 'plus one' take their seats. She recognises Vladimir, but doesn't recognise his friend. She hadn't invited either of them to the funeral yet here they are. He introduces his latest 'girlfriend' as Lola, who is easily the ugliest woman she's seen since his last one. If she is a woman. Even if she's a man, he's pretty scary. At least they're both dressed in black, although most of it appears to be leather. Festooned with tattoos and piercings, the pair of them lend a vaguely unsavoury air to proceedings and she makes no further effort to engage with them. She doesn't have time to seek out the mystery woman at the back of the room as Mandy's signalling that she's about to begin.

'Ladies and gentlemen, welcome. Please join with me as we celebrate the life of our good friend, Robert Smith.'

Pamela finds it hard to engage with the ceremonials. Everything about them seems half-cocked, contrived even. Robert had always tried to avoid talking about death and last wishes and funerals and had left her with no clues as to what he might have wanted to commemorate his life. Mandy's skills as a celebrant paper over the cracks to some extent but it's a poor showing overall. Monty's eulogy proves to be both rambling and irreverent, striking all the wrong notes and veering dangerously close to a best man's speech. At least it's short. A piece of solemn organ music plays the coffin out, although the recorded music switches off too early, leaving just the squeaking of the trolley wheels. A deeply unsatisfactory send-off it seems, despite Mandy's best efforts. They don't stand on ceremony in Spain, so the body is on its way to the crematorium within minutes. She's arranged to pick up the ashes later, although she has no idea what she's going to do with them. Scatter them? Where? Never mind, she'll think of something vaguely appropriate.

She's pre-booked some taxis to ferry the guests across town to her hotel, where she's hired a private function room and some catering for the wake. She sticks her neck out and asks Vladimir and Lola if they'd like to join the party but they decline. He tells her he'll be in touch very soon, 'regarding a few outstanding matters of business', as he puts it in his impeccable public-school English. At close quarters, Lola looks every bit as grim as she looked from a distance. Let's leave it at that, shall we?

*

As luck would have it, Pamela shares a taxi with the mystery woman, who tells her she's one of Robert's business acquaintances. She lives in San Sebastian and describes herself as an art consultant who's been working with him on some recent projects. Her name is Marissa Sanchez. Pamela is quite taken with Marissa and is delighted she's agreed to join them at the wake.

Throughout her life, Pamela has tried her level best to dodge occasions such as this – funerals, memorial services, wakes etc. The hotel has laid on an excellent spread for them but the attendance is sparse and hardly anybody has anything in common. The atmosphere is dire, even for a funeral. Through no fault of her own, she's been hit upon by one of the 'Daves', behaviour she finds deeply offensive. What's more, this particular Dave has bad teeth, halitosis and dandruff and must be pushing seventy, so he isn't even a great catch. She's suitably rude, disparaging and dismissive towards him and he eventually gets the message and leaves the event, presumably to hit the town bars. His friend, Dave, joins him.

Simon and Joanna continue to work their way through copious amounts of free booze and food. At some point, Pamela and Simon meet up during a ciggy break in the smoking area outside. As he prepares a rather sorry-looking rollup, he regards her vape pen with the lip-curling contempt he thinks it deserves. Having lit up, he ploughs straight in, brazenly seeking assurances regarding his future, which, with Robert gone, has become much less secure.

'So, Pamela, what happens now? I didn't see this coming, no way.'

'You and me both. I'm still on the back foot, I'm afraid. Haven't had time to think things through yet.'

'I saw Vlad at the funeral. What the fuck's he brought with him this time? It's worse than the last one.'

She makes a mental note to tread carefully. Simon and Vladimir seem to have a lot to talk about all of a sudden, judging by a long and animated conversation they engaged in after the funeral.

'I don't know what to say about Lola. Whatever I say, someone, somewhere will disapprove I don't doubt.'

Pamela had been called out on more than one occasion for being outspoken on such matters. Simon continues to make his case.

'Are you going to put the house on the market?'

'Oh, probably. The last thing I want is another house. Especially something fackin horrible like his place.'

'It's unique, I'll give you that. So unique that it might take a while to sell don't you think? How about me and Jo sticking around and keeping the place shipshape. While you find a buyer, you know. Help you get the best price.'

'Thanks, Simon. I'll give your kind offer my full and careful consideration and get back to you.'

He regards her with some suspicion as well he might. Her preference would be to put both of them on notice. Never mind, she has another question, a pressing one in the circumstances.

'Have either of you seen Varvara since Robert died?'

'Yes, just the once. She made a brief appearance at Highfield on the day we found out about his death. Since then, nothing. She seems to have disappeared. Completely.'

'Any idea where she might have gone to?'

'Not really. Her car's gone as well, although the big car's there, gathering dust. Me and her never did talk much. I don't think she likes me. Us.'

Bully for her, she thinks.

'Anything else?'

'Well, over the years, she's hardly ever left the house and grounds. Spends most of her time in her workshop doing the jewellery. On the day we heard Robert had died she'd gone out very early. According to the CCTV, she returned before lunchtime but didn't stay long. I haven't seen her or her car since. My reckoning is that with her bloke gone, it might become more difficult for her to remain in England. She might be heading for home as we speak. Could be out of the country by now.'

He could have added that she'd had a passenger in the car with her when she returned, although the CCTV footage from the gate wasn't clear enough to identify who it was. He's saving that little nugget for another time.

Simon and Joanna leave soon afterwards as they have a plane to catch. Pamela always had the feeling that Robert's loyalty to Simon was ill-advised – she doesn't trust him, or the dislikeable Joanna for that matter. She'd been one of the cleaning team in the early days but is now running her own cleaning and events company. She's also recently moved in with Simon in the staff annex – with Robert's blessing it seems. Rent free no doubt. Something didn't smell right about it. Despite her misgivings it might be wise to hang on to them to keep the house and grounds clean and tidy and deal with any visitors, at least until the house is sold.

She looks across at Monty, who looks significantly wasted, even by his standards. She persuades him to go back to his room and have a lie down. Desmond and Lizzie head for the exit, promising to keep in touch. Only Marissa remains and seems eager to talk to her. Pamela finds her exceptionally attractive but needs to find out more before exploring the possibilities. As an example, she hadn't been invited to the funeral so what is she doing here? As the wake seems to have dribbled to an end, she asks Marissa if she'd like to join her for a drink in the bar. She didn't think she'd accept but was absolutely thrilled when she did.

Chapter 24

The two women settle into their seats. A Gin and It and a large glass of Rioja arrive. The complimentary bowl of nuts and nibbles is positioned between them.

'So, you and Robert. Were you and him, you know, an item?'

Marissa takes Pamela's rather impertinent question in her stride.

'He was without doubt a handsome man but no, sadly. Strictly business. From the way he spoke about Varvara, I could tell he was very much in love and would not dream of doing anything to ruin that. He showed me pictures of her, so you cannot blame him. Sorry.'

'That's OK. We were married, but I'm not convinced we were ever in love. He was a difficult man to love and we were never that close. His laid-back ways and lack of engagement drove me to distraction and there were times I couldn't work out whether to hug him or throttle him. Our relationship was fun while it lasted but it died a death after he told me about The Girlfriend.'

'You mean Varvara?'

'The very same. I must stop calling her "The Girlfriend". It doesn't seem fair anymore.'

They return to their drinks, each of them waiting for the other to continue. Pamela tries her best not to stare too hard at Marissa but it's a difficult ask. She needs to say something to break the spell.

'Let me guess. You're the woman he consulted about digital art.'

'Yes. Did he mention me?'

'Only in passing. He and I didn't see eye to eye on the digital stuff. You mentioned you live in San Sebastian?'

'Yes, I have a small apartment not far from here. A couple of streets away on Casa san Bartolome.'

'It's such a beautiful town. I envy you a lot, living here.'

'I was born here. When I married, I moved to Majorca with my husband. When I became a widow back in 2009, I moved back.'

'You're a widow?'

'Yes. My husband was killed by a car bomb planted by ETA. He was a policeman, so he was targeted. One of their last victims.'

'I'm very sorry. Did you have any children?'

'We tried, but no.'

Pamela reaches across the table and holds onto her hand. She's noticed a profound sadness within Marissa, hidden from sight but close to the surface. They sit in silence for a short while until Pamela can't help herself.

'So, digital art. A travesty. I hate it with a vengeance, I don't mind saying, and I dislike all the technical and financial shit that's grown up around it. Sorry, I know it's your bag, but really? Fack's sake.'

'Cards on the table, Pamela. I am not an expert on digital art. I am not an expert on any art for that matter.'

'You're not?'

'No. It was a play I used to get closer to Robert and find out more about what he was doing.'

'So, what do you do? Sounds a tad cloak and dagger to me. Are you allowed to tell me?'

'Not really but I will, some of it anyway. I actually work for Europol. I am a policewoman on secondment as an agent. I specialise in financial crime, money laundering, that sort of thing. If I tell you too much more, I might get into trouble.'

'Tell me what you can. I need to make sense of what happened to him. Please, it's important. I'm on the hook to sort his estate out.'

'OK, I will try. When he got into digital art, he stumbled into something that took him into perilous and unpredictable territory, especially when the Russians moved in. It brought him into our orbit and I was tasked with getting close to him with a view to recruiting him. When I told him what was going on and implied that he was being set up, he agreed to help us. He was assisting us in building a case against some very dangerous criminals who were looking for new ways to hide large quantities of money.'

'Oh, God. Robert, you idiot!'

'Please. Do not be too hard on him. He was a great help to us but seemed to lose his nerve, just as we were getting close to a result. We were building a complicated case, a sting if you like and it took time to set up. When I last saw him, I got the feeling he was about to, as you say, jump ship.'

'Did he intend to do anything illegal?'

'Nothing that we know of. It seems he was involved with some very bad men doing some very bad things. Would you be willing to carry on where he left off and help me build a case?'

Pamela catches the waiter's attention and orders some more drinks. When they arrive, she tells Marissa she needs to think long and hard about helping her. Whether she helps or not, she's keen to see her again for purely selfish reasons. At the end of the evening, they're both rather tired and ever-so-slightly sloshed. They exchange contact details and part with a rather clumsy hug and kiss.

Pamela emerges from her pit the next morning feeling very much under par. After forcing down some breakfast, she finds a quiet perch in the lobby and runs through the things she needs to do. The first priority is to pick up Robert's ashes. After that, she'll call on Morales and check whether he's got any further with the investigation. When she returns to England, she'll start dealing with the estate. It would be logical to kick this off by putting the ridiculous mansion on the market and get that eyesore out of the way asap. She calls up an old friend at Country Life who gives her the number of a suitably well-heeled estate agent in the West Midlands. She's spending one more night in San Sebastian and calls Marissa to see if she's around and up for a night out.

She is.

*

After enjoying some food and wine together, they meander around the town for an hour or two, getting to know each other. They'd previously agreed there'd be no shop talk. Later, Marissa asks Pamela to walk home with her. They come to a halt in front of an unassuming apartment block just around the corner from the hotel. They kiss briefly and it feels right. It feels good, exceptional even. They go up to the apartment, pour some wine and continue where they left off. Slowly, gently. Pamela is aware Marissa's taking her first steps sexually with a woman and doesn't want to ruin her chances by overdoing it. Since her recent brush with mortality, she's been re-evaluating her rather freewheeling – bordering on cold-hearted – approach to relationships and friendships. This new friendship with Marissa feels different to the others, much more serious, longer term even. Before heading back to her hotel, Pamela agrees to help as best she can with the ongoing Europol investigation. It's the least she can do in the circumstances.

Chapter 25

In the morning, Pamela collects Robert's ashes from the funeral home and puts the rather inadequate container in a carrier bag. She calls into the police station to see if there have been any developments. She asks after Morales and finds him at his desk, working his way through a mountain of papers. He seems pleased to see her and her arrival gives him an opportunity to escape from the paperwork for a few minutes. They enjoy a smoke/vape and a chat outside. He says he's sorry for missing the funeral, citing pressure of work. Unfortunately, there's no further news regarding the investigation. Before she leaves, he gives her a small evidence bag holding the items Robert was carrying when he was killed. He then gives her a holdall containing his belongings, including the contents of his room safe. She's halfway down the road when she realises she's forgotten the carrier bag holding the ashes. Having doubled back and retrieved them, she accepts the inspector's offer of a lift across town in a squad car. She has some time to kill before travelling to the airport, so returns to her room. She has rather a lot of extra luggage to deal with.

Being unsure about the required protocol for carrying such things on aircraft, she settles for wrapping the flimsy ashes container in bubble wrap and bringing him home in her suitcase, hoping it's not searched at the airport. She empties the evidence bag onto the bed. The contents are mostly unremarkable – his passport, wallet, a broken watch stuck on the time of his death. The wedding ring she'd given him in happier times – why did he keep that? Some house keys. As she examines each piece, her emotions get the better of her and she ends up in a bit of a mess, shaking and weeping silently.

'C'mon Pamela, get a grip woman.'

She puts the belongings back in the bag and goes to the bathroom to fix her face. She then turns her attention to his holdall.

It contains some crumpled clothes, a spare pair of shoes, some clean underwear, a toilet bag and very little else. Robert travelled light, no question about that. There's a sealed plastic bag in there – presumably the contents of his hotel safe – containing three items. An iPad, a USB cable and a small electronic gizmo. The latter is smaller than a smartphone. It has a tiny screen and a couple of buttons and it's obvious even to a techno duffer like Pamela that it plugs into a computer and enables something. What? No time to dwell on it – her airport taxi arrives in ten minutes so she'll have to get cracking. Her suitcase is packed and ready. She crams the clothes back into the holdall and squeezes the iPad into her flight bag, noticing that Robert, the great security maestro, has written the password on a small sticky note stuck to the bottom of it. She pops the gizmo in her handbag, checks the room and heads for the lifts.

*

Back at her studio, she unpacks the suitcase. There's a thin deposit of grey powder in the bottom. Without thinking, she grabs a handheld vacuum and cleans it up. When she realises what she's done, she's horrified. Never mind, there's plenty of Robert left in the container although how much of it is actually him is anybody's guess. To assuage any residual feelings of guilt, she'd used her time on the flight to sketch out a design for a smart, modern funerary urn for his remains. Next time she speaks to Grayson, she'll ask if he'll be kind enough to make it for her as he owes her a favour or two. She adds Robert's clothes to the pile of washing in the kitchen as she wants them clean before donating them to the Sally Army. For now, she stows the iPad and the gizmo in the safe she keeps under the bed. She's too tired to do anything else, so turns in early.

She doesn't get anywhere near enough sleep during her first night back at the studio. Her mind's teeming with half-cocked theories regarding Robert's death, his legacy, his fiancée, his shady business dealings etc. She hasn't heard anything from Varvara since the exchange of texts a few days ago. She's remained true to her word and has remained off-grid. There's no point in looking for her as she wouldn't know where to start. She's toying with the idea of seeking help from a professional, somebody with the right skills in missing persons cases. Someone who would know where to start. While she thinks about it, she adds private detective to her list. Maybe Marissa knows somebody – she'll mention it when they next talk. So much to do.

Now, Robert's estate. As his widow, she stands to inherit all of it, whether she wants to or not. She's decided to set up a separate bank account to deal with the proceeds from his assets as they are realised. She has more than enough money of her own and doesn't need or want any more. The money from the estate can remain untouched until Varvara chooses to break cover, as surely she must. Talking of money. When they first got married, Robert appointed his wife as his executor, thereby making her both judge and jury for what happens to his estate. She has the key to a safe deposit box and a letter of introduction. The box is at Coutts in The Strand and that's where she's heading this morning. What happens next depends very much on what she finds when she opens that box.

*

Safe deposit boxes. They're not very fashionable these days, are they? Having said that, Coutts is an old-fashioned private bank, although it's no longer independent. It's part of the Nat West Group, which, as RBS, had to be rescued by the UK taxpayer after playing fast and loose with their customers' money. Pamela's never visited Coutts and wouldn't be seen dead banking with them, given their antediluvian image and inflated fee structure. She carries a picture in her head of a splendid old building and liveried staff in top hats waiting to attend to her every need over tea and home-baked biscuits. The reality is different but not by much.

Coutts' head office occupies a large piece of real estate on The Strand. The newish reception area presents an impressive wall of glass to the visitor although if you bank with Coutts, you're unlikely to be intimidated by it. Once inside, Pamela is greeted politely by a man in a purple greatcoat, but that's about as far as it goes regarding tradition. She presents her letter to a young, business-like Asian girl in a smart suit who checks it out and escorts her to the vaults before leaving her to it. She locates the numbered box, inserts the key and extracts it from the wall. She takes a look inside.

She'd been hoping to find a will in the box. She doesn't. There's a list of names and contact details and some other papers. More about these later. Most of the money from the sale of his company had been placed with Coutts who appear to have done an excellent job as wealth managers. As his executor, they've kindly provided

Pamela with an up-to-date valuation of his investment portfolio. Taken with his art collection and his house, her late husband has accumulated a net worth in excess of £100 million. She knew he wasn't poor but she obviously had no idea. Not a bad result for a man who'd endured such a struggle during his early life.

There's also the question of the more recent investments in digital art, about which she knows very little. It's also a complete mystery to Coutts, who hadn't been prepared to sully their hands with the likes of cryptocurrency investments. She thought the cryptocurrency had been relatively small beer but Robert had hinted it might have changed somewhat when they spoke about it. She's keen to play everything by the book so she'll contact his solicitor, one of the names on the contact list.

Chapter 26

Claire Shorter had been Robert's solicitor for many years and she'd been genuinely upset when Pamela told her about his untimely death. She works out of a suite of offices squeezed into a very old building in Sheep Street, Stratford-upon-Avon. When Pamela arrives for her appointment, there's an atmosphere of quiet bustle about the place. It's a stiflingly hot day, the portable fans are struggling and there's no air conditioning. Claire is red in the face and is fanning herself with a sheaf of papers. She's about Pamela's age, plump, smartly turned out. She has a kind face and an emollient voice, perfect for matters of probate.

'I was very sorry to hear about your husband's death. He was a lovely man and I'll miss his occasional visits. I liked him.'

'So did I. There was The Girlfriend of course. Sorry, Varvara I mean.'

'Yes. He seemed utterly in love with her. Besotted even. No offence.'

'None taken. Do you know she's disappeared? Completely, it

seems. You haven't heard from her by any chance?'

'No, I haven't. Perhaps she's grieving, withdrawn into herself for a while.'

'You could be right. I hope you're right. I'd like to think she's not in any danger.'

'Danger?'

'Sorry. I'll spare you the details. It's her family background – weird doesn't come close to describing it. Take her brother for example.'

She gives Claire the edited highlights of the little she knows about the Sokolovas and her husband's various entanglements with them.

'I had no idea. He seemed such a careful man. How did he let it happen?'

'He fell in love, I suppose. Nothing else seemed to matter to him.'

Tea is ordered and when it arrives, the two women start talking about probate.

'You know Pamela, I'm surprised. I thought that of all people, he would have left a will. Especially after he got together with, erm. Sorry.'

'Don't worry. As soon as I heard about her, I admit I was angry and upset but I did offer to get out of his way and give him a divorce. He thanked me for the offer but wanted us to stay married. He may have been concerned about her nationality or her family. Or something we'll never know. There is no will, I can assure you.'

'How can you be so sure?'

'It would have been in the safe deposit box. I'm as sure as I can be.'

'With or without a will, the probate is straightforward. You're his wife and it all goes to you. The entire estate.'

'Fine, but I'm also his executor. Although the probate's a done deal legally, would you mind sticking around as my advisor on legal matters. Just in case?'

'It would be a pleasure. How about going through the detail for me. What have you found out so far?'

She updated Claire on what she knew. It didn't take long. There was Highfield, with the house and grounds valued at up to £10 million. There was the art collection with a recent insurance valuation of £12 million. Coutts valued the investment portfolio at close to £80 million.

'So, there you have it. I propose to sell the house and the art collection and put the proceeds in a high interest account where it can wait for Varvara's reappearance. I have no idea what to do with the investments, other than to leave them with Coutts and bank the profits until I make up my mind.'

'Does he have any other assets?'

'Ah, yes. He has a rather flashy sports car that he bought for cash – completely out of character. Thought I might put it up for auction and give the net proceeds to his favourite charity.'

'Good idea. Go for it.'

'I will indeed. Then there's the digital art collection. By choice, I've steered well clear of this and don't know a fat lot about it. It's tied in with an investment in cryptocurrencies and is complicated by the involvement of Vladimir, Varvara's brother. Don't ask. The value of the investment is currently unknown – to me, anyway – and it appears to be off the books. Coutts are too up themselves to get involved. I need to find out more about this stuff before deciding how to play it.'

After the meeting, Claire drives her to the station and she gets the train back to London. There are two types of train available on this route – slow and extremely slow. Plenty of time to have a drink and make a couple of calls. The first is to Lewthwaite and

Lewthwaite, instructing them to put the house on the market, price on application. They already have the keys, which she'd found in the safe deposit box. The second is to Monty, who doesn't answer. She leaves a message suggesting they meet to discuss Robert's art collection and options for selling it. A lunch would be good and she'd ask Monty to pick up the tab for a change.

Regarding the house, she'd reluctantly left Simon and Joanna in situ so they could keep the house and grounds up to scratch and deal with the comings and goings of the sale. Pamela is less than keen on visiting Highfield unless she absolutely has to. She's never liked the place to put it mildly and would probably stay somewhere else if she needs to visit the area.

She'll get the odious Simon to clean and polish the Porsche. That was about as far as she'd trust him. She'll arrange the sale herself and knows an art dealer friend who likes fast cars and might be inclined to give her a good price. Should make six figures with any luck.

The contents of the safe deposit box are now in her handbag. In addition to the list of contacts, there's a small padded envelope containing a mysterious metallic plate with a load of letters on it. The metallic plate has a sticky note stuck to it with some handwritten scrawl, possibly login details. The weird thing is, a similar-looking plate was recently delivered to her studio by courier. She popped it in the safe. She's guessing that the plates go with the gizmo and have something to do with the digital art.

There's an intriguing entry on the contacts list. It's not a name as such but she's sure it's connected somehow or other with the crypto/digital shebang.

Chapter 27

Eleanor and Thomas Lanchester are enjoying an early breakfast. She's showered and dressed and is attacking the day with her usual vim and vigour, tapping away furiously at her phone. He hasn't showered and is still wearing his dressing gown. He patently isn't ready to attack anything beyond the next cup of coffee. She's just come off a shouty call with somebody or other – you know how it is with these people. Ellie glares at her phone as if it's to blame for something.

'I'm afraid I won't be able to join you for the house viewings today, love. Work stuff. Sorry.'

There's a brief hiatus while the occupant of the dressing gown processes the information and formulates a response.

'Can't one of your minions cover it?'

'I wish. I don't have any minions. Hangers-on, more like.'

'So, what's the big deal all of a sudden?'

'I told you but you probably weren't paying attention. I'm bringing out a new range of tantric massage oils. They need me urgently in

London to help with the launch. The face of the label and all that.'

'Bummer. As a matter of interest, what the fuck's a tantric massage oil?'

'Oh, God! It's a massage oil, but instead of ...'

Tom can't help himself and he's tuned out before she reaches the end of the first sentence. His wife's holistic thingummy business remains a complete mystery to him but it's becoming ridiculously successful. It's grown so big, she might have to focus full time on it. Which is a great shame, as that means he'll be looking for a new agent. How do you even do that?

Him and Ellie had got together at the RSC when they were both struggling young actors. Cramped accommodation and close proximity had thrown them together and they'd fallen in love. They got married. Money was in short supply so it was a registry office do and a few friends. There were a couple of drinks afterwards at the Dirty Duck then back to rehearsals. There were some hard years of reputation-building on the stage amid a smattering of minor roles in films and TV. Their world changed when Ellie blagged Tom an audition for a supporting role – a villain, inevitably – in a major studio superhero franchise. He didn't get to play the villain, but landed the lead role instead. The irony of a lauded Shakespearean stage actor playing a comic-book character with a cool line in astral projection – but precious little emotional presence – was not lost on him. Or his fellow thesps, who mocked him mercilessly despite being consumed with envy.

As the studio expected, the franchise got huge and made him a big star. From then on, he and Ellie were a team. He did the acting and she did the rest, putting her own acting career – such as it was – on hold to be his agent, riding the wave while they could. A golden couple. No kids – they'd agreed there wasn't enough time to do them justice.

They're spending some rest and recreation time at a friend's house near Stratford-upon-Avon after enduring a gruelling global publicity tour for the third and latest film in the series. There are proposals in place for a fourth. Since the second, he's been on a percentage of the box office, making Tom Lanchester Inc. a very wealthy outfit. There's just one quirk about the whole circus – the prosthetics and make-up required for the role render him barely recognisable on screen. This works well for him, allowing him to remain comfortably below the radar when he's off screen, flying much lower than his wife these days.

Ellie has finished pitching the tantric oils – again. She's also feeling a bit guilty about missing the house viewings.

'I've seen the videos for the houses so I'll go with whatever you decide.'

'Are you sure about that?'

'Yes, I am. As long as there's plenty of space for entertaining and we can get people in to look after everything. I mean everything, Tom. Cooking, cleaning, the lot.'

'Understood.'

The toot of a car horn announces the arrival of her taxi. She grabs the overnight bag she keeps ready for last minute stuff like this and moves in for a quick hug and peck.

'See you tomorrow, darling. Love you.'

She wipes the lipstick off his cheek and leaves him to it. As the taxi draws away, she takes a discrete glug from her LARQ water bottle. She's testing this item with a view to adding it to her portfolio of products. Today, it's filled with designer gin and a splash of botanic tonic, also from her range. To keep her going, you understand.

*

Another morning, another mansion to look around. This particular mansion promises to be far more interesting than the more traditional Cotswolds one he's got lined up for the afternoon. Lewthwaite and Lewthwaite's slick promotional video had whooshed him and Ellie through a mind-boggling layout, a secluded location, plenty of land and a giant overdose of what can only be described as bling. It's the sort of place that might have been dreamed up by a EuroMillions lottery winner or a successful West Midlands businessman – a scrap dealer, perhaps.

One of the ironies about Tom's recently acquired wealth is that you can live in the lap of luxury without breaking the bank. Or even bothering the bank for that matter. Take the car he's driving today for example, a McLaren 570S, which was loaned to him free of charge after he lent his name to a recent promotion. He pulls the McLaren up in front of a serious-looking wooden gate, the sort that slides sideways on wheels when it opens. As he does so, he notices a battery of security cameras taking a sudden interest in his arrival. One of the desirable features – among many – of this particular property is the extensive high-end security system installed by the previous owner for reasons unknown. Privacy has become a big deal for Tom of late. Something worth protecting.

He leans out of the window and presses the only button available to him. After a tiresome delay, he gets a terse response.

'Name please.'

He discerns a broad Brummie accent amid the static and crackles. His Brummie had been bludgeoned out of him at stage school, although he could deploy it convincingly if the role demanded it.

'Hi, I'm Tom Lanchester. I've an appointment to see Gill Lewthwaite at ten-thirty.'

'You're expected, Mister Lanchester. Follow the drive until you see the house then park by the ornamental fountain in front of the garages. Mrs Lewthwaite will meet you at the front doors, under the portico.'

Yes, this house has a portico.

There's a buzz and a click and the gate opens in its own time, revealing an elegant, tree-lined drive. The place is only a few years old so the trees – English limes – have yet to mature properly. He drives on, the vast engine burbling and popping as the car crunches over the pea shingle, struggling to cope with such sedate progress. The house eventually emerges and he draws up behind a large Audi something or other. In front of this is a dirty, battered pickup truck. On the other side of the fountain is an impressive, newish Porsche wearing a layer of dust, seemingly abandoned.

A careworn, mid-forties woman in a smart business suit is waiting for him. Dyed blond, double chin, chubby around the midriff, too much make-up. He dreams up a quick thumbnail sketch for her:

Young, ambitious estate agent, works all hours, falls for one of the partners, gets married, has a couple of kids, returns to work when they go to senior school. Not as good as she used to be – in more ways than one.

'Good morning, Mister Lanchester. Welcome to Highfield. I'm Gill Lewthwaite and I'll be showing you around the property this morning.'

Very formal. Posh accent, probably put on, the flat vowels a dead giveaway. An undercurrent of nervousness. Enough of this.

'Excellent. I'd prefer it if you called me Tom.'

'How much do you know about the property, Mister, er, Tom?'

'I've watched the sales video a couple of times and read the particulars. My wife has outlined her requirements and I'm keen to have a look round.'

'Nice car by the way. Great colour.'

'You're too kind. The colour's called "volcano orange" if you're interested.' Tom's not in the mood for small talk today. 'Shall we start?'

'Oh, yes, of course. Follow me.'

He follows her into a vast, opulent reception area with rooms off. Marble and polished wood everywhere. Splendid décor, replete with artworks. He feels completely overwhelmed but quickly realises it's exactly the feeling the architect was looking for.

'We're at the entrance level, which is the top floor of the house. There are three extensive floors, but you'll have noticed how the property adopts a low profile within its hillside setting. Perfect for a high-profile person who might want to adopt a lower profile from time to time.'

Visibly pleased with her turn of phrase, which sounded rehearsed to him, she leads Tom off to the right. The tour proper has commenced, as has the agent patter and accompanying flamboyant arm gestures. It's round about now that Tom gets the uncomfortable feeling they're not alone in the house.

'The impressive drawing room. Note the dimensions of this superb space, which has access to a large balcony from which you can enjoy far-reaching views across the rolling Warwickshire countryside.'

'Is all the furniture staying?'

'Yes. Subject to a separate negotiation.'

Tom isn't sure about the furniture. Most of it looks like it's never been used and has more than a hint of 'Middle-Eastern dictator' about it. The drawing room is, indeed, impressive. He reckons their entire Beverly Hills condo would fit comfortably within it. Which begs a question.

'How big is this place, Gill? Overall, I mean.'

She taps and swipes her tablet.

'Nineteen thousand square feet, give or take. Well over twenty if you include the staff quarters.'

'Staff quarters?'

'You'll need staff, won't you? There's a lot of house to look after.'

This will be a major plus point for Ellie. Staff. Bloody hell. He has no idea what twenty thousand square feet looks like, but it's a big number.

'How much land is there?'

'Fifteen acres, more or less. There's a small lake in the grounds. A helipad close by.'

A helipad, but of course. What every home needs and simply has to have. Tom has a thing about helicopters, regarding them as fundamentally unstable, never more than a split second away from a disastrous malfunction.

'Helicopters. You'll never get me up in one of those things. Death traps.'

'Could be useful for some of your visitors though.'

'I'll give you that.'

They sweep through the mega-equipped kitchen and the palatial dining room amid a flurry of Gill's factoids and copious gesticulations. They reach the sunroom, which is big but less than half the size of the drawing room. As he settles back into one of the large sofas, Tom tries to relax in the first room that could almost be called cosy. In truth, he's experiencing a growing sense of unease. It's difficult to be sure but it feels very much like somebody's shadowing them, tracking their progress around the house, remaining just out of sight. He feels the need to mention it.

'You might think I'm losing it, Gill, but it seems like somebody is following us around. Perhaps some staff are working today?'

'Strange, I'm not getting that feeling at all. It's the wrong day, anyway. For the cleaners, I mean.'

For Tom, the unease is tangible, making it hard for him to focus. Gill forges on.

'Such a beautiful room, don't you think, more intimate than the rest? A bolthole even.'

'I agree with you. I like it very much. It's the only room I've seen so far that isn't trying too hard.' A charming, almost-normal room, devoid of the overt sumptuousness seen elsewhere.

They don't linger in the adjacent staff quarters as Gill clearly doesn't expect her prospective clients to spend any of their valuable time in there. On their return to the reception area, they use the lift to visit what she describes as the bedroom level. They head towards the picture window on the landing.

'In front of us is the large open terrace, ideal for entertaining guests when the weather permits. Once more, it goes without saying – fantastic views.'

It's a humongous terrace. You could fit well over a hundred people on it – great for parties. The vastness of the place is starting to intimidate him. After all, they're only two people so what are they going to do with all the space? He convinces himself he's almost certainly missing the point.

While admiring the view, Tom senses some movement behind him. He spins around quickly but there's nothing to see.

'Is everything OK, Tom?'

'I'm not sure. You're certain there's nobody else in the house?'

'Not to my knowledge. The housekeeper went out to buy supplies. The caretaker is the only other possibility.'

He tells himself he needs to relax a little. Get a grip. Maybe all that astral projection stuff in the films is getting to him?

'I have another question for you, if you don't mind?'

'Go ahead.'

'The house has many elegant paintings and sculptures dotted around. They look like originals. What's the story?'

'The previous owner collected modern art and displayed it in this house. His widow is arranging for the entire collection to be removed when the place is sold. Any minor damage to the décor will be made good, so no need to worry on that score.'

'OK, thanks. Hang on a minute. That sculpture over there on the plinth. Is that what I think it is?'

'I'm afraid it is.' Gill appeared to be blushing. 'To our right, we have a corridor with four guest bedrooms, all with en suite facilities.'

Each guest bedroom is large, luxurious and beautifully equipped. On each side of the corridor, he notices some flat screen TVs, begging another question.

'What's with the TV screens? Are they part of the security?'

She taps away at her tablet.

'Ah, yes, those. I'm told the previous owner had a number of digital artworks in his collection. The screens were intended to display a selection of them. They're due to be removed soon and, as I said, any damage will be made good.'

They move across to the wing housing the family bedrooms. They stop briefly in front of a closed door.

'This provides access to the equipment room. The equipment drives the swimming pool and other facilities in the house – the underfloor heating, air conditioning, lighting, sound system, intercom, security etc. Simon can brief you on that stuff should you be interested.'

Tom's about to ask a question about running costs but decides against it. He's still getting used to being a man for whom such questions are irrelevant.

'On our right are three family bedrooms with balconied views to the rear of the house.'

Superb bedrooms, no doubt about it. What's not to like? A different bedroom for every night of the week and staff to clean up after them.

'Do you have any details on the security system? I'm particularly interested in that, as you might expect.'

'No, I don't, sorry. The people who maintain the system will be able to give you a full rundown on it, should you be interested in proceeding. I have their number.'

'How about the guy who operates the gate?'

'Simon. The gate and door security are on a separate system. He only knows how to let people in and out.'

'Great. Thanks. What's next?'

'The master bedroom. Follow me.'

She adopts the manner and purpose of someone about to deliver the jewel in the crown. The master bedroom turns out to be a small suite of rooms, commodious and suitably luxurious, with its own balcony and 'his' and 'hers' dressing rooms and en suites. Decorated with signed, limited edition Roy Lichtenstein prints, part of the collection. Tom's a big admirer of Lichtenstein's work.

'Shall we take the stairs down to the lower floor?'

As they descend, Tom enquires about the previous owner.

'I haven't been told much about him and there's not a great deal online. He was an intensely private man by all accounts. From what I could find out, he was a wealthy guy who used his fortune to build this house and collect art.'

The staircase delivers them onto the dance floor. No kidding, a proper dance floor with its own bar area and cellar. For entertaining, of course.

'And through these double doors, we arrive at the splendid swimming pool complex.'

It hardly ever happens, but Tom's lost for words. 'Magnificent' wouldn't come close to describing it. The entire lower floor has been given over to relaxation and pleasure, pure and simple. He's sure Ellie's going to love all this. Product launches, parties, that sort of thing.

'Then there's the fitness area. Over here.'

In other words, a fully equipped gym, sauna and steam room with a changing room and showers.

'Could I have a quick look, please?'

'Of course. Follow me.'

Tom is knocked out by the fitness area – it's superb. Although the place is a few years old, all the equipment looks new and untouched with the exception of one exercise bike. One of the showers looks as if it's been used recently. He's now convinced there's somebody else in the house but decides not to pursue it with Gill as she might think he's losing it.

'There's more to come. This way.'

They double back across the dance floor and reach the billiards room complete with a full-sized snooker table and a pool table. On the snooker table, a game of billiards is in progress. It's difficult to define the feeling, but it's like somebody has just left the room, leaving the game unfinished. He points at the table and looks at Gill who shrugs her shoulders.

'Simon?'

'Listen, could you have a word please. If I was inclined to buy the place, I wouldn't want the staff playing fast and loose with the fixtures and fittings. Or using the gym and swimming pool for that matter.'

She's suitably contrite and agrees to have a word. They finish the tour of the main house with a visit to the cinema.

'... boasting a large screen, Dolby sound and top of the range projection facilities. Somewhere to sit back with your popcorn and admire your latest release.'

'I don't think so, Gill. I only ever watch myself during production – in the rushes. By the time the film's released, I've sat through it so many times I've lost interest.'

She looks crestfallen, as if a bubble's been burst.

'Would you like to have a look outside?'

He would. During their tour of the extensive landscaped gardens, he spots something purporting to be a miniature Grecian temple in a far corner of the lawn.

'Is that a folly, Gill? Looks a bit peculiar on its own, doesn't it?'

She taps and swipes.

'Right. That's a garden shed, disguised as a temple I suppose. It's where Simon keeps his mowers and gardening stuff.'

The folly strikes Tom as being a bit random. A bit forlorn. Never mind.

Finally, they visit the extensive garage block which has space for at least eight cars. It should have been more, but a couple of the larger garages – the ones closest to the house – have been converted. The door's locked and the security looks extensive. The windows are covered up, so they're unable to look inside.

'Any ideas?'

She consults her tablet again.

'It's not mentioned in what I have here. I'll find out for you from the vendor.'

Time is getting on. They return to their cars and Gill announces the end of the tour. It's taken them the best part of two hours to get around and they've hardly scratched the surface.

'So, what do you think? Interested?'

'Definitely. I have a few things for you to work on though. I need to know what you're asking for the place as a basis for negotiation. I'd very much like to find out more about the security system from the experts, as its high on my wish list. There's the mystery room or rooms in the garage block – what's that all about? Oh, and one last request.'

'Yes?'

'Have a word with the staff about wandering around the house. We don't want them taking liberties, do we?'

*

As expected, Ellie was knocked out by the place and they bought it. Cash. They'd have to wait for the art to be removed and the walls made good before moving in. No chain to worry about.

Tom had checked out the security system and what they'd told him ticked all the right boxes. Although they didn't particularly like the cut of his jib, Simon passed all the background checks so they would keep him and Joanna on the payroll, although they'd bring in their own chef. The mystery area in the garage block turned out to be a workshop of sorts, completely empty. The reason for the high level of security installed in and around it would remain a mystery. The Lanchesters didn't own any cars and had more than enough living space in the main house, so they left the workshop in situ for the time being. Finally, when questioned, Simon had vigorously denied using any of the facilities in the main house.

Chapter 28

Pamela has been prevaricating about the sale of the art collection, her main bugbear being the excessive commissions charged by auctioneers. She believes her mission is to get the best prices she can while minimising the amount of commission. What other trade would take as much as forty-five per cent of the value of an item in commission and costs? A case of taketh with one hand and taketh with the other as well. Plus VAT.

She confronts Monty Gallimore with this very question as they enjoy aperitifs in the bar. They're lined up for what promises to be a long, leisurely lunch at the exquisite Cotswolds pile, Buckland Manor. Monty likes this place a lot and has booked a private dining room at considerable cost. He did this as soon as he found out she wanted to talk about selling Robert's collection, a collection he knows rather well, having contributed his fine art expertise while it was being assembled. Pamela's decided to stay the night and has invited her latest squeeze, Katrina, to join her for a light supper and, with any luck, some nocturnal fun and games.

‘Fifty fackin per cent, Monty. I ask you.’

Her approach has one objective – to put Monty on the back foot and keep him there throughout the afternoon.

‘That’s a bit of an exaggeration and you know it. For a start, you’ve included VAT, which goes straight to the government, bless ’em. Then there’s the disbursements, passed on at cost.’

‘Cost plus a handling fee. Don’t make me laugh.’

‘Well, yes, there’s a certain amount of work involved in totting them up and passing them on.’

‘By one of your minimum wage minions, no doubt. I hope you’re not thinking of passing this one on by the way. I can’t remember the last time you bought me lunch.’

‘Don’t change the subject. I entirely refute the aspersions you’re casting about the humble auctioneer’s honest pursuit of a decent living.’

Humble auctioneer. As an aside, Monty’s wine collection runs to several thousand bottles and is worth well over a million quid. It would have been more, but he’s incapable of keeping his hands off the better bottles.

‘OK, let’s call it forty-five per cent. It’s a hefty wodge for doing close to bugger all. Half of that’s basically the buyer’s premium. What’s that all about?

‘Erm. Tradition?’

Pamela looks like she’s about to explode. Monty’s in a hole but sees no reason to stop digging.

‘Seriously, my dear, there’s a lot of expense involved in shifting artwork. I have premises to maintain, staff to pay, bills – you name it.’

Pamela’s no longer going to explode, but she remains very much on the offensive. She’s about to wade in again but Monty’s spared for now by the arrival of a smartly dressed head waiter reeking of cheap aftershave. Adopting the right level of obsequiousness, he offers to escort them to their dining room.

She's considered any number of options for selling the collection. The best way to minimise fees and commissions would be to sell the collection herself using every means at her disposal. Online in other words. Although she's a mover and shaker in the art world, it would require an immense amount of effort. She'd also have to lean on somebody like Monty who knew the market. Alternatively, she could use a top fine art auctioneer and hope the gains in prices would outflank the exorbitant seller premiums. She'd still need somebody like Monty to work with her as a consultant. Finally, she could place the whole collection with a top auction house like Bonhams and swallow the ginormous premiums, hoping for a big payday because of the prestige. This would be the least effort and she wouldn't need Monty. During a lunch of epic proportions, she runs all of these options past her dining companion, who doesn't like the look of any of them. They continue their verbal sparring over the vintage port.

'As I said before, my dear, none of your ideas sound like the way to go, although you know I'd be delighted to work with you on selling the collection bit by bit.'

'So, I should go with Bonhams?'

Monty had learned his trade at Bonhams and had clawed his way up the ranks until the death of his father brought him back to run the family business in Yorkshire. After taking charge, he moved the entire business to the Cotswolds and focused on the fine art and antiques, establishing an excellent reputation. In other words, he knew his stuff and was more than able to take Pamela's joshing in his stride.

'Hold your horses. Do you know how rich those people are?

They're so bloated, they move at a snail's pace. You'll be looking at twelve to eighteen months to get anywhere near a slot on their schedule. Can you even wait that long?'

Monty's holding the stub of his cigar and gesticulating wildly. A large chunk of spent ash falls into his lap but he doesn't seem to notice. He's right about one thing though – she can't wait that long. With the house as good as sold, she'll soon need to get the artworks out of there and into storage. She's desperate to get on with her life, what's left of it – her recent brush with cancer still looms large.

'No, I can't, darling. Any suggestions?'

'Why don't you give the whole shooting match to Gallimores? I'm sure we could agree some very favourable terms, you being an old and valued friend.'

'Thanks, Monty, but forget it. Gallimores is too small, too provincial. Wouldn't attract the right types or the right wallets. Sorry.'

This gets right up Monty's nose, which was exactly what she'd intended.

'Cheeky bugger. You'd be surprised at our reach and our reputation, especially in the field of modern and contemporary art. Miles better than Bonhams if I might be so bold.'

A deal is tantalisingly close. She throws a few numbers around in her head before continuing.

'OK. What exactly do you mean by "very favourable terms"?'

'Oh, I don't know. Ten per cent selling commission. Plus VAT. Insurance at cost. Removal and storage at cost. No hidden extras, that's all you pay. Any items that aren't sold, I'll buy them from you at reserve.'

'Tut, tut, Monty. You sound like I'm forcing you to cut your own throat. For sake of argument, let's say the collection sells for fifteen mil, hammer price. Let's also say your buyer's premium, which you neglected to mention, is fifteen per cent – it might be more for all I know – who cares? As a result, you stuff upwards of two million pounds in your back pocket. Are you really going to charge me a grubby little extra ten per cent? Another million? You could retire on this one deal, no problem. Focus on your wine or your property or your cars.'

'Well, it's a big collection. It'll take a lot of ...'

'Oh, please. Hold it right there and stop whingeing. Here we go. Five per cent sales commission, which I will pay direct to a charity of your choice on your behalf. Insurance? OK. All reasonable costs associated with removal and storage? OK, but don't you dare add anything that even smells like a handling charge.'

She's held up by some spluttered protests from an outraged Monty. When he's finished spluttering, she carries on.

'Think about it. With this deal, I get a quick and efficient sale of the entire collection and you get a payday north of two million pounds. Cancer Research or whoever get half a mil. What's not to like?'

After a bit more spluttering, they shake hands on the deal and order some more port. Within an hour, there's a taxi driver waiting at reception and Monty rises rather unsteadily to his feet, his teeth firmly clenched on a rather damp and dishevelled cigar, long since extinguished.

'Bye, Monty. Safe journey. Don't forget to send me the contract before I change my mind.'

'Cheerio, Pamela. I'd like to say it's been a pleasure doing business with you but ...'

'If it makes you feel any better darling, I was going to give you the business anyway.'

*

She sees Monty safely off the premises, but only after confirming he's paid the bill. He practically has to be poured into the taxi. There's enough time for her to find her suite, grab a quick shower, apply a few dabs of make-up and add a few pieces of jewellery. A little black dress will suffice and not much else. In the mirror, she looks as good as it gets these days and feels surprisingly spry considering the demanding afternoon she's just endured. She positions herself at the bar, orders a sparkling mineral water and waits eagerly for Katrina to make an appearance.

She'd got talking to Katrina, a fellow artist, at a recent exhibition at Tate Britain and they'd hit it off immediately. They'd gone on to spend an energetic, largely sleepless night together at Pamela's studio. During that sleepless night, she'd found out her new lover boasted a significant collection of tattoos and piercings. Those adorning her tongue and labia were particularly exotic and had brought an exquisite extra dimension to soixante-neuf. Twice.

What about Marissa? In her own defence, Pamela would say that her and Marissa were on a slow burn, a work in progress for the longer term. She'd feel bound to add that Katrina is an opportunity too good to miss. She'd then defy you to argue with her.

Chapter 29

Following the sale of the house, Pamela had arranged for the art to be removed from Highfield and put into temporary storage at Gallimore's warehouse. The decorators had been into Highfield to tidy up and the plasma screens had been removed. The new owners would be moving in soon.

It might have had something to do with the two million pounds, but Monty could move rapidly when it suited him. By twisting arms and calling in favours, the catalogues had been produced, reviewed and despatched within a month. The collection had been dusted down and hung in Gallimore's splendid new exhibition hall in Cheltenham. When Monty proudly showed Pamela around, it was the first time she'd seen the entire collection in an exhibition setting. She'd been mightily impressed and had felt a pang of regret that Robert had gone – he would have been immensely proud. She almost felt guilty for driving such a hard bargain with Monty. Almost. Any residual guilt was washed away when she discovered – through a prospective buyer – that the old devil had loaded the buyer's premium somewhat.

The week of viewings is launched on the back of a veritable blitzkrieg of publicity. Local TV and radio, social media, numerous prestigious art publications. Pamela has done her bit by drumming up support among her highfalutin, well-connected contacts in the art world and she's recruited Desmond to bombard his media pals with the big news. All in all, quite a stir has been drummed up around the collection and they've had hundreds of expressions of interest. The equivalent of a full house is expected for the invitation-only gala opening of the viewing exhibition.

About an hour prior to the opening, Pamela's running a rule over a guest list that numbers well over a hundred people. She recognises some of the names – a smattering of her friends and colleagues, Desmond and Lizzie, art dealers, local celebrities. Plenty of publicity and media people. A couple of camera crews. One name leaps out at her for all the wrong reasons. Vladimir Sokolova – plus one, no doubt. She isn't sure what to make of this so buttonholes Monty about it. He's caught up in the thrill of it all and gives her short shrift.

'What's the problem? He's a Russian and he's probably seriously loaded. Anyway, it's quite in order for anybody to register an interest in the collection. You should know that my dear.'

He's right on one thing. She doesn't have a leg to stand on regarding the suitability of the guests. She steels herself for a potentially difficult evening. An early glass of bubbly wouldn't go amiss.

The exhibition has been organised into a number of subcategories, genres if you like, reflecting the way in which the collection had been assembled. When they first started it, she and Robert had sketched out some broad categories to help focus their search for suitable pieces. He had a keen interest in pop art but later broadened his scope, leaning towards the work of the YBAs and street art. He hadn't been particularly taken with sculpture but grew to admire the work of Lynn Chadwick, among others. For her part, Pamela recommended artists to him based on her specialism – British artists active after World War Two. She also recommended a look at the surrealists, especially Leonora Carrington. As the collection grew, Robert realised he would have to double his budget to at least ten million and increase his maximum per piece from a hundred thousand to two hundred and fifty thousand. Even then, much of the art he aspired to own was well out of his price range. Despite this, the finished collection comprised more than ninety works of art, all of them by well-regarded and collectible artists.

*

Monty opens the evening with a speech that's garbled, pompous and overly self-congratulatory. He barely mentions Robert and fails to mention Pamela at all. At one stage, he loses his thread, forgets where he is and takes a hasty, very public swig from his hip flask. Never mind, there are plenty of people milling around and Monty hasn't stinted on the food and drink, although the champagne is probably from the bargain basement end of his substantial collection.

He's hired a local catering company to provide the food and the waiting staff. Several attractive young men and women in uniform attire are circulating among the guests, topping up glasses and serving canapés. Pamela is wearing a name badge and is soon engulfed by a small swarm of enthusiastic art lovers, keen to hear what she has to say about the exhibits, a couple of which are hers. The swarm provides her with some protection against any approaches from the likes of Vladimir although she hasn't spotted him yet.

About an hour later, all her admirers have moved on. She's now doing nothing much in a corner of the hall. There's a waitress nearby and she waves her empty glass at her, hoping for a refill. The waitress walks over and takes her glass. She offers Pamela one of the two drinks on her tray and takes the remaining one herself. She puts the tray down on a nearby table, clinks glasses with a frankly gobsmacked Pamela and sinks about half of it.

'It is tasty, no? English at a guess. Good to see you, Pamela. It has been a while. Can we do some talking before the boss man catches up with me?'

The waitress smiles. It's a dazzling smile. She knows that smile and recognises the voice and the accented English. She's changed her hair colour and downplayed her looks, but still looks fantastic.

'Varvara. What a lovely surprise. Where have you been hiding yourself?'

'If I told you, I would have to kill you. That is a joke, do not worry yourself. We should find somewhere a bit quieter to talk. Outside? Do you still smoke?'

'After a fashion.'

'I will see you in five minutes. Outside the main doors. It is a pleasant area of town and we can take a quick walk around the streets.'

'You're on.'

The waitress downs the rest of the bubbly, picks up the empty tray and quickly melts back into the melee of people. Pamela finishes her drink, visits the ladies and heads for the main doors. She manages to fend off the people who want to talk to her, including a distinctly wobbly Monty.

*

Varvara's waiting for her outside and has just lit a cigarette. It might be late summer but it's a cool evening. She hasn't got a coat but doesn't seem to notice the cold.

'I didn't know you smoked. It's bad for you, my dear. I should know.'

'I had not smoked since I was a teenager. Then I heard that Robert had died. It was very upsetting for me, as you can only imagine.'

She is very close to tears and for the first time ever, Pamela feels sorry for her and feels like putting an arm around her. She can't quite bring herself to do it, so takes a good long pull from her vape pen instead. The sweet-smelling steam envelops them.

'Smells good. Perhaps I should switch to e-cigarettes. I do not enjoy these.'

She stubs the cigarette out and asks to try the vape pen. As they set out on their walk around Montpellier, she takes a pull from it.

'Yes, I am liking this. Now, I am on a fifteen-minute break, so I do not have much of a long time to bring you up to date. How much do you know?'

'Not much. Robert had asked me to sort out his affairs should anything happen to him. I've found a buyer for the house and as you can see, I'm in the process of selling his art collection. He has amassed a small fortune in conventional investments. I know virtually nothing about the digital stuff.'

'Hmm. You get to keep all of this?'

'Officially, yes. The thing is, I don't want or need any of it. In fact, I'd be much happier without it. I would be more than content to push some of it your way.'

'I am surprised. Am I not the woman who ruined your marriage?'

'I'm over that now, don't worry. I've moved on.'

'You know, he always liked you. He would never speak badly about you.'

She takes another pull on the pen and emits another cloud of steam. They carry on walking.

'Did you say you have sold the house?'

'Yes. Have you heard of a chap called Tom Lanchester? He's a film star apparently. Him and his wife actually like the place, would you believe?'

'I have never heard of him. When does he move in?'

'Soon. I'll let you know if you like.'

There's a brief gap in the conversation, during which she sends Pamela her new number.

'You saw Robert when you identified him. Was he badly damaged?'

'No. I only saw his face. He just had a few scratches and bruises, that's all. He looked to me like he was asleep.'

'Do you think it was an accident?'

'Why do you ask? Do you think somebody took him out? Your brother? The police don't seem to think so.'

'I think it is very unlikely. He needed Robert alive, especially after certain developments in their joint enterprise.'

'Interesting. When we spoke on the night he died, he said he'd done something stupid.'

There's a sudden flash of anger.

'The only person who has done something stupid is my fucking stupid brother. To add to all the other stupid things he has done in his useless life.'

She's not in a good place. Pamela waits patiently for her to calm down and continue.

'Robert was a kind, beautiful man but he behaved like an idiot sometimes. Sleepwalking into a deal with my brother was the worst thing he could have done. It rapidly spiralled out of control, putting all of us in great danger.'

She stops suddenly and takes another pull on the vape pen.

'He double-crossed Vladimir over the cryptocurrency, putting both of us on a hit list. Thinking about it, I was probably on that list already. To protect ourselves, Robert and myself put together a plan to disappear completely for a while. When I heard he had died, I thought he had been killed deliberately. Be aware that my family have a certain reputation in this area.'

'So, you carried on with the plan, thinking you might be next on the list?'

'Yes, although the plan has changed. There is a teenager, a Russian boy who is very dear to me. He has joined me in hiding for his own safety. We are both secure but I cannot reveal to you where we are living.'

'Is anybody else in danger?'

'Not yet. My family are likely to focus on the digital investments. If they cannot get what they want, they may turn their attention to his other assets to help them cut their losses. I will keep you informed.'

They stop walking. She gets her phone out and presses and swipes a few times.

'Have you received one of these?'

On the phone is a photo of a small metal plate, exactly the same size and shape as the ones she has.

'Yes, I have. One was among his possessions but I received another one through the post a couple of days after he died.'

'Did it have a note attached to it? Did you keep the note?'

'Yes, and yes.'

'Good. Get rid of the one he left for you. It is now useless. Put it in the recycling if you like. Guard the one you got though the post with your life. It is very important.'

'OK. Anything else?'

'I have found out Vladimir has been called back to Moscow so he will not be attending the viewing tonight. I think Igor is getting nervous about his cryptocurrency losses and is thinking about backing out. But Robert has also done the double-cross.' She starts to smile. 'It is not as straightforward as it seems and I am starting to appreciate the new situation. Enjoy it even.'

Pamela glances at her watch.

'Your boss might notice you're gone. Shouldn't you be getting back now?'

'Maybe not. I am not comfortable serving food and drink to people and the money is shit.'

'Wait, please, just for a moment. How do I find out more about how much trouble we're all in?'

'Do you have a number for Link?'

'Do you mean Link_03? If so, yes. It's on the list of contacts he left for me.'

'Call him. I have asked him to brief you on the digital investments and why they are now so important. I will be in touch soon. Do not come looking for us.'

She's been standing adjacent to an unremarkable car parked on the road. She disposes of the parking ticket, gets in and squeals away at some speed. Pamela had meant to mention Marissa during their brief chat but didn't get the chance. As she makes her way back to the event, she's mightily relieved that Vladimir's a no-show. While she's pleased Varvara's safe and well, there's a lot for her to get her head around. Who's the teenage boy for example?

Chapter 30

Within a month of moving into Highfield, Tom and Ellie had to pack their bags and move out. Rehearsals for the fourth film in the franchise were about to start in Hollywood. As an expedient, they stuck with Simon and Joanna to look after the place while they were away. Meanwhile, Pamela has an art collection to sell.

For a provincial auctioneer – fine art or otherwise – the Gallimore's premises is quite something. It occupies an unassuming site on the outskirts of Winchcombe, a largely unremarkable Cotswolds town. Many of the bidders have taken advantage of a 'nostalgia' package that brings them from nearby Broadway on a steam train and ferries them to the auction on an early sixties' Midland Red double-decker bus. Monty's used a wafer-thin slice of his estimated two million pounds to give the place a good clean and a lick of paint. He's able to accommodate at least a hundred people in the room and has the technology on board to support a horde of telephone and internet bidders.

On her arrival – via taxi rather than steam train – Pamela grabs a coffee and asks one of Monty's people to show her the full list of authorised bidders. Unfortunately, Vladimir – plus one – is on the list of people who are attending in person. The most striking aspect of the pre-registered phone and internet bidders is the amount of international interest, especially North America. Must be the pop art. One name in particular catches her attention – Tom Lanchester – who'll be phoning in from the States. Monty has thrown in some up-market catering for the in-person bidders. As he rushes past, she grabs him to ask who's doing the catering this time, hoping she might bump into Varvara again. She doesn't recognise the name he gives her.

About half an hour before the start, her phone pings. It's a text from Varvara telling her she won't be attending. She cautions that Vladimir has gained a 'minder', a present from her father who no longer trusts him. In a follow-on text she warns her that despite appearances, the minder is dangerous and unpredictable to say the least and should not be approached. She scans the crowd quickly but doesn't see them. During the scan, she catches a glimpse of Monty taking a surreptitious swig from his trusty hip flask, which doesn't augur well for the auction. He's seen fit to lead from the front and will be the auctioneer today. This is not good news, believe me. She takes one of the few spare seats at the back of the hall, finds and skim-reads Lot 1 in her catalogue and waits for the fun to start.

Around two o'clock, an alarmingly florid Monty bounds on to the makeshift stage and takes up position behind a rather grand lectern. Not grand enough to preclude a tilt to the left and a slight wobble. Across the stage from him is a small team who are there to manage the telephone and internet bids. Around fifty lots are due to be auctioned in the afternoon session, which will focus on the lower value pieces. After a break for food, the early evening session will commence at about six-thirty, with pop art as the main attraction.

Monty is struggling with the only moving part – an on/off switch – on a recalcitrant microphone when there's a brief commotion in the hall. A couple of weird-looking punters elbow and jostle their way towards two spare seats a couple of rows in front of Pamela. The lanky, vaguely threatening one is Vladimir. His minder looks about half the size of the person he's minding. He has long, lank hair, a boyish face and an apology for a beard, no more than a wispy tuft. When they're seated, the room settles down and Monty, who is grimly hanging onto the lectern rather than leaning on it, opens proceedings.

'Ladies and gentlemen, Gallimores welcome you to the auction of the entire collection of the late, lamented Robert Smith, who was a personal friend of mine.'

A couple of young, fit-looking people are waiting in the wings to fetch and carry the artworks as they're introduced into the auction, bid for and sold. When Pamela started attending auctions many years ago, their equivalent had been a couple of slow, elderly blokes wearing faded cow gowns. Monty was keen to get underway. He didn't even have time to say 'without further ado'.

'Lot 1. An original John Piper abstracted landscape from the late 1950s executed in watercolours, gouache and pastels. Around this time, Piper was working on the stained glass for the new Coventry Cathedral, making the work interesting on several levels. I'll start the bidding at forty thousand.'

Pamela notes that forty grand is significantly higher than the reserve, demonstrating that Monty's in a bullish mood today. She hopes he's not being too ambitious. She'd recommended John Piper's work to Robert when they were building the collection and it had taken them an age to track this one down and buy it. There must be some Piper enthusiasts in the auction as the hammer comes down at forty-five. Plus Monty's buyer's premium, don't forget. She recognises the buyer and gives him a wave. Nice chap, a dealer, absolutely loaded. He's interested in the Porsche as well. She's sure he'll hang around for at least the afternoon session, so she'll seek him out during the break and remind him about the very desirable, low mileage sports car she has for sale.

The most surprising aspect of the afternoon session is that Monty remains reasonably compos mentis throughout. Vladimir stays quiet and doesn't bid for anything until one of Pamela's pieces comes up – Lot 22. It's a smallish, semi-abstract sculpture called *Vagina Dentata*, executed in bronze and mounted on a marble plinth. She'd charged Robert fifteen grand for it. He'd liked the piece very much and had displayed it proudly at Highfield. She didn't have the heart to tell him she'd fashioned it as a reaction to his relationship with Varvara. She'd literally broken the mould after the first casting, making the piece unique. Vladimir has clearly taken a shine to it and gets involved in a bidding war with a collector. He wins the battle and it's eventually knocked down for thirty grand. As the hammer descends, the victorious bidder turns around and smiles at her. He repeats the favour a little later by bidding successfully for one of her mixed media abstract paintings, *Persona Non Grata*, Lot 30. This time the hammer price is twenty grand, netting her a cool fifty in all, which she's already decided to donate to Robert's charity, 'Who Cares?' She's pretty sure the Russian isn't bidding for entirely altruistic reasons and he'll want something in return. Quid pro quo.

At the end of the first session, Pamela has a quick tot up. The lots have made a combined hammer price of about six million pounds and Monty has trousered his first million in commission. Not bad for an afternoon's work. As he brings proceedings to a close and heads for the wings, he gets disorientated and has to be helped off the stage. The evening session might still prove too much for him.

*

Pamela's enjoying the break, which includes a half-decent meal served at the table in a temporary marquee. She's every reason to feel pleased with herself as she's just shaken hands on the sale of the Porsche for an excellent price – no commission, no fees. The food is good and the wine is excellent. The latter is from Monty's collection, the fine wine cellar that keeps on giving. She finishes her meal and waits patiently for the coffee to be served. Her fellow diners have departed, eager to grab the best seats at the evening session. She browses the catalogue. There are some star-studded lots coming up and the limited-edition Lichtenstein prints are expected to reach record prices if Monty keeps his act together. She's about to take a sip of coffee when she receives a couple of unwelcome visitors. They sit down opposite her.

'What were you on, Pamela, when you produced that vagina piece?'

'Oh, the usual. I'd like to say it's a pleasure meeting with you again. Who's your friend?'

'This is Apti. He works for my father. Looks after the security and related matters. He is from Chechnya.'

Pamela is grateful for the warning she got from Varvara. Her first instinct would've been to pat him on the head and tell him to be a good little boy.

'Thanks for your generous bidding earlier, by the way. The net proceeds from my pieces will go to one of Robert's charities. Hope you don't mind.'

'And here I am thinking I am doing you a good turn. As the English say, one good turn requires another.'

'I'm not entirely sure how I can help you today.'

'I am told that you are the executor of Robert's affairs after his unfortunate accident. Do you know that he and I were in business together? Digital art. NFTs.'

'That shit? Do me a favour! I had nothing to do with it and, in the immortal words of an imaginary man from Barcelona, I know nothing. I wouldn't touch digital art with a barge pole. You must know that.'

'Well, be that as it is. Since his untimely death, I have had a few problems accessing our joint investment fund, which is held in a cryptocurrency account. I am keen to check on the funds and see how they are doing. Make sure they are still there. Do you have access to a wallet?'

'I do not, whatever one of those is. I advised my late husband against getting involved but he didn't listen.'

He's also done something stupid and it's starting to dawn on her what it may have been. She remembers something that might get her off the hook, if only temporarily.

'He did leave me a mystery object. It's a metal plate about the size of a small iPhone. It seems to have a code on it. Might that be useful?'

He looks at Apti, who nods almost imperceptibly.

'It might. Do you have it with you?'

'Of course I don't. I can send it to you if you like. By courier, if it's that important.'

'As quick as you can, madam.'

Apti has entered the conversation. He has a reedy, heavily accented voice, which doesn't sound like it has properly broken. Vladimir hands her one of his business cards. It has a London address on it.

'I'll do it tomorrow when I get back. By the way, when you've sorted out the cryptology, make sure you send Robert's share to me. It's part of his estate.'

'I will certainly do that. I hope for your own sake you are not pissing about with us. That would be most unfortunate. Goodbye for now.'

'Aren't you staying for the evening session? It promises to be great fun and not a vagina in sight.'

'No. I have no interest in the pop art. Americans leave me cold, as you can imagine. One more thing.'

'Yes?'

'Have you been in contact with my sister? I have been unable to locate her since Robert died. I am worried about her state of mind given what has happened to her in the past.'

'Sorry, I haven't. We're not exactly the best of friends as you might expect.'

'Well, let me know if you locate her. I am keen to catch up with her – we have a lot to talk about.'

The two men make as if to leave.

'I will be in touch with you soon regarding Robert's share. I would not like you to miss out on anything.'

Pamela shudders as she watches them leave. She would send him the metal plate as agreed but he wouldn't be best pleased when he finds out what it contains. She finishes her coffee and heads for the auction room.

*

There's much more of a buzz about the evening session. There aren't as many people in the hall but there's plenty of activity on the phones and online. Too much activity for Monty who isn't used to running auctions with quite so much online action. During the bidding for Lot 60, it all gets too much for him. He suddenly lurches sideways, makes a desperate grab for the lectern and launches himself and the lectern off the stage, demolishing Lot 60 and bestowing cuts and bruises on the guys flanking the exhibit. As Pamela rushes forward to help, she hopes and prays that Monty's insurance is fully paid up. Lot 60, a rare original painting by Leonora Carrington, had just received a telephone bid close to £1 million when Monty collapsed, the excitement of it no doubt tipping him over the edge. The Carrington is now in several pieces and each piece has to be solemnly withdrawn from sale. Like motor cars, the painting is a write-off. The insured value will be nowhere near a million pounds.

The cry of 'Is there a doctor in the house?' produces a gaggle of doctors, all of them retired, some of them looking old enough to remember administering leeches. They reach a consensus and an emergency call is made. More to the point, is there a half-decent auctioneer in the house? Thankfully, the answer is yes. After the removal of Monty on a stretcher to the waiting ambulance, there's a break in proceedings while the injured team members get some first aid and the new auctioneer gets briefed. Pamela slips him a cheque for a couple of grand – for his trouble.

The evening session restarts and is a huge success, pushing the hammer price for the entire collection beyond fifteen million pounds. The set of Roy Lichtenstein original prints (Lot 75) is snapped up by Tom Lanchester for close to a million pounds. Pamela reckons these will go back into the house, reminding her that she must meet with Tom and thank him personally for buying the damned carbuncle. Monty's payday has more than doubled while he's been lying prone in intensive care, recovering from a suspected heart attack. It isn't his first.

It's close to midnight when the auction closes. A fleet of taxis rapidly disperses the remaining bidders to their hotels. As Pamela had predicted, every lot has been sold and some record prices have been realised. After including the insurance payment for the Carrington disaster, Pamela will be able to pay nearly £16 million pounds into the holding account. The account is being updated with nearly a million pounds every month from Robert's investments, nudging it towards thirty million after including the proceeds from the house. A solid return, although tax and death duties will take a fair chunk. Whatever the amount, she'll do nothing with the money until Varvara's prepared to come out of hiding. The chances of that are negligible while her brother is prowling around looking for his share, whatever that might be.

Talking of Vladimir, she had to field a rather angry call from him a few days later when he found out the metal plate she'd sent him was completely useless. He flew into a rant and she ended up having to cut him off. It was about time she made that call to Link_03.

Chapter 31

Pamela was baffled by Vladimir's increasingly unhinged behaviour. She'd called Marissa to ask if she'd heard anything through her connections. She said she hadn't and there was no compelling reason to disbelieve her. While speaking to her, she realised how much she'd missed her new friend. Her recent fling with the much-decorated Katrina had fizzled out as quickly as it had started. It was Katrina's lack of warmth and her over-physicality that had put her off in the end. Pamela still enjoyed sex and lots of it but was now looking for the cuddles and commitment to go with it. Feeling her age perhaps, even if she didn't look it. She took the opportunity to re-establish her connection with Marissa and reset their relationship. She got the ball rolling by inviting her to England to spend a long weekend together at a rather splendid country house hotel. To her delight, Marissa accepted straightaway.

She'd read in the newspaper that Tom and Ellie Lanchester were back in the country, taking advantage of a break in filming that was due to last until the end of the year. She'd got in touch with Tom and arranged to meet them for lunch, a small thank you for buying Highfield.

She's chosen a tiny restaurant in Stratford-upon-Avon called Salt, which has a Michelin Star and an excellent reputation. Lunch is on her, the least she can do to show her appreciation. During an excellent meal, she warms to Tom, finding him utterly charming and charismatic in an understated way. His wife, however, is difficult to like. In addition to an obvious booze problem, she's loud, pushy and seriously up herself – Pamela's words. In the past, she might've been tempted by a desirable man like Tom but males no longer rang her bell. Thinking about it, the last time she'd been penetrated by a real man rather than a sex toy was by Robert on that fateful day a few years back. The day he'd confessed to her about his new girlfriend.

As they're being helped into their coats by the staff, Tom insists that she and Marissa visit them at Christmas so they can return the favour. Despite her barely concealed disdain for Highfield, Pamela accepts for both of them. She'd spoken enthusiastically about Marissa during lunch as if they were already a proper couple. She hopes she's not getting ahead of herself.

*

The Ettington Park Hotel is quite something. It's a few miles south of Stratford, set back from the road in what used to be a deer park. It's an imposing Grade 1 listed, neo-Gothic mansion, approached via a long, sweeping drive. Pamela has secured the Shirley Room for the Friday and Saturday nights. It's a large 'feature room' that will provide her and her potential lover with plenty of space, wonderful views, a four-poster bed and a slipper bath. When looking at the bath online, she imagined there'd be plenty of room for two in there. There are a couple of bottles of vintage champagne in the fridge, cut glass flutes on the table. All is set for a night of romance and she can barely contain her excitement.

The excitement, like the champagne, would have to remain on ice for another hour or two. There's urgent and pressing business to attend to and Pamela has booked one of the small meeting rooms in the hotel. It's called, rather grandly, The Oval Office. She's been in touch with Link_03 who has set up a Zoom meeting to brief them on the cryptocurrency investments and bring them up to speed on the latest developments. They might even discover why Vladimir is so wired about this stuff just now.

Link has insisted on them hooking their laptops up to a secure VPN of his choosing as he doesn't trust the hotel to have anything like the right amount of security. A couple of minutes into the Zoom session, Pamela and Marissa have been accepted into the meeting and are occupying the top right-hand and bottom left-hand boxes on a screen divided into four. The top left box displays one of Link's CryptoPunk avatars. Link is chairing the meeting and looking after the technology. He wastes no time in getting underway.

'HI, PAMELA. WELCOME TO THE CALL.'

'Hello. Can I call you Link?'

'SURE. EVERYBODY ELSE DOES. DON'T THEY, MARISSA?'

'Wait a minute. Do you two know each other?'

'We do, yes. Link is on Europol's approved list of suppliers. He often does paid work for the organisation, although I cannot tell you the details. Are you well, Link?'

'AS WELL AS CAN BE EXPECTED IN THE CIRCUMSTANCES. VERY TRYING CIRCUMSTANCES RIGHT NOW IF I MIGHT BE SO BOLD.'

Pamela was trying to recover her composure after hearing about Marissa and Link. She feels like she's surrounded by shape-shifters, and it doesn't end there. A black box appears at the bottom right of their screens.

'HOLD ON A MO. WE HAVE ANOTHER PERSONAGE JOINING US. SHE SAYS SHE ONLY WANTS TO LISTEN IN. DON'T WORRY, HER CREDENTIALS ARE IMPECCABLE.'

The box stays black and no name appears.

'HI, VARVARA. I HAVE MARISSA AND PAMELA ON THE CALL. DO YOU WANT TO SAY ANYTHING BEFORE I KICK OFF?'

At Ettington Park, Pamela and Marissa turn to look at each other, quizzical looks on their faces.

'Hi, Link. Ladies. I know most of what Link is about to tell you two. I am here to ensure that by the time we finish the call, we are all on the same page as you say and each of us is aware of the danger facing us. That is all. Please carry on.'

She switches to mute. Her box remains stubbornly black and blank.

'THANKS. HOW MUCH DO YOU TWO KNOW ABOUT THE CRYPTO SHENANIGANS?'

She's not sure about Marissa now but Pamela's certain she knows considerably less than the other attendees. She outlines the story so far from her point of view, mentioning her recent encounter with Vladimir and what she'd done so far to fend him off.

'THANKS, PAMELA. THE FIRST PROBLEM IS THE LATEST VALUE OF THE CRYPTO FUND. ALTHOUGH THE EXCHANGE RATE VEERS AROUND FROM TIME TO TIME AND SOMETIMES FALLS OFF A CLIFF, THE POUNDS STERLING VALUE OF THE INVESTMENT FUND IS AROUND ...'

They hear the tapping of keys.

[11/11/2019: 1 ETH = 148.12 GBP (Source AOEx): Fund value: £134 million]

'... a hundred and thirty million pounds. Ether is struggling right now for various reasons. Goes with the territory. The value has dipped by about a third since Vladimir upped his family's stake.'

Two sharp intakes of breath from the Ettington Park attendees. They're genuinely shocked by the amounts involved. Marissa is the first to react.

'How did that happen? He'd hinted that Vladimir had upped his stake, but that's a hell of a lot of money.'

'From what Robert said, it seems like he tried to impress his dad by opening up a new channel for money laundering. Crypto is unregulated so it's good news for launderers. The downside is it's a very unreliable investment, to say the least. However, if the crypto is invested in something like NFTs, the investment side starts to look much more promising. His dad decided to take a punt for whatever reason. He'll be regretting it big time and he'll probably want to cut their losses.'

'Why doesn't he?'

'Which brings me to the second problem. Robert did something we both agreed was very risky, dangerous even. He transferred all the crypto to a new wallet and reset the private password. He omitted to tell Vladimir.'

'Meaning what exactly?'

'Meaning Vladimir has a wallet that doesn't work anymore. He's unable to access the investment fund and is powerless to arrest the slide in value.'

'Why did Robert do it? He must have known it would have repercussions. Serious ones.'

Varvara chooses that moment to unmute and step in. Her Zoom display remains black as coal, which seems to match her mood.

'I have given that a lot of thinking time since he died. He was seriously pissed off by the behaviour of my brother and the way he was being, how do you put it, stitched by my family. Sorry Marissa, but he had felt he could not wait for the Europol slowcoaches to get their act together. He worked out a simple way to put a huge chunk of dirty money beyond use and then did it. At the time, he did not tell me the amounts involved but we both recognised the danger and arranged to disappear for a while. His sudden death was not part of the plan but the rest of it has worked so far.'

'What do you mean, so far?'

'There will be consequences. I almost feel sorry for my idiot brother. In his eagerness to impress his father, he offered him what he thought would be a win/win investment opportunity. When he made his case, he may have over-egged the pie. Either Igor did not read the small print or he was setting his son up to fail, giving him an excuse to dispose of him and make way for a new protégé.'

'Why did Igor throw so much money at it?'

'Good question. He is usually more careful. I would guess that the family business was scaling up and the deals were getting bigger. Narcotics probably. My contacts think there was a big deal going down, they had to process a huge influx of cash and needed to make it safe quickly. They also needed to spread their bets to deflect attention. The crypto investment is about a third of what they were looking to launder. The double-cross with the wallet has done two things. It has prevented my brother from withdrawing funds to fix a big slide in the exchange rate. It has also put the entire fund out of his reach. They stand to lose the equivalency of £200 million.'

'Isn't that a good thing?'

'It depends where you stand, Pamela. I know my family too well. They will stop at nothing to restore their access to those missing millions. It is not as if the money has been incinerated. It is out there on the blockchain somewhere and all they need is the new wallet. The new recovery seed would be useful to them but only as a fallback. Three of the people on this call have pieces of the solution. All of us are now targets.'

'Could I make a suggestion?'

'Go ahead.'

'I assume that none of you are interested in running off with tens of millions of pounds worth of crypto and pissing it all up the wall anytime soon?'

Link's turn of phrase is a bit unfortunate given that three of the four participants are women. Despite that, there are nods around the table. A thumbs up icon emerges briefly from Varvara's blackness.

'You have a binary choice, I suppose. You can leave the crypto 'lost in cyberspace' and walk away, putting the seed phrase beyond use by destroying all references to it, including hardware on which it's embedded. The millions would be lost for ever.'

'Go on.'

'Or you can retain access to the funds on one device — the new crypto wallet — and keep it secure until such time as it's safe to use. The millions of pounds can still remain at large as long as everybody plays the game. There's a chance that Vladimir could get his hands on it I suppose.'

'It is Varvara again. Whatever we do, we are in the same shit. Even if we walk away, we will still be open targets. My family will not believe we have not kept a route open to the funds. We might as well hang on to it. I am not capable of memorising the seed phrase, so it could not be beaten out of me. Pamela?'

'Same here. But pardon me if I feel the most exposed of all of us. Marissa is police and you and Link remain well hidden whereas I don't have a secret hideout or identity to fall back on. That said, I would prefer to stay with the new setup, as suggested. It looks like we're damned if we do and damned if we don't. It seems such a waste to chuck it all away.'

'OK. Let's work this through. Robert would have generated a new seed phrase when he set up the wallet. What happened to the wallet? Pamela?'

'Well, there was a small electronic gizmo in his hotel safe.

'Can you describe the aforementioned gizmo please?'

'Smaller than a mobile phone, tiny screen, a couple of buttons. I've found a safe place for it.'

'Great. That's the new wallet. Do you have his laptop?'

'Yes. Well, I have his iPad. Does that count?'

'Did he take it to San Sebastian with him?'

'He did, yes. He kept it in the safe in his hotel room.'

'In that case, you have the only path to the currency. The key is embedded in the wallet. Wherever you've put that wallet, please find somewhere safer asap. Do you have the PIN?'

'I'm not sure. What does it look like?'

'Four numbers. Like a PIN for your debit card or

WHATEVER. EASILY REMEMBERED.'

'Yes, I have it. I'm guessing I shouldn't keep it written down on a sticky note attached to the iPad?'

'CORRECT. DON'T TELL ME, ROBERT ...'

'Did exactly that. Yes.'

'OK, LET ME SUMMARISE. PAMELA HAS THE NEW WALLET WITH THE LATEST PRIVATE KEY AND A PIN WITH WHICH TO ACCESS IT. THIS IS THE ONLY ROUTE TO THE FUNDS AND SHE WILL TAKE STEPS TO PUT IT IN A SAFE PLACE. BETWEEN YOU, VARVARA AND PAMELA, YOU HAVE A MANUAL RECORD OF THE SEED PHRASE. TWELVE WORDS EACH. BY THE WAY, HOW DO WE KNOW WHO HAS THE FIRST TWELVE AND WHO THE SECOND TWELVE?'

'We don't. Oh, hang on. There's a small stick-on dot at the top of the plate. It's got a '1' on it.'

'VARVARA?'

'Yes. My dot shows '2', the second set of twelve.'

'AS YOU HAVE A FUNCTIONING WALLET AND A TWO-PART MANUAL BACKUP FOR THE SEED PHRASE, I AM PLANNING TO END MY INVOLVEMENT IN THE ACCOUNT. TRUST ME. I'M NOT RUNNING AWAY BUT THE LESS PEOPLE IN THE KNOW, THE SAFER IT WILL BE FOR EVERYBODY.'

'It is Varvara. I agree with Link. Please be careful everybody as there are some very bad people out there. I know this.'

A bit like Igor's afternoon board meetings, there are no minutes. Link's last action before closing the meeting is to set up another Zoom call.

*

As they leave The Oval Office, Pamela and Marissa look at each other. It's a look that says there's a lot of night left and there's chilled champagne waiting for them upstairs. They could have gone to the bar first but why waste time? As soon as they're back in their suite, they're out of their clothes and onto the vast bed as quick as you like. At one stage, they break off to enjoy some champagne. Later, they try out the slipper bath, where they prove beyond doubt that two women can fit in there with plenty of room to manoeuvre.

In the morning, the two lovers enjoy a deluxe hotel breakfast in bed. They concoct a couple of flutes of buck's fizz from some leftover champagne and juice. Despite feeling hungover and tired, they can't stop giggling.

'What a night. I will never make love to a man ever again. I mean it.'

'Are you sure?'

'I am. Would you agree we have something special here?'

Pamela has to agree. Marissa is a very special lady. Ridiculously attractive, great body. Loving, kind and very affectionate. This is becoming the real deal for her, a proper loving relationship, no less. She can't remember being so happy.

The 'Do Not Disturb' sign stays on their door for an hour or two more. When Pamela's phone rings later, they're both half asleep, sprawled across the four-poster. She has no intention of ruining the moment by answering it. Five minutes later, it rings again.

'You had better answer it. It might be important.'

She answers it. She wishes she hadn't.

Chapter 32

The call had been the police, reporting there'd been a break-in at the studio the previous night. It'd been reported by a neighbour. Marissa and Pamela had sprung into action and were packed and checked out of the hotel within half an hour. A taxi got them to Moreton-in-Marsh station in less than twenty minutes, where they picked up the intercity train to London Paddington. It would be more accurate to call it an intervillage train during the Cotswolds stage of its journey. It does, however, speed up substantially after Oxford and the two of them arrive in good time to meet with Geoff Andrews at Pamela's studio.

Geoff is the SOCO or scene of crimes officer. You might have thought a SOCO was a police officer but that's not the case anymore and Geoff isn't wearing a uniform. He starts by removing some of the police tape from the doorway. There isn't a great deal left of the door.

'Don't worry, ladies, we've run the rule over the crime scene and extracted what we can. It's one hell of a mess in there, I'm afraid. Sorry about that.'

He does a lot of apologising. It goes with the territory, I suppose. They walk down the entrance hall and enter the main studio. It's the first time Marissa's seen the studio and she's taken aback by the chaotic jumble facing her. Pamela initially sees nothing out of the ordinary. Closer scrutiny reveals that some of the canvases have been damaged, slashed with a knife or similar. A couple of bronzes have been toppled from their plinths and one or two of her ceramic works have been smashed. A solitary bronze sculpture remains intact on a plinth in the centre of the studio. It's the *Vagina Dentata*. More than that it's a calling card, a crude warning from an angry Vladimir. It chills her to the bone but she's not prepared to explain it to Geoff. She'll discuss it later with Marissa and get her take on it.

'They've really taken it out on my artwork, whoever they are.'

'Have you any idea who may have done this. It seems personal to me, that's all.'

'My work isn't universally popular, put it that way. Nobody in particular springs to mind.'

'It looks like the break-in was carried out by a professional team. Our people have been through the entire apartment and have found no forensic evidence. Nothing that's useful anyway.'

'Why might that be important?'

'Professional teams are expensive to deploy. They're used by people with deep pockets who are looking for something specific and valuable. Think governments. Think organised crime. Anything spring to mind?'

'No, not really. Hang on a minute, I keep a small safe under the bed.'

She bounds up the staircase to the mezzanine. She looks under the bed then leans over the rail to tell him it's missing. After a further cursory search, it appears to be the only item that's been removed.

Geoff's phone rings and after apologising yet again, he takes the call. It doesn't last long.

'I'm needed at another incident. Sorry ladies but I need to leave you to it. Sorry about that.'

*

Pamela was quite relieved when he left – off the back of a further apology. He's handed her a number to ring when she feels up to making a statement about the break-in and reporting the missing items. Marissa is looking askance at the one sculpture still standing.

'Is that what I think it is?'

'Yes. Read the brass plate, why don't you?'

She reads, then nods her head.

'Ah, right. OK, I get it. It is very – I am struggling to find the right word – visceral is it not?'

'It's meant to be. Let's get a drink before we talk about all this.'

Regrettably, she's run out of the ingredients to make a Gin and It. They have to settle for a couple of beers, the only alcoholic drinks in the fridge. As usual, it's freezing cold in the studio and it'll take a couple of hours of groaning and gurgling from the ancient heating system to get up to temperature. The bed's equipped with an excellent electric blanket and Pamela sets it to max. Soon, they're both naked and snuggling under the covers. The beers remain on the bedside tables, untouched for now. Too bloody cold.

'You must be upset about the robbery and the damage. I have booked a few days off, meaning I can stay around for a while, keep you company, help you sort it out. I am happy to help, you know that.'

'Thank you, darling. I wouldn't be human if I didn't feel scared but I also feel pretty fackin angry. Let me tell you what I think.'

The room temperature has struggled up to a tad more than tepid, so they adjust the pillows and assume semi-seated positions, the covers pulled up under their chins. Neither of them is minded to make love right now, especially given the current state of the front door. As they sip their beers, a watery winter sunshine spills into the studio through the large picture windows. Cold comfort it seems, as it'll be dark within an hour.

'First up, the damage. Spiteful, don't you think? The slashed paintings. The toppled sculptures. The smashed ceramics. All that work. Mindless and cruel. How very Russian. At least they didn't leave a pile of excrement in the wastepaper bin.'

The incredulous look on Marissa's face demands a further explanation.

'It's what happened when my house up north was burgled a few years back. The police said it was not uncommon during robberies. The shitting in the bin trick I mean. Fackin people.'

'OK. What else?'

'Second, Geoff said it was a professional job so they must have been looking for something valuable. We found out yesterday that the wallet-type-thingummy could be worth a fortune. It might also be a life-or-death matter for Vladimir who'd have no problems funding a professional team from what I've heard.'

'Agreed. Carry on.'

'Thirdly, the stolen safe. It's not massively secure but it would have been noisy and time-consuming to rip it open on site. So, they lifted and shifted it. Unless, of course, they got disturbed.'

'Was the, er, thingummy in the safe? Please say no.'

'It wasn't. As luck would have it, I didn't think it was safe enough in there so I moved it and some related stuff to another location. Good job I did.'

'Clever you. Is there more?'

'Well, there's a substantial part of my jewellery collection gone

AWOL in the safe. They're insured but I think I've seen the last of them, dammit. There were some very nice pieces in there, heirlooms and the like.'

'Anything else?'

'The vagina piece. The one sculpture left standing.'

'Why did they leave it alone?'

'For a start it hasn't been in my studio for some years, so the robbers must have brought it with them. You're aware we had a big sale of the art collection a few weeks ago. Vladimir bought this work and paid well over the odds to my mind.'

'So, you think he was here during the break-in and left you the sculpture as a very expensive calling card. A warning, in other words.'

'Thereby upping the ante. Putting the frighteners on me, as I'm the only remaining player very much at large.'

Marissa thought her friend was putting a brave face on it, but there was no mistaking the danger she was in.

'I cannot do a great deal for you, Pamela, but I would take it personally if you came to any harm. I can arrange some discreet surveillance for you when I am not around. The budgets will not run to twenty-four hours or anything like it but it might make a difference.'

'Thank you, my darling. It wouldn't go amiss in the current circumstances. I'll take whatever you can offer on that front.'

'Consider it done. I will make some calls.'

They lay together in the gloom for a while. After what seemed like an age, the studio warmed up. Later that evening, Pamela ordered a pizza delivery. When it arrived, Marissa squeezed into one of Pamela's dressing gowns and dealt with the delivery guy. He didn't seem at all fazed by the fact there was no front door to speak of.

Chapter 33

Another month, another board meeting in Moscow. It's the afternoon session – off the record – and the top players in Igor's business empire are enjoying the spa facilities at his dacha. Vladimir is also there. There's a self-congratulatory feel to the proceedings as they've managed to disperse an immense amount of cash in record time. More than a third of it has gone into cryptocurrency but his son's vague updates have done nothing to reassure the oligarch. He'd recently asked Valery to take another good look at NFTs and he'd concluded the big bucks were still a couple of years away. Given the ongoing plunge in Ether's value, he'd advised Igor to cut their losses as soon as possible.

It's normal for Igor to break off for a private chat with his security director and this month is no different. He and Apti head for the jacuzzi. Between the steam room and the jacuzzi, Igor's demeanour darkens considerably and he's now wearing his 'Leonid Brezhnev' face. He lowers himself with some difficulty into the bubbles while Apti takes up a position opposite him.

'Item one: Piotr. Where the fuck is he, Apti? I had his university course booked and we were ready to go. How can he just disappear?'

'I have no idea, boss. He emptied his flat and vanished. None of my contacts in England know where he is. Believe me, if they did know, they would have told me.'

'I believe you. Any theories?'

'What about your daughter? She has not been seen since the day after Robert Smith was killed. I observed her and Piotr together in Oxford and it did not look like a chance meeting. After that, I made Piotr's girlfriend a very good offer to go back to Canada, clearing the way for the next steps.'

'So, your theory is?'

'Varvara and Piotr have gone into hiding together. They did this after Robert Smith was killed. It must be a very good hiding place because we have expended a lot of effort trying to find them with no success. Is there a connection between them?'

'The only connection is me.'

'She hates you of course, which makes her dangerous. Extremely dangerous given her training and background.'

'Absolutely. Redouble your efforts. Whatever it takes. You understand?'

'Yes, boss.'

'Item two: Vladimir. My cretinous son is hanging by a thread but he's still there – mainly because you've been unable to find Piotr. I should never have listened to him regarding the cryptocurrency investments, although I blame Valery as well for getting carried away. Anyway, I am seeing my son later. I want what remains of the cash back now, but I don't trust him. He has become very evasive. Shifty even – more than normal. He is hiding something, Apti, and I may have to call on your services again. A family matter, you understand?'

'Yes, boss. Can I mention something else?'

'Shoot.'

Only Igor could get away with saying something like that to Apti.

'I heard through my sources there was a robbery at the London home of Robert Smith's wife. Although some serious operators were involved, Vladimir was also there. It was bungled, basically. I can only guess at what he was up to. They got away with a portable safe containing some of her jewellery and papers, nothing useful. They didn't get what they were looking for, I am told. Wasted effort. They trashed the place instead.'

'And what were they looking for? According to your sources.'

'They think Vladimir has been double-crossed by Robert Smith. It was probably intended as a temporary measure to get him to back the money out. When Mister Smith had his tragic and untimely accident, the temporary measure became permanent. I can only conclude that your son has been locked out of the account and the robbery was an attempt at fixing that.'

'How safe is our investment?'

'Very safe, what is left of it. Ether has plunged in value in the recent past but the tokens are still there on the system. All we need to do is find the new account. Find the account, find the money.'

'Thanks very much. Can you stick around for a while? I might need to talk tactics with you later.'

'Yes, boss.'

'I'd like to go to the sauna now to finish off. Could you help me get out of here?'

Igor's physical wellbeing has deteriorated so much that he now needs an electric hoist to get him out of the jacuzzi. He'll need the same device to help him get in soon. Apti is happy to oblige on this occasion.

'Could you tell Vladimir to join me in the sauna? Only him, nobody else.'

'Yes, boss.'

*

'You wanted to talk to me, papa.'

Igor was wearing the sort of look that the term 'hatchet-faced' was invented for. Even on the rare occasions he tried a smile for size it usually came out close to a scowl. As Vladimir settled himself on the pine slats, a scowl was what he got. It could have been worse.

'Yes, I did son. I wanted to talk to you about our investment in the cryptocurrencies.'

'OK. What is the problem?'

'It seemed like a good idea when you pitched it to us and we went for it. Unfortunately, we are too soon to market for the NFTs according to the money men and we now have an unlimited exposure to the downside of cryptocurrency. I have decided to derisk the whole investment and get out before the market screws us big time. I want you to withdraw our funds and we will reinvest them somewhere a bit safer. US dollars. Valery reckons the Virgin Islands have some safer options for us. Equally discreet and backed up by none other than our good friends in the UK government.'

'How long have I got to do this?'

'A week, two at the most. The exchange rate is killing us so every day counts. That may change but we should not depend on it recovering any time soon. Valery tells me the investment has halved in value.'

Vladimir thought it might be worse than that.

'OK. There might be a problem.'

'There usually is with you. Before you start whining, spare me the details. Apti has already briefed me on the unfortunate business with Robert Smith and the cheap trick that he has played on you. I could chew you up and spit you out for being such an idiot but I would be wasting my time. As they say in the West, you are down the shit creek with no paddle.'

It's blisteringly hot in the sauna – exactly how Igor likes it. His son is feeling the heat in more ways than one and has started to squirm. He makes a big effort to appear calm but he knows exactly what his father is capable of. The silence persists for what seems an age. Eventually, Igor emits a huge sigh.

'Here is what you are going to do to rescue this unfortunate situation. The first thing you need is a good team. Apti will be with you the whole way and he will handpick a couple of suitably skilled people – deniable freelancers, I expect – from Yevgeny's agency. They will travel to England using false papers and you can use one of my London apartments as a base. You target the people who were around Robert Smith. Your mission is to rescue as much of our money as you can. Focus for now on the cryptocurrency. Don't let me down.'

'How ...'

'Enough! Apti has all the detail and will brief you later. You leave for England tomorrow. One more thing.'

'Yes, papa?'

'In the immortal words of Robert Burns. Do or die, son of mine. Do or die.'

On that note, Igor waves him away. As he basks in the baking heat, he chuckles to himself about the Robbie Burns' thing. It was his tank crew's motto during the war. Do *and* die would be more accurate given the churn among his comrades, which is why he'd put Apti on the team. He'd lost count of the number of last chances he'd given his wayward son. Despite him being family, the loss of all those funds would seriously undermine the business. It saddened him but his son had become a dead weight he wasn't prepared to carry any longer than necessary. He's also started to speculate about how much time he has left given his own deteriorating health, which has started to embarrass him. Being winched out of your own jacuzzi is not a great look.

Securing the funds is only the first part of Apti's assignment. The second is to hunt down Varvara and remove her from play. Igor fears his daughter far more than his other enemies as he's sure she intends to take him down at some stage. There is no doubting the strength of her motivation – as Apti said, she hates him and with good reason. Her military skills – several years as an elite paratrooper and officer, including combat experience in South Ossetia – are quite something. A force to be reckoned with. When they find her, he's sure they'll find Piotr and he's already looking forward to welcoming his son to the family business.

Chapter 34

Since the break-in, Marissa had made a credible case for some affordable surveillance around Pamela. When proposing this, she'd been careful to leave out the important detail about them being romantically involved. The arrangements are necessarily low key – so low that Pamela hasn't noticed any difference. There's also a panic alarm. According to Marissa, just one touch of the button and a SWAT team will be climbing the stairs to her studio within fifteen minutes. She's not sure whether to believe her or not but it makes her feel a tiny bit safer.

Only last week, Pamela had received a call from Coutts about a failed attempt by some shady-looking no-life to get access to Robert's safe deposit box. It was serious enough for her to catch the next tube into Central London. At Coutts, she'd looked at the remaining stuff in the box and had removed just the one item, placing it in her handbag. Keeping the crypto-wallet close to hand appeared to be the only remaining option and would enable her to keep tabs on the account. The exchange rate of Ether had stabilised after recent precipitous losses – a few percentage points, a couple of million down. When she'd checked it yesterday, it didn't look too bad.

[25/12/2019: 1 ETH = 98.95 GBP (Source AOEx): Fund Value: £89 million]

She'd shared the information with Marissa who thought the danger to them would be less while the value held. If the exchange rate took another big nosedive, all bets were off given the people they were dealing with. Great. Pamela didn't tell her she was keeping the wallet close by as she's sure Marissa wouldn't have approved. She could have handed it over to her for safekeeping but didn't want to lose control of it, although she would have been hard-pressed to explain why. At least she hadn't started calling it 'my precious' yet. Seriously, it's now the big prize. Put it this way, all Vladimir has to do is get his hands on it and he's back in business. The new seed phrase would be a bonus but not essential for what he needs to do to get back in his papa's good books.

*

Just now, the wallet is nestling in her tote bag on the floor between her and Marissa. Pamela takes another gulp of some very nice wine. It's Boxing Day. She and Marissa are enjoying a sumptuous evening meal with Tom and Ellie at Highfield. The food had been prepared earlier by their chef and all they have to do is heat it up and keep it warm until they're ready to tuck in. They're currently enjoying the main course, which is beautifully presented and involves a goose, some roast vegetables and a sauce or two. The chef had suggested pairing it with a 2014 Barolo and a 2019 Pinot Gris from Alsace. Pamela's on the red, which tastes nothing like Monty's Christmas present this year – a good thing, by and large. Talking of Monty, he's now fully recovered from his latest heart attack and doing his best to hasten the onset of the next one. He now regards himself as semi-retired, whatever that means.

In a nice touch, the Lanchesters have hired a smart young waiter from a local catering company to serve the food and wine to them. The waiter is polite and very good at what he does. He doesn't say very much but it's enough to detect a slight accent in his excellent English, possibly Eastern European. Ellie, who's been hitting the wine in a big way, can't help drooling and commenting on how handsome he looks even though he's very young. Tom carries on eating and tries his best to ignore his wife's poor behaviour.

They finish the main course. All the plates have been licked clean except Ellie's, which has hardly been touched. The waiter is attending the table, cleaning away the plates and cutlery. He drops one of the forks with a clatter right next to Pamela and apologises profusely while retrieving it. As he heads for the door, laden with precarious piles of plates, cutlery and food waste, there's a bright flash and a loud explosion outside that shakes the house and rattles the windows. He deposits what's left of the pile of plates on a sideboard and scarpers as fast as he can. Pamela is the first of the diners to react.

'What the fackin hell was that?'

Tom shoves his chair back and springs into action.

'I've no idea but I'm keen to find out. Sounds like it came from the front gate. Where's that waste-of-space Simon when you need him?'

As he rushes out, he looks across at Ellie but she's slumped down in her seat and in no fit state to spring into anything, let alone action. Except, perhaps, to throw up – which is exactly what she does. Marissa gathers her up and drags her to the nearest bathroom to get her cleaned up.

Pamela's left on her own, so does her bit by wrapping everything left on the table – including Ellie's stomach contents – in the tablecloth and depositing it in a corner of the vast kitchen. On her way back to the table she hears a heavy truck pull up outside followed by a chorus of shouting in a babel of languages. This doesn't sound at all promising. When she gets back to the table, she dips into her bag for the reassuring feel of the crypto-wallet. She can't locate it immediately and starts scrabbling frantically. Eventually, she empties the bag out onto the table. It's no longer there. Somebody must've half-inched it. There's no time to dwell on it however, as there's quite a commotion in the hallway outside the dining room.

Chapter 35

First to appear is Tom, staggering forward like he's just been pushed. He has been pushed. For some reason, he has both his hands on the back of his head. He appears calm but bear in mind he's a good actor. He aims a question at Pamela.

'Friends of yours by any chance?'

She doesn't have to answer. The next person to appear is clad in black leather. He looks and sounds pumped and for once in his life feels like he's in charge. A potent mix of adrenaline and narcotics is fuelling the fire, adding a dangerous edge to his behaviour. He doesn't have any weapons and doesn't need to as Apti's next to arrive, armed to the teeth. He's dressed in worn, faded combat fatigues to complete the look. Vladimir needs no introduction but introduces himself anyway, his arrogance well to the fore amid the faux bonhomie.

'Pamela. Great to see you again. I am a bit late to the party it seems. I have brought some friends with me, so I hope you have saved some of your leftovers.'

He reaches across to the Barolo, scrutinises the label and takes a large glug from the bottle, wiping his mouth on his sleeve. He offers the bottle to Apti who waves it away contemptuously. He might be a vicious and indiscriminate killer but he's also a devout Muslim.

'I see you've brought your little minder with you. I'd really like to say it's a pleasure to see you both but I'm struggling.'

Apti lifts his venerable GSh-18 service pistol and points it at her. She refuses to cower. Despite being terrified, she's deploying her best regulation stiff upper lip. She remains in her seat. Two more items of bad news are about to enter the room – Bogdan and Fedor, Apti's handpicked recruits from the shadowy Wagner Group. Mercenaries basically. These guys are less overtly well-armed than Apti, but each of them is about twice the size of the Chechen. It's mainly well-tended sinew and muscle by the look of it. Bogdan's in plain clothes, has a holstered pistol about his person and is carrying a laptop. Fedor has grey camouflage fatigues and he too has a sidearm. In addition, he has a heavy, tube-like weapon slung over his shoulder and the tail fins of some RPGs protrude from the rucksack he's carrying. The heavy weapon is the latest RPG-7, borrowed from Wagner's extensive UK-based armoury and is prime suspect for creating the earlier explosion at the gate.

Although using the buzzer hadn't occurred to them, it turns out Simon would've been more than happy to wave them through. The handyman is the next person to enter the dining room and it's pretty obvious he's betrayed them to the Russians. For money, no doubt and plenty of it knowing him. Pamela loathes Simon with a vengeance, so the betrayal comes as no surprise.

'Hello, Simon.'

'Pamela.'

'I heard your missus kicked you into touch and went back to

Poland. Can't say as I blame her. How much did they pay you? Not nearly enough, if you ask me.'

Simon shrugs his shoulders – water off a duck's back as far as he's concerned. His response is brief and dismissive.

'I'm not very likely to ask you, am I?'

Vladimir's sympathies are with Pamela on this one, which is why he lets her get away with it. He's on a roll right now, enjoying himself even.

'Oh, wait a minute. I think we are missing a few people. Simon?'

'There's Mister Lanchester's wife and there's Pamela's girlfriend, the policewoman.'

'Pamela? Would you mind enlightening us as to their whereabouts?'

'I would mind ac ...'

Apti's pistol cracks and an elaborate vase explodes on the sideboard behind Pamela. It's more than enough to trigger her survival instincts.

'Ellie was a bit worse for wear, so Marissa took her to the loo to get cleaned up.'

'Bogdan, could you collect the ladies? I would hate them to miss anything.' Vladimir isn't finished yet. 'Is that it? Simon?'

'There was a young guy they hired. He came in to help serve the food.'

'Where is he? Pamela?'

'He legged it when he heard the explosion. Wish I'd done the same.'

'Must be hiding somewhere. Apti?'

'On it.'

Within fifteen minutes, Ellie, Marissa, Pamela and Tom are sitting around the dining table, all of them firmly tied to their seats with industrial strength cable ties. They've been thoroughly shaken down and anything capable of communicating with the outside world has been taken and disposed of. Pamela's bag and its contents have been inspected and moved well away from her. She's racking her brains about what might have happened to the bloody wallet. She thought Marissa might have taken it – she'd been sitting next to her throughout dinner. It seems unlikely now as the Russians had searched them all thoroughly, although she may have hidden it in the bathroom somewhere.

*

Vladimir sits at the head of the table. He's leaning back on his chair and man-spreading. Think Alan Rickman as the Sheriff of Nottingham. He has a captive audience and is clearly enjoying himself. He dictates his terms.

'Listen to me carefully. I liked Robert Smith and I know he loved my sister very much. I thought he was a good friend. Instead of this he double-crossed me big time and stole an enormous quantity of hard-earned cash. Now I want it back – what is left of it – and at least one of the people around this table can provide me with the solution.'

'We don't have what you want, believe me.'

Pamela feels it needs saying but there's an air of desperation about it.

'It has not escaped my notice that the crypto investments have tanked while I have been locked out, knocking a big portion off the value. Give me the wallet, the new PIN and the seed phrase now and, subject to Bogdan's technical checks, we will leave you in peace.'

'We don't have it. What don't you understand?'

'Call me cynical, Pamela, but I do not believe you. I am so sure you can help me, I am proposing an incentive scheme.'

He makes a great play of looking at his watch, which, as you might expect, is big and complicated.

'It is just after midnight now. Every hour, on the hour, one of you will be released from your bondage, taken outside and shot. This will continue to happen until I get the wallet and it is proven to work. Understand?'

Pamela is powerless to intervene. Her one bargaining chip, the wallet, has gone and people are being lined up to die needlessly.

'We don't have the fackin wallet.'

'I think you do or you know where it is. What is more, I am persuaded to leave you until last. See how long it takes for you to remember where you have put it. Now, we will eat our supper and leave you to think.'

He turns to leave, then remembers something.

'Simon? Stay here and watch over our hosts. Shout if anybody tries anything. When we've finished eating, I have another important task for you.'

Simon's main preoccupation during his oversight of the hostages is to avoid eye contact with them. Especially Pamela who, as we know, has a good line in death stares.

Chapter 36

Before she'd been removed from the bathroom at gunpoint, Marissa had realised exactly what was happening and got a coded emergency call off to the security services. When she heard the hammering on the door, she'd dumped the phone in the toilet cistern. Within half an hour, a security team had been scrambled. Soon afterwards, a control centre had been established and a team comprising senior officers from Europol, MI5, SIS, Home Office, Counter Terrorism and the NCA had been hastily assembled, some already on site in Warwick and some online.

The Europol rep provided them with an overview of the case and what had led up to the potential hostage situation at Highfield. Three of the five men involved are known to the authorities and they're urgently trying to identify the other two, believed to be mercenaries. A team of heavily armed police are hunkered down at the entrance gate, awaiting orders. Although a hostage negotiator has been chosen and is on her way, she faces an immediate challenge – there are no demands and no established way of contacting anybody. Until they find out more about what they're dealing with, there's no alternative but to secure the area and sit it out.

*

After legging it, the waiter hurries back to the safe room where he and his mother have been hiding out undetected since Robert's death. The safe room is actually a small complex of rooms embedded deep beneath Highfield. It was designed and specified by Robert and installed during the recent security upgrade.

Varvara has been glued to the latest action via the extensive CCTV network – night vision-enabled – watching events unfold in the house. Danger is everywhere but she can scarcely conceal her delight at the turn of events. After months of hiding, the novelty had worn off long ago and life beneath Highfield had started to pall for her and her son despite a few brief moments of freedom. The one saving grace is that it'd given her and Piotr plenty of time to build their relationship.

'Did you get the wallet, dahling?'

He waves the small device at her.

'Is this it? It was in Pamela's handbag. She was so intent on smooching with her new girlfriend, she didn't notice what I was doing.'

'Shall I check it out?'

He throws the wallet across to her. She switches from the CCTV to the wallet app and inserts the device into the only spare USB port on her laptop. She taps in the PIN and is soon looking at the tokens. She ignores the NFTs and focuses on the currency.

[27/12/2019: 1 ETH = 97.08 GBP (Source AOEx): Fund value: £88 million]

The news isn't great for her brother. Ether's been in the doldrums for some time and the investment is looking less than healthy. Oh dear.

'How is it doing?'

'The tokens are well down and my brother will do well to clear £90 million. The fool has lost more than half of the original investment. Our father will not be pleased.'

'What happens now, mama?'

'Well, here we are. This is our moment – our one big chance to take the fight to them. We must take it. Tell me truthfully, my son – are you ready for this?'

'I am. You just have to say the word. I hope I don't let you down.'

She stands up and embraces her son briefly. She's dressed simply for the task ahead – monkey boots, lightweight combat trousers and a vest top. Her hair is tied back, the ponytail emerging from the gap at the back of her military-style peaked cap. She's wearing no make-up, no jewellery. Combat ready. For the next few hours, she'll need to think on her feet, knowing she has to stay only a second or two ahead of Vladimir and his cronies. When he suddenly showed up and laid down his terms, he'd created the best opportunity she'd ever have to destroy her family.

'Would you stay here for now. Keep a careful watch on what is going on around the house. I am going to look around, get some idea of what they intend to do. I am a little bit short of firepower, so I will check what they have left lying around. I have my earpiece and mike on, so keep me advised. It is very important you let me know if the team near the gate look like they are about to enter. If they come in too early, it will ruin everything. Wish me luck.'

'Good luck, mama. What happens if ...'

'Do not worry. I have had the training. If anything does happen to me, I am sure you will make the right calls. You are a big boy now.'

Despite keeping exceptionally fit since she left the army, she'd be the first to admit her military training hasn't been used very much lately. She might be a little ring rusty but she'd always back herself in any one on ones. Some weaponry would be welcome as it would even up the odds a touch. The first part of her plan will hopefully address that. As she heads for the lift, a thought strikes her. If something does go wrong, she'll need something to bargain with – assuming she's still alive. She walks over to her laptop, disconnects the wallet and pockets it. You never know. Her first port of call is the serious-looking military vehicle parked outside on the drive. She might take a look inside, see what they've brought with them.

*

Vladimir is in a huddle with Fedor, discussing next steps. They have some serious ordnance in the back of their Tigr-M armoured vehicle, including a number of small but powerful mines that can be linked together and detonated remotely. There are enough of these to raze Highfield to the ground, providing him with his very own 'James Bond' moment before he makes his escape. If any hostages survive the executions, they'll be wiped out when the house goes up.

Working quickly, it will take two of his people less than an hour to plant the charges and wire them up. With Apti on a mission to find the waiter, he can only spare one of his core team for this task so he'll have to call on Simon to help out. Fedor and Simon are soon on their way. As he looks across at Pamela, he points at his watch and smiles. He has yet to choose the first victim.

*

When she gets outside, Varvara's first act is to disable the automatic lights on the driveway, tipping the odds slightly in favour of her local knowledge. As she approaches the no-nonsense vehicle abandoned near the ornamental fountain, she recognises the Tigr from her military service, although this one is an upgraded model. It'll be a piece of cake to break into and she hopes to find some usable weaponry inside. As she's thinking this through, the double doors to the house swing open and she has to leap quickly into the bushes.

Two men wielding powerful torches stride across to the vehicle and open the tailgate. One of them is Simon. She dislikes him intensely but she's weirdly grateful to him for betraying her friends and unwittingly delivering her enemies to her doorstep. She consoles herself with the fact it's all going to end in tears for him – or worse, given who he's dealing with. The other guy must be a mercenary and even in the poor light, his attitude and demeanour mark him out as a Wagner man – a simple killing machine with the emphasis on simple. From her position in the bushes, she has a great view into the back of the Tigr, giving her a glimpse of what they might be planning. They set about their work in silence – probably a language barrier thing. The Russian stows what looks like a weapon and a rucksack in the Tigr – interesting.

After a lot of banging and crashing, the Wagner guy slams the tailgate shut. They have a large holdall with them and take a handle each. Some heavy ordnance no doubt, as they're both struggling with the weight of it. When she's sure they've made it back indoors, she emerges from her hiding place. As expected, the arrogant bastards have left the vehicle unlocked. Their first mistake, albeit a small one. She'll need more than one.

*

Fedor knows his way round explosives, that's a given. Simon is there to do as he's told, something he's been doing all his life. The Russian has already studied the floor plans for the house so Simon's local knowledge won't be required. They get on with their work, which entails the planting of mines at regular intervals and daisy chaining them together with lengths of cable. The plan is to plant the explosives on the top and middle floors only. The lower floor will be consumed by the two floors above collapsing in on themselves. Due to the quantity and weight of the ordnance, they're doing the work in two stages, the middle floor first. They'll then return to the vehicle and collect the stuff for the top floor. After that, it's 'job done'. Fedor will be able to complete the final wiring and electrical connections himself and will require no further input from Simon.

*

Back at the Tigr, Varvara is rummaging around in the back. She unzips a holdall and sees at least a dozen mines, a big coil of cable and a wireless network base station with detonator. There's no longer any doubt that her brother and his team intend to destroy the house and everything and everybody left inside it, come what may. Typical behaviour from her brother and how very Russian – if he can't have it, nobody can. She can't do much about the explosives and will have to let them get on with it. Of more immediate interest is the RPG launcher and the RPGs. The launcher is a newer model but hasn't changed much since she last used one. She takes it and slings it over her shoulder and removes just one of the RPGs, which should be enough for what she has in mind. She doesn't know Fedor's name at this stage, so christens him Idiot1. Ideally, she would have liked a handgun, but can't find one in the vehicle – they're obviously keeping them close.

Before the two men emerge from the house to collect the second bag, she's shut the vehicle and moved on. While they're collecting the rest of the explosives, she risks a quick visit indoors. She descends the stairs and has a quick look at the charges in situ. If and when they're triggered there'll not be a lot left of the house, that's for sure. She knows from the CCTV that the hostages are being detained in the dining room and is tempted to get a little closer and listen in. She rejects this as being too dangerous. Piotr has whispered in her ear that the small guy is still roaming the house. She remains on full alert as she picks her way towards the billiards room in the semi-darkness. There'll be plenty of time later to reacquaint herself with Apti.

*

In the safe room, she drops off the RPG kit and tells Piotr to lock it away. Time for a toilet break. As she sits and thinks about her next move, her heart racing, there's a banging on the door and she gets the 'hurry up' from Piotr.

'Something has happened down by their vehicle. Two people walked out there and there was a flash, a gunshot perhaps. Only one person walked back indoors.'

She rushes back to her laptop, grabs the mouse and switches to the dining room camera. There's a gap where Marissa had been sitting.

'It looks like Vladimir's made his first move. I need to get out there now. I hope I am not too late.'

She'd have preferred to have a gun or two but would have to improvise for the time being. She grabs a canvas tool roll from her jewellery-making bench and runs for the exit. Mindful of the fact that Apti's on the loose she avoids moving through the house and is grateful the rain has abated somewhat. She takes a shortcut, making her way through the garden borders close to the house. Nearing the Tigr, she's on high alert. As she approaches the driveway, she stumbles across a body and almost loses her footing.

Chapter 37

She kneels down next to the body. A quick feel of the neck confirms it's a dead body, still warm. On closer inspection, she recognises Simon. He has a neat, red bullet hole in the middle of his forehead. Executed by Idiot1 she supposes, having outlived his limited usefulness. No great loss to the human race in her view.

She whispers into her mike, asking Piotr if he knows where they've taken Marissa. He's pieced together a route that makes the terrace the most likely destination for the execution. She's about thirty seconds away, and arrives as Fedor emerges onto the terrace, pushing Marissa in front of him. Luckily for both women, the idiot has a sense of theatre embedded in his thick skull and pushes her into the exact centre of the fan-shaped space. He forces her to kneel, facing away from him. Marissa stays brave, stays tough, refusing to beg for her life. By the time he points his MP-443 Grach at the back of her head, Varvara's within a pace of him. As his trigger finger starts to apply pressure, she's on him.

Her weapon of choice is one of her jewellery files, a vicious-looking item called a round needle file, a Vallorbe 7.5mm. It's like a stiletto but a bit rougher around the edges. She grabs a handful of hair, pulls his head back and rams the file up through his neck, mouth, sinuses and brain, the point bursting out of the top of his skull. She's not entirely sure this will kill him outright but it doesn't matter, he might as well be dead and there's a lot of blood. Marissa slowly looks over her shoulder and sees her rescuer, who's holding a finger to her lips. She takes Fedor's gun and fires one silenced shot into his head. She decides to leave him there. One more thing. She removes the file from his head. It makes a horrible scraping noise as it's withdrawn. She wipes it on her trousers, removes the handle and returns it to the canvas tool roll. She unties Marissa's wrists and offers her a hand. They jog back to the billiards room. On the way back, there's no sign of Apti.

She moves the sliders on the snooker scoreboard until there is a click and a whirr and a panel slides aside in the wall, revealing the entrance to a lift. They get in and the lift descends quickly. When the doors open, they enter the living quarters of the safe room. The young lad who'd recently been serving at the dinner table is staring intently at his laptop. He looks up and waves. Varvara explains.

'Welcome to the safe room. This is Piotr, my son, my beautiful boy. I owe you an explanation. When we started to feel the heat from my family, Robert had this safe space built with the intention of disappearing completely if we ever needed to. As you know he unfortunately died in Spain. I thought my son was in danger of being kidnapped so I took him in and stayed with the plan. We have been hiding out here since Robert died. Nobody seems to have noticed us, although having Tom and Ellie in the house has complicated matters for us.'

'I thought I was going to die out there. Thank you for stepping in and saving my life.'

'You were very brave. I admire that.'

'I had no idea you had a son. Did Robert ...'

'He knew about Piotr but he did not know he was my son. I did not get the chance to tell him. They would have been good together.'

'That is a great shame.'

'Yes.'

'How can I help?'

'Stay here with Piotr and keep your eyes on the CCTV. There is a secure channel available for you to establish contact with your people and tell them that you are OK. Can I ask you please to keep them at a distance while I deal with this situation.'

'But they can help, surely?'

'Let me just say it is personal. If I go down, you can call them in.'

'There is no chance of her going down, do not worry. Welcome to the Batcave, Marissa. Could you take a headset and keep watch while I make you a coffee?'

'Thank-you, Piotr. Black, no sugar.'

'Coming up.'

Marissa dons the headset and tunes in to the CCTV, swapping around between the camera points and getting used to the controls. She turns to Varvara.

'I will hold them off as long as I can. Do you have any idea where the wallet is? I'm curious, that's all.'

'Do not worry, I know exactly where it is and it is safe for the time being. I think I will join you for coffee first. After all, the next victim is forty-five minutes away. No pressure.'

*

Apti has made his way around the entire house and has found nothing out of the ordinary. He's also drawn a blank regarding the whereabouts of the young waiter. He's impressed by the house even though it's far too extravagant for his taste. He sits down on the steps in front of the main entrance facing the garage block. Simon told him earlier that Varvara used a workshop over there to run her jewellery making business. It's a potential hiding place so there's no harm in him taking a look. No harm at all.

Simon has left this part of the house open, so Apti walks in. The workshop takes up about a third of the garage space although it's difficult to tell what's inside. There's some sophisticated-looking security on the doors so he deploys a more direct approach. He removes the pin from one of his grenades, rolls it along the floor towards the door and takes cover. The explosion rips the door off and collapses some of the structure. He rushes in, hoping to find the missing waiter, dead or dying. As the smoke disperses and the dust settles, what's left of the interior reveals itself. Empty – time to move on.

Behind the garage block and built on to it is the house for the servants, people like Simon. After giving it a quick eyeball, he heads for the grounds. Nothing unusual to report, although he stops by the helipad to make sure there are no obstructions or hazards. They have a helicopter and pilot on standby, ready to take them to a Wagner safe house when they've secured the device. He hasn't yet decided when to deal with the Vladimir problem.

He takes a detour to check out the terrace before returning. He wants to make sure the first killing has been completed to his satisfaction. Sure enough, there's a body lying in the darkness but something doesn't look quite right. He approaches the body warily and realises soon enough that it's Fedor lying there. He immediately gets down into a crouch, shoulders his weapon and looks around, suddenly alert. On closer inspection, he notices his ex-colleague has some seriously weird head injuries and may even have been killed twice. His gun has been taken. He drags the body to one side – no point in advertising they're a man down. He has plenty to think about as he backs away cautiously and goes indoors.

*

In the dining room, Pamela's having trouble keeping it together. She'd fallen for Marissa in a big way only to have her brutally snatched away by this clown.

'If I had the fackin thing, I'd give it to you. I'm not interested in the money, believe me. It's not worth anybody's life.'

'I don't believe you, Pamela.' He glances at his watch. 'Another thirty-five minutes until I make my choice.'

To tell the truth, he's feeling much less sure of himself now. Apti has been away for a long time and Fedor hasn't returned from his latest mission. There's also been an unexplained explosion across the way. As he continues to fret about what might have happened, Apti appears at the doorway.

'No sign of the waiter. Could we have a word?

*

In the safe room, Marissa is reporting in to Control, telling them to hold their SWAT team back as there are three hostages who remain in great danger. Deploying the team now could do more harm than good in her judgement. She advises them that enough explosives have been installed to bring the whole house down, requiring only the touch of a button to trigger it. She assures them she's safe but can't tell them exactly where she is. She doesn't mention Varvara and what her intentions might be. She lets them know that the only demand from the Russians is for the cryptocurrency wallet and that they believe somebody among the hostages has it. Her recommendation is to let events play out and to wait for her OK before sending anybody in. As men – and women – of action, the people at the top take some persuading to sit on their hands but they do it. They're really struggling with the fact there are no demands to be met and nothing to negotiate. They order a holding pattern and tell the SWAT team to remain in position at the gate.

*

Apti and Vladimir leave Bogdan to keep watch on the remaining captives. They sit opposite each other in an adjacent sitting room while Apti describes what he's found out there. They talk in Russian.

'I took a look inside your sister's jewellery workshop.'

'I heard the explosion. What did you find?'

'Nothing unfortunately. Empty.'

'What about Fedor? Where is he? Have you seen him?'

'Yes, I saw him. He was lying dead on the terrace. He'd been stabbed through the head with something sharp and pointed and shot with his own gun. There is no way the policewoman would've been able to overpower him and do that.'

'Where is the policewoman?'

'Gone. No extra blood or brain matter that I could see. We must assume she's alive and hiding somewhere.'

'Which means what exactly?'

'Until I found Fedor, I didn't know what to think. Now I'm sure we have a highly trained ex-soldier roaming the building. A worthy opponent judging by the mess she made of our late colleague.'

'She?'

'Why not? Varvara has lived in England for a long time and she was in the Russian military for years. Elite battalions mostly. You've probably done her a big favour by coming here in force. She sees an opportunity to keep the money out of our reach, destroy us and take her father down as a bonus. A final fight to the death. Are you up for it?'

Apti may have been ready for a fight to the death but Vladimir wasn't. Far from it.

'I'm only interested in the money. When we have secured the wallet and I've seen the tokens we're out of here. Understood?'

'Perfectly. It will soon be time for you to choose the next victim. Please allow me to do the necessary this time. No more fuck-ups. Shall we?'

As they stroll back to the dining room, Apti's mind is focused on the mission. For him, it's never been about the money. He's certain that Varvara is armed and roaming around the house and if she is, Piotr can't be too far away. A big part of the solution has just dropped into his lap. He's sure she'll attempt another intervention when he gets the next execution underway. This time, he'll be ready and waiting for her.

Chapter 38

Back in the dining room, Tom's reflecting on his life, what's left of it. He'd been less than impressed by the behaviour of his wife, even before the Russians turned up. Her drinking has got steadily worse and her erratic behaviour of late has been threatening to turn 'the golden couple' into a laughing stock. If they ever get out of this in one piece, he'll leave her for sure. It'll cost him dearly but it'll be worth it, although he'll have to find a new agent.

There's been a change of tack from Vladimir, who still insists on leading the group despite not being in charge. He's chosen Tom and Ellie to be the next victims and Apti will be their executioner. Ten minutes left. Tom speculates on who'll be the first to go. Although she's sobered up somewhat, Ellie's sobbing uncontrollably. He's tempted to say, 'pull yourself together woman', but his heart's not in it.

*

Piotr is watching carefully as events unfold on the CCTV. The time has arrived for the latest execution and Vladimir is nowhere near getting his hands on the crypto wallet. This time, he's chosen two victims – perhaps he has his eye on the clock. The chosen ones are the film star and his wife. Tom, poker-faced. Ellie, all over the place. She even makes a forlorn attempt to make a run for it but only succeeds in running into Bogdan who restrains her and ties her hands behind her back. When they're both under control, Apti forces them out. He has his service pistol in one hand and a battered World War Two bayonet in the other. His AK-47 is slung over his shoulder and his pockets are bulging with grenades.

'As soon as you know where they are going, dahling, whisper in my ear. There are two of them this time and Apti won't be as careless as his late comrade.'

She's pretty sure Apti's guessed who his opponent is and might well be setting her up. With this in mind, she's persuaded Marissa to accompany her. They have one pistol between them plus the lethal jewellery files. During her police career, Marissa has had regular firearms training and knows how to handle weapons. After a quick tutorial on the Grach, she gets the gun.

*

Apti has chosen the terrace again as a suitably theatrical setting for the double execution. He has plenty of space to play with and no known hiding places for the expected gate-crasher. He suspects that Fedor was attacked from behind, so he positions himself close to the double doors at the terrace entrance after making sure they're locked. He positions Ellie on one side of the terrace and Tom on the other, on the basis that his adversary can't be in two places at once. He waits patiently and watches over his tethered goats, both of them drenched and bedraggled. He's in no rush to kill them.

*

Visibility isn't great but Piotr has described Apti's setup as best he can to both women, who have only one tactic – to focus on one hostage each. They've agreed that if a hostage is secured alive, the rescuer will return with him or her to the safe room rather than hang around. The far end of the raised terrace can be accessed from the lawn via two flights of metal steps, something that Apti had overlooked. Between the two flights of steps is a steep grassy bank. Marissa and Varvara take up their positions, each of them at the top of one flight of steps, crouching out of sight. They're as close as they can get to each hostage without breaking cover.

The rain has stopped and the moon has put in a fleeting appearance, helping illuminate the scene for the benefit of Apti. There are a lot of unknowns so Varvara focuses on the knowns. She knows that the little shit is trying to entice her into a mistake. She knows that he'll kill both hostages, whatever happens. She knows that he'll want to take her alive and use her to get to Piotr. She's gambling on him not expecting two protagonists as they can only surprise him once. She'd give anything to have another gun but what the hell. No time like right now.

She breaks cover but remains out of sight, positioning herself directly behind Tom. When she reaches him, she whispers some instructions and doesn't waste any words. Tom helps her immensely by not reacting and staying stock still. Great acting.

'Wait for your moment. Throw yourself down the grass bank. Find some cover. Get to the billiards room.'

She steps out from behind Tom, deliberately placing herself in the line of fire. She walks slowly towards the Chechen, both arms in the air. She speaks to him in Russian. He drops the bayonet and shoulders his AK-47.

'Good morning, Apti. It's been a long time. You haven't changed.'

'I guessed it was you. No further.'

'I'm unarmed. What do you want with these people?'

'Useful idiots. A means to an end. Talking of which.'

He swings his rifle around to where Ellie is kneeling, launching a hail of bullets as he does so. She isn't there. When he brings the gun back to bear on Varvara, Tom has seized his chance to escape. He's lost both hostages in the blink of an eye. How very careless, but he doesn't seem overly concerned.

'Clever. Of course – the policewoman. Never mind, I will shoot you now and go after them.'

'Wait. Before you do anything, I might be able to help you if I choose. I know exactly where the wallet is and I know exactly where Piotr is. Go back to Igor with both of them and he'll reward you richly. You'll need to dispose of Vladimir as well, which I assume is part of your mission.'

'I can see why Igor has such respect for you. You're so unlike your brother. I have to admire your daring, given that I hold all the cards.'

'You hold the advantage but you have none of the cards. You need me, Apti. Shoot me and you end up with nothing. Take your time.'

He spends a few moments weighing his options. Varvara remains motionless.

'Very well. I saw what you did to Fedor – very impressive by the way – so first I will search you for weapons. Turn around.'

He stows the AK-47 for now while retaining his handgun. He uses his free hand to search her thoroughly and finds no knives or firearms. She'd already made up her mind that 'no weapons' would be a better look than 'some weapons' in the circumstances and had disposed of the jeweller's files before revealing herself. Expecting to be searched if caught, she'd given the crypto wallet back to Piotr for safekeeping. Apti doesn't find any weapons but he does remove her earpiece, crushing it underfoot. The search is a deeply unpleasant experience for her as he chooses to linger on the more intimate parts of her body. Having satisfied himself in that respect, he holds out his free hand, palm upwards.

'The wallet please.'

'It's not about my person, as you well know. I am not that crazy.'

'Then take me to it. Please, no trickery.'

'Follow me.'

*

Marissa and Ellie have arrived back in the safe room after a brief detour to the gym area. Ellie has calmed down somewhat and is coming to terms with the fact they've been sharing their house with a couple of strangers, one of whom had lived in the house before them. Marissa reports the current situation to Control, telling them that another hostage has reached safety. Piotr is following the progress of Apti and Varvara on CCTV as they make their way towards the lower floor.

Tom reaches the billiards room and Marissa sets off to collect him. She'll need to be quick. As the lift door opens, she beckons to Tom to join her, stressing the urgency with facial expressions. They can hear voices, Russian voices, meaning Apti and his captive are getting close. They make it into the lift just in time. With Tom and Ellie reunited, Marissa has a decision to make. Does she stay put or does she re-emerge to help her comrade? It's a tough decision – she's no longer armed, so doesn't have a great deal to offer.

*

The atmosphere in the dining room has grown poisonous. They all heard the earlier burst of gunfire and have to assume that Apti has carried out his orders to the letter, although he hasn't yet returned.

Vladimir's convinced that Pamela knows more than she's saying and is delivering on his promise to leave her until last.

'It is carnage out there, Pamela. Time you came clean and produced the wallet. It is your only way out.'

'I refer you to my last statement on the subject. I don't have the fackin thing. If I did, you'd have it by now. Funny thing is, I don't think you ever intended letting any of us live, whatever happened. If you end up empty-handed, you're as dead as the rest of us.'

'Shut the fuck up, Pamela. Perhaps you don't have the wallet. It might be for the best that you go next. It is another forty minutes but only if I want to wait that long. I might even take a personal interest in your execution.'

'How kind of you. If you have the balls you were born with.'

Pamela's putting on a brave face but her situation is increasingly desperate. She has no idea that Marissa is alive and playing an active role in the fightback. She doesn't know the authorities have been alerted and are waiting nearby, ready to move in. If she had known about them, she might have been forgiven for wondering why they hadn't intervened.

Chapter 39

Varvara's mind is working overtime, interrupted now and then by a painful poke in the back from the barrel of Apti's gun. She's very much on her own. The last thing she wants is to give this creature the two things he needs – the wallet and her son. Knowing the way people like him operate, serving them up to him on a plate won't be enough to save her life. Her one advantage is that she knows every centimetre of the house. She badly needs a way of tilting the odds in her favour. In a straight fight and with no weaponry at his disposal, Apti would be as good as dead. She's decided on the swimming pool and gym in which to engineer a kind of showdown. Plenty of options available and if she dies, she'll be past caring and Apti will be no further forward. They push through the doors to the swimming pool.

'Very impressive. Now, where's the wallet?'

'It's in the changing room. It's stored in my locker.'

'Please forgive me if I don't trust you. I'll be right behind you.'

They enter the changing room and she heads towards one of the lockers, the only one with its metal door ajar. She reaches inside.

There's no wallet – she knows that. There is, thankfully, a loaded MP-443 Grach semi-automatic pistol, placed there earlier by Marissa. Given his lack of height, Apti can't see what's going on so steps back a couple of paces.

'No tricks, Varvara.'

'No tricks, Apti. Here it is.'

She swings around and gambles that Apti won't shoot immediately. Picture the scene. A cramped changing room. A small man and a tall, athletic woman. The man is pointing a loaded pistol up at the woman and the woman is pointing a loaded pistol down at the man. The man's AK-47 is leaning against a wall in the swimming pool area. He has several grenades stashed in his jacket pockets but can't get to them easily. She starts to smile.

'The odds have shifted, Apti. We're both armed now. You need me. I don't need you.'

The Chechen takes a second or two to consider this.

'I can offer you a deal. Would you like to hear it?'

'What could you possibly have to offer, Apti? I don't think so.'

She takes a slow, deliberate step forward. As she does so, she watches his trigger finger for signs of intent. He backs off – her lack of fear has installed her in the driving seat. The slow motion, stop-go danse macabre continues for a few more steps until they return to the pool area. Apti looks for the AK-47, but it's not where he thought he left it. He backs off further in the face of his opponent's steady, relentless assault. He's about to risk the first shot when he loses his bearings and backs into a poolside recliner. As he shoots, he tips backwards and the bullet flies upwards where it becomes embedded in the ceiling, releasing a shower of powdery stucco. His backward momentum and trajectory launch him into the deep end of the pool. When I say 'deep end', we're talking two metres, possibly a bit more.

*

Marissa has decided to rejoin her comrade despite her lack of firepower. She knows Varvara has led her adversary to the swimming pool and hopes she's located the handgun. After easing her way through the double doors, she hears voices in the changing room. They're talking in what she assumes is Russian, recognising the sounds but not the words. About five or six metres to her right, there's a large automatic weapon. She might as well take it, although she hasn't handled firearms like this before and doesn't trust herself to use it properly. The door to the changing room swings open and she ducks behind a pillar, taking the gun with her.

*

Varvara had known exactly what she was doing when she started to force Apti backwards and out of the changing room. Taking that first step had helped her seize the initiative and had forced her opponent – literally – onto the back foot. The timing had been perfect, as she was well aware Apti was about to shoot her at point blank range. As they'd emerged from the changing room, she'd caught a brief glimpse of Marissa holding the AK-47. This had given her the confidence to persist with her high-risk tactics.

Apti appears to be struggling to stay afloat. He tries to aim a shot at her but his old service pistol lets him down for once. Probably waterlogged. He'd hit the water awkwardly, well away from the side of the pool and even two metres has put him out of his depth. She sees the desperation in his eyes. She had no idea he couldn't swim. What a shame. His heavy canvas fatigues become waterlogged very quickly, weighing down his slight frame, dragging him under. Finally, the *pièce de résistance*. The grenades. She'd forgotten about the grenades, heavy grenades, dragging him down and deeper. She takes a seat on the lounger and watches impassively as the slow, dramatic death struggle of Apti Yamadayev, director of security for the Sokolova family business, runs its course. She rests the gun on her lap and it remains there. After a couple of minutes, he's an inert dark shape at the bottom of the pool, pinned there by the waterlogged clothing and the now useless grenades.

She feels a hand on her shoulder. It's Marissa and she's holding the AK-47.

'Can I swap mine for yours?'

The tension dissipates. They swap weapons then they laugh. Before they leave, Varvara strips down to her underwear and dives into the pool, heading for the inert shape nestling at the bottom. When she reaches Apti, she grabs his head and jerks, breaking his neck instantly. She surfaces and heads to where Marissa is waiting with a towel.

'Do you always have to kill people twice?'

'I wanted to make sure with this one. I had a close encounter with him in a dark room many years ago – an experience I will never forget. Now he is out of the way, we can all breathe more easily, believe me.'

She strips off her wet underwear and throws it on one side. Marissa throws her the towel and she dries herself off before squeezing back into her clothes and ruffling her hair. She's getting 'hurry up' looks.

'What?'

'We have less than half an hour until the final execution. It's going to be Pamela. What is the plan? Do I call in the team?'

'No, not yet. Let us return to the safe room and I will tell you what I have in my mind.'

The safe room is getting rather crowded although there's space for a couple more. They've all been lucky so far but there's no guarantee of success. Vladimir will be getting desperate by now although he still has a hostage and the capability to hurt them. As usual, Varvara is planning on a direct approach. High risk, high reward – maximum danger.

Chapter 40

Varvara works through the next steps with Piotr and Marissa. She then takes Tom and Ellie on one side and delivers the bad news she's been waiting to tell them.

'They have planted explosives throughout your house and plan to destroy it. I am very sorry for you. It is too difficult to try and stop them doing this so you must be prepared to lose this beautiful place. Do not worry yourselves about your lives. This complex has been designed to be both bombproof and fireproof. You will be safe here, even if the main house is completely destroyed.'

Tom's calm about the whole deal and Ellie isn't. She seems on the verge of another hysterical outburst and Varvara's seriously considering sedating her – or worse. Ignoring his wife, Tom seizes a brief opportunity to clear something up. Something that's being bugging him for a long time.

'When I was looking round the house before buying it, I got the distinct feeling somebody was following us, keeping an eye on us. It was blamed on the staff at the time. Was it you?'

'No, Tom, it was not. It was Piotr, practising his skills. If it had been me, you would not have noticed anything.'

'I can believe that.'

'I would like to thank you for sharing your house with us, even without you being aware. It was not our intention to do this. The death of Robert took all of us by surprise.'

'You're welcome. You're an exceptionally brave woman, Varvara.'

She can't spare any more time. She turns to Piotr.

'Apti told me they intend to bring in a helicopter, so there is a slight change to the plan.' She glances across at one of the storage cabinets. 'We are close to the finish now.'

He nods. She kisses her son, takes the wallet from him and pockets it. She then grabs the AK47 and beckons Marissa to join her for what she hopes will be the end game.

*

'Fifteen minutes to go, Pamela. Should you not be making peace with your maker?'

'Spare me the religious crap why don't you? Do your worst, whatever that is.'

'I'm looking forward to this much more than you might think. I never did like you to be honest. Your English pomposity. Ridiculous.'

'So, as I have nothing to lose, why don't we talk about how well this is going?'

'You could always cough up the wallet, you know. Save yourself.'

'I'm not going there. As a matter of interest, any idea what's happened to the rest of your team? I haven't seen the bomb man for a while.'

He feigns disinterest and focuses on cutting some lines of coke.

'Then there's the little chap with all the weapons. What's

happened to him? Are you being abandoned?'

'The wallet, Pamela. That's all I want.'

He returns to the white lines. Bogdan looks on in disgust as he hoovers up half of them.

'Ten minutes, Pamela. The wallet if you would be so kind.'

*

Pamela is about to respond when the missing wallet makes a sudden, dramatic appearance. It hits the highly polished table and slides towards Vladimir, scattering the remainder of his coke, covering him with the white powder. Varvara takes a seat at one end of the table, directly opposite her brother. She's pointing Apti's AK-47 in his general direction. She speaks to him in Russian.

'Hello brother. Is that what you came here for? Was it worth all those deaths? You always were a fuckwit.'

Bogdan is about to spring into action but comes up short. Marissa has a gun held to his head and quickly disarms him.

'Sit down and pay attention to what the lady has to say.'

Pamela is overjoyed to see her lover alive and in rude health. Marissa doesn't seem particularly pleased to see her and lets her know why.

'If you're wondering who took it from you, it was the waiter, not me.'

'I'm sorry, Marissa. Please forgive me.'

'I will think about it.'

Varvara continues.

'The new PIN is on the sticky note. I'm giving it to you in exchange for your remaining hostage.'

'How do I know it's the real deal?'

'Get your grunt to check it out. He's got a laptop, hasn't he?'

'Bogdan? You know what to do.'

He throws the wallet over to him. He plugs it in and presses some keys. Marissa continues to hold a gun to his head. A minute passes although it seems longer. Eventually:

'It works. Come here and have a look.'

He walks across, looks at the screen then looks at his sister. She nods. He should be overjoyed but he's not. Far from it, churlish even.

'Ninety million GBP. Well down. Fucking cryptocurrency!'

'Could have been worse. Why don't you take the wallet and the PIN and leave us in peace.'

'I want the recovery seed as well. Just in case.'

'Sorry, brother, no can do. You're not really in ...'

Bogdan's obviously no amateur. He's managed to overpower Marissa and wrest the gun from her. A gun that's now pointing at her head rather than his.

'You were saying?'

Varvara remains calm. Too calm it seems to Pamela who isn't enjoying this one bit.

'I was about to say that we don't have the recovery seed. When he set up the new wallet, Robert didn't note it down. Sorry. I can blow you away with this little item.' She waves the AK-47 at him theatrically. 'Used to belong to Apti. Remember him? Little guy? Stupid beard?'

'I presume you did for Fedor as well.'

She shrugs her shoulders.

'You should be thanking me, brother. Apti was under orders from our beloved papa to rub you out when you'd secured the currency. Right now, he's lining up your replacement. Did you not know?'

'Bogdan? Kill the policewoman.'

'OK, OK. No more killing. Here, take the gun.'

She slides the weapon across the table, gouging out a significant chunk of the expensive veneer and scattering more of the coke. Vladimir picks it up and points it at her. She can tell he's never handled a weapon like that before. Even if he could, there's no ammunition in it. Just in case.

'Call the helicopter in, Bogdan. Time to leave. The seed phrase is a minor detail and no longer matters to me.'

'Is that it?'

'Not quite, dear sister. I wouldn't want you or your friends to miss the big finish.'

'Don't tell me. You're going to blow the place up. How pathetic is that?'

'And I'm going to give you all a grandstand seat. The big bang. Tie our two latecomers to the empty chairs, Bogdan. Start with the policewoman.'

Within ten minutes, the helicopter is on the ground. Varvara and Marissa have joined Pamela at the dining table. All tied up.

'Farewell, dear sister. I hope you enjoy the fireworks.'

'Farewell, dear brother. They're going to blow you out of the sky as soon as you take off.'

'They will not risk it. We have people out there feeding them a line about hostages on board the chopper. We will be long gone before they work it out. So will you.'

Bogdan's getting twitchy.

'Hurry yourself. The helicopter cannot hang around for ever.'

The Russians leave. As they go, Vladimir makes a big play of showing them the remote-control detonator.

'Not long now, folks.'

*

The authorities are apoplectic about the helicopter that's just arrived and is sitting idling on the helipad. The ongoing threat to destroy the building and kill the remaining hostages had persuaded them to let it land. They've now been told there may be hostages about to board it and they're undecided about what to do next. They have people dotted around who're ready and able to take it down, awaiting orders.

*

Piotr glances at the CCTV then looks across at Tom.

'Time to go. Are you ready?'

They both rush towards the lift. For the sake of the mission, they've had to bind and gag Ellie.

When they're sure it's safe, Piotr and Tom enter the dining room and busy themselves releasing the hostages, using sharp knives to slice through their bonds, working quickly. Realising the cramped lift won't cope with all of them, Marissa and Varvara peel off to get away from the building as quick as they can. Piotr and Tom lead Pamela at a run to the billiards room, where they all squeeze into the lift.

Chapter 41

Vladimir can't believe his luck. He had no idea his sister would be in the house until Apti suggested it. After all the drama and death, she just walks in and hands over the wallet. How very careless. Her getting the better of Apti and disposing of him is another bonus.

The two remaining Russians get a bit lost on their way down – it's a big house – but they're now walking across the lawn to the waiting helicopter. Vladimir has the detonator but he's waiting until he gets to the helipad before he activates it. This will give him a great view of the big mansion's last moments, a final payback for Robert's treachery. They're close to the helicopter when Bogdan stops and points. He's spotted something lying on the lawn.

'There's something over there on the grass. Not sure what it is. Shall I go over and check it out?'

'No, there is no time. We are almost there. Stay with the plan.'

The stuff that his sister said about Apti and his intention to kill him was playing on his mind. Lamely going back to his papa and handing over the cash now feels deeply unattractive to him. Cashing in the cryptocurrency would make him a rich man. Rich enough to strike out on his own. The more he thinks about it the more it appeals to him.

They reach the helicopter. He turns round, takes a deep breath and presses the detonator. Nothing. Has the late Fedor – much vaunted Wagner explosives expert – fucked up? He jabs again at the button and a second or two later the pyrotechnics commence. The house erupts in a series of heavy explosions and collapses in on itself, the flames lighting up the sky.

'Fuck you, Robert Smith!'

He punches the air and dances a preposterous little jig but there's barely time to savour his moment of triumph. Bogdan grabs his arm and drags him towards the helicopter.

*

Tom and Piotr get Pamela back to the safe room just as the explosives are detonated. The safe room gets a belated stress test and passes with ease. Unfortunately, the upper parts of the lift are badly damaged, having borne the brunt of the collapse. No way out, apparently.

*

After separating from the rest of the hostages, Marissa bursts through the front doors of the house and runs down the drive towards the SWAT team who have been told to expect her. Her plan is to stay with the armed police and act as their guide when they get the order to go in. She's about halfway down the drive when there's a series of loud explosions behind her. She sincerely hopes everybody has found safety.

*

As soon as she's set free, Varvara checks with her son that he's carried out her latest instructions. Suitably assured, she gives him a quick kiss, then turns and sprints towards the terrace. As she reaches the far end, the explosives are detonated and she has to hurl herself down the steep grassy bank on to the lawn. There isn't much time. As instructed, Piotr has placed the RPG launcher exactly where she asked and has loaded the single grenade. The weapon is protected from the damp by a green tarp. She guesses Vladimir and Bogdan had walked right past it in the dark.

She's only allowing herself one shot. No margin, no second chance. She harks back to her training on RPGs. From a distance of fifty metres an experienced soldier will hit the target every time and destroy it. Fifty metres is a bit too close for comfort here. From a hundred metres, the hit rate decreases to 96 per cent and then tails off substantially. She reckons she's over a hundred metres from the target, no more than a hundred and twenty, reducing the odds to something like 90 per cent. Any closer and she risks being spotted while she prepares. Any further away and there's a good chance she'll miss. The passengers are seated and belted in, waiting for the helicopter to take off. Ignoring the chaos and secondary explosions behind her, she shoulders the weapon, takes careful aim and fires. She hopes and prays that the helicopter doesn't move during the 0.6 seconds it will take for the grenade to reach it.

When a grenade launcher launches an RPG, the projectile takes a bit of time to get warmed up, only reaching maximum velocity when it's halfway to the target. When she presses the trigger, a brief flash of flame is emitted from the grenade, lighting up her and the area around her. For the occupants of the helicopter, this is the first sign that they're going to die a horrible death. It's too late to defend themselves – think about it, what can you do in less than a second apart from watch the grenade home in on you? Assuming of course that her one shot is accurate.

*

Vladimir's sitting next to the pilot, who is initiating lift-off procedures. He's so busy admiring the demise of Robert's house that he fails to notice his sister taking up position directly in front of them. The first thing he sees is the flash from the rocket ignition and immediately realises his moment of triumph will be just that – a moment. Bogdan is the only person in the helicopter who reacts to what is happening. He's only just got his belt undone when the grenade penetrates the cockpit and explodes, obliterating the three Russians. A small crypto-wallet is also destroyed in the inferno.

As she stands and admires her work, she knows that killing them once will be more than enough this time. Again, no great loss to the human race in her view. She lets the launcher drop to the ground and looks up at the wreckage of the house. What she could do with right now is a fast, hard half an hour on a proper exercise bike.

*

Marissa had no idea what Varvara was planning to do when they parted company. Her first inkling is a bright flash of light from behind the jagged outline of the house. This is followed quickly by an explosion, which is followed by an even bigger explosion that sends a ball of smoke and fire into the sky. She takes a guess that the remaining Russians have been targeted by her comrade, meeting a fiery end with any luck. If that's the case, she hasn't a clue where the weaponry came from.

She's given a full briefing to the SWAT leader and has agreed to accompany them when they're cleared to go in. Her remaining concern is for the hostages gathered in the safe room, thinking they might have to be dug out of there. The SWAT leader and one of his team find a vantage point up on the wrecked wall, giving them a clear view across the house and grounds. After a few seconds, the leader mutters a command.

'Gimme the bins!'

'Boss.'

The leader whips off his night vision goggles and raises the powerful binoculars. As he tunes in, the scene becomes much clearer. In what's left of the house, part of the gym is exposed to the elements. Set amid an exposed jumble of blackened furniture and equipment, one static exercise bike has survived the carnage. Remarkably, the bike is in use. He blinks a few times, then zooms in. He captures a few seconds of video for the record. He pans across to the helipad where the tangled remains of the helicopter continue to smoulder and takes another video clip.

'Download that lot to HQ. ASAP.'

*

In the safe room, Piotr unlocks and opens a door which looks like it might provide access to a store cupboard. He reaches in and flicks a switch. Bright lights reveal a short flight of steps and a tunnel ahead. The tunnel ends at the shed posing as a Grecian temple where a concealed trapdoor leads to the outside world. The late Simon Vickers had never twigged his shed was being used by Varvara and Piotr to come and go as they pleased during their months in hiding.

Having untied Ellie, Piotr leads his charges to safety along the tunnel. As they emerge on the lawn, a reddish glow from the remaining flames provides them with a hellish glimpse of destruction. There isn't a great deal left of Highfield. The smouldering pile of wreckage on the helipad might have been a helicopter in a previous life. Piotr presses a button and seals the tunnel exit before leading the ragtag group of survivors across the lawn towards the driveway and safety. Tom catches him up and asks him what's happened to his mother. He points towards the ruins of the house where a figure on a static bike is silhouetted against a fullish moon, which has broken through the clouds. The cyclist is pedalling like mad, oblivious it seems to the destruction around her.

'She is up there, cooling down. Mission accomplished. She likes to exercise first thing in the morning so this is normal. She will join us later, I have no doubt.'

The group stop and stare at the remarkable scene. They break into a spontaneous round of applause for the moonlit cyclist, receiving a brief wave in return.

*

The leader jumps down from the wall and looks across at Marissa. It's been a long, dark night but they'll be going in soon. He's sure of that now.

'Are you ready?'

Instructions crackle through his earpiece. The team are good to go. They shake themselves down, shoulder their weapons and head towards the house. Marissa follows them in.

Chapter 42

The remaining hostages are quickly gathered in and escorted to waiting ambulances. They'll be checked over for any physical injuries before being transferred to a local hotel to get cleaned up and grab some sleep. The hotel is well protected by detachments of the security services. Debriefs have been arranged for the following day and they will then be free to go, but only if they want to. The Russian nationals are of particular interest to the powers that be and will be taken to a safe house as soon as they're ready.

*

After receiving assurances that the wrecked house is safe to enter, Marissa makes straight for what's left of the gym, where isolated pockets of fire are providing a flicker of orange light. Varvara has finished her workout and is doing some stretches. She looks up and smiles at her comrade in arms. She's dripping wet and steam is rising from her body. The two women embrace. No words are exchanged for a couple of minutes as they hold on to each other. The Russian breaks the silence.

'I thought you were going to arrest me.'

'I did think about it.'

They both laugh, although it doesn't last long.

'What happens now?'

'I suggest you start with a long, hot shower. If you can find one.'

They look around them. More laughter.

'So, what *does* happen now? Piotr and myself. Homeless and helpless. I am afraid they will deport us. Send us back to Russia.'

'Relax. You are much more in control than you think. The authorities will want to know what you know about the Sokolova businesses. The less said about the cryptocurrency, the better. It might exist on a blockchain somewhere but it is out of reach and that is the main thing. One thing is certain – Igor is already on borrowed time.'

'All very well. But what about Piotr and me?'

'I cannot speak for the UK – not any more it seems. We can arrange for you to stay in any European Community country of your choice for as long as you like. New identities are available if you need them. A clean slate, as they say.'

'What about the people who were killed?'

'What people?'

'You are right. What people.'

Another brief embrace, then Varvara's off to find her son. Her beautiful son.

Chapter 43

'Welcome to DC!'

Marissa and Pamela are taking a short break in America and Varvara is at Dulles Airport to meet and greet them amid a flurry of hugs and kisses. In the ten weeks since the events at Highfield, Piotr and his mother have been deciding where to set up home. They've yet to make up their minds, but one thing's for sure – it won't be the UK. There'd been only grudging sympathy from the Home Office to their plight and no guarantees were given. The few officials they met seemed to be stuck in a 'hostile environment' mindset, determined to make it difficult for them. The US has been much more welcoming, although it's not a permanent thing.

There are plenty of other options available to them. They currently favour a move to Poland and Marissa is assisting them with their application for permanent residence. In the meantime, Varvara's secured a part-time research job at Georgetown University. It's an assignment that affords her son the time and space to explore the university and what it has to offer. It also provides the

CIA with an opportunity to chat to her informally about her past and explore mutual interests.

The three women are getting together to deal with the cryptocurrency fortune that is out there somewhere on the Ethereum blockchain. There is an added complication – a potentially deadly, flu-like virus that is playing havoc with international travel. They got into the country easily enough but they need to remain vigilant to ensure they can get out again. In the meantime, they're determined to enjoy their time in America, Donald Trump notwithstanding.

Her visitors accompany Varvara to her car. They load up and are soon on their way to the city. She's in a relaxed mood. They all are. She glances in the rearview mirror.

'Have you two loving birds named the day? We are expecting invitations.'

Pamela responds.

'Not yet, no. We thought we would find a new home first – in Spain most likely. Might take us a while to find the right place so don't hold your breath.'

Marissa has some good news for her friend.

'There is no problem with you and Piotr moving to Poland. The process is close to completion and there is plenty of time to decide where and when. Take your time.'

'Thank you.'

'Why Poland?' Pamela was genuinely curious.

'I have friends there, I know a little Polish language and it is very convenient for travel to Russia and the Ukraine.

'How about Piotr?'

'He does not have to join me yet. If his plans start to fruit, he will spend the next four years studying in America.'

'And your jewellery business?'

'We only intend to stay here for six months, which is not enough time to set up properly. I might buy in some kit and materials to keep my hand going. We will see. Anyway, here we are.'

Varvara has rented a superb five-bedroom town house in a select area close to the university. She pulls into a space at the rear of the house. There are more hugs and kisses as Piotr welcomes them, takes their luggage and shows them to their room. Tea is served and they make plans for the next few days, knowing full well virus restrictions might intercede at any time.

*

Tonight, Piotr's at the local cinema with some of his new friends, providing his mother and her visitors with an opportunity to discuss the cryptocurrency. They've finished off the pizzas and are well down their second bottle of Zinfandel. Varvara tops up their glasses and gets straight to the point.

'Are we going to leave it there, sitting on the blockchain?'

'Why not? None of us need it.'

Pamela's right. She's gifted Varvara all of the net proceeds from the house and art collection, making her a very wealthy woman. She and Marissa have plenty between them and she's keen to set up a charitable trust with Robert's investment income. His legacy, if you like.

'Are you not just a little curious, Pamela?'

'Not in the slightest, my dear.'

'Marissa?'

'I have to admit that I am. As a civilian rather than a policewoman. What harm would it do?'

That makes two yeses and a qualified no. Varvara's done her research and is keen to go for it.

'Link has told me how to reinstate our access to the tokens. Did you bring your half of the seed phrase?'

Pamela scrabbles around in her bag and places the small metal plate on the table. Varvara puts her metal plate beside it. The seed phrase is complete – twenty-four words. She unwraps a new wallet and fires up her laptop.

'Can we not tempt you, Pamela?'

'I'm going for a vape. How long do you need?'

'About thirty minutes.'

'Then do your worst. Nothing good will come of it, mark my words.'

They do their worst and check the tokens. Things are looking up.

[09/03/2020: 1 ETH = 150.58 GBP (Source AOEx): Fund Value: £136 million]

Ether is enjoying a significant renaissance and their curiosity has been satisfied for the time being. When Pamela returns, they resolve to meet up somewhere in the world every year and review the cryptocurrency. Marissa offers to be the honest broker and is entrusted with the new wallet. Pamela and Varvara will retain each half of the key phrase. Just in case.

Unfortunately, their time together in Washington is cut short by new travel restrictions. Pamela and Marissa get back to Europe on one of the last flights out. The human race is about to hunker down and wait for the vaccines to arrive.

*

A year later, lockdowns are the order of the day and the virus – COVID-19 – has already claimed over a million lives and counting. Travelling is out of the question, so the three of them hold their annual meeting on Zoom. Varvara calls in from her splendid new home in Lodz and she uses her phone to take her friends on a rather wobbly virtual tour. Marissa and Pamela join in from their new place near Pamplona, which is far too extensive for the virtual tour treatment.

Just that day, they'd discovered the value of the cryptocurrency had soared to a breathtaking billion pounds – and counting.

[08/03/2021: 1 ETH = 1,246.59 GBP (Source AOEx): Fund value: £1.12 billion]

Ether has become the darling of the cryptocurrencies and is on a steep upward trajectory. Nobody's prepared to guess how long it'll last. Perhaps Igor should have been more patient with his son and allowed him to stay in the game. Hold on – don't even go there. With cryptocurrency, normal rules don't apply.

Talking of Igor. Varvara has received an update from some reliable sources in Russia. Her father has been missing for some time and she's now willing to bet he's dead. Causes unknown. A combination of mislaying a significant amount of money and losing Apti's security presence – particularly the latter – had left him vulnerable. She's heard the vultures are squabbling over the entrails of the business and more bloodshed is on the cards. Mission accomplished as far as she's concerned.

Chapter 44

Pamela and Marissa's new place is a small working vineyard in Navarra, just south of Pamplona. They've called it *Vina San Sebastian*. 'Small' doesn't do it justice – the main house has six bedrooms and there are extensive grounds that include the vineyards and a winery. Marissa has quit the police force and is starting a new career in viniculture. She's working alongside Pablo – their retained manager – until she feels confident enough to take over the reins. Pamela contents herself with her art blog and an occasional piece for *The Times*. Most of her time these days is spent organising the new Robert Smith Foundation.

Given the success of vaccination campaigns – in the Western world at least – there'd been an easing of the rules around international travel. Now was as good a time as any to get married and invite their friends to Spain to help them celebrate it. Among the guests are Tom and his new girlfriend, Varvara (plus one), Piotr (plus one) and Monty. All of them would be staying at the vineyard for a few days. Of all the people on the invitation list, Varvara's 'plus one' is causing the most speculation. When the guests arrive in Navarra, they're shown to a large table in the courtyard, shaded from the fierce sunshine. Bottles of wine and plates of pintxos are available. Pamela welcomes everybody.

'Before we start, I see a few new faces. So, Varvara, who is the mystery man?'

'This is Dmitro. He is from the Ukraine and is my "teenage sweetheart". He thought he had escaped from me but I tracked him down. I am so happy I found him. He is staying with me in Lodz and helping with the jewellery.'

Varvara gives him a huge, sloppy kiss. He's a handsome, bearded, fit-looking chap as you might expect and has something of the warrior about him. Right now, he manages to look both pleased and embarrassed.

'Welcome to our celebration, Dmitro. Tom?'

'This is Amanda, but she answers to Mandy. She's a film director and producer. We met on the set of a small indie I did recently. She barked orders at me all day and we fell in love. How about that?'

'Am I allowed to ask about Ellie?'

'You are. Positively thriving the last time I checked. She went into rehab, and is clean as far as I know. Her business is now worth half a billion dollars.'

'The house?'

'The remains of it were bulldozed. We claimed the insurance after a long argument over exactly what an "act of war" was, then sold the land off and split the proceeds. I'm living in LA now – with Mandy of course.'

'Have you finished being whatshisname?'

'Most definitely. The franchise has run its course. Whisper it quietly but the last one wasn't very good even though it turned a profit somehow. I'm thinking of doing some more stage work, going back to my roots. Off Broadway maybe. Mandy's got a few interesting ideas. I'm just hoping I don't end up like Michael Keaton's character in *Birdman.*'

'And Piotr?'

'This is Alex and she's from Chile. I met her on the course I'm doing at Georgetown and we share an apartment in DC.'

Piotr is picking up the first hints of an American accent. Young, smart, healthy, good-looking, their whole lives ahead of them. What's not to like? With the introductions out of the way, Pamela moves on.

'Welcome to our beautiful vineyard, one and all. Help yourself to wine – our very own – and tapas. After that, Marissa and Pablo will give you the tour. Dinner at nine in the courtyard. Ceremony at eleven tomorrow morning. No need to dress up.'

Monty has lost some weight somehow and is looking quite spry by his standards. His garb is very much 'Englishman abroad' – voluminous shorts, thick socks and sandals, silly hat. He sidles up to Pamela, a large glass of red to the fore, some of it spilling.

'Nice stuff. If you're looking for a way into the UK for your, er, produce, look no further. There's an acquaintance of mine in Broadway. Dabbles, you know how it is.'

'Sorry, Monty, but you'll need to talk to Marissa. I'll mention it to her. Let's get the wedding out of the way first, shall we?'

'Of course, totally understand. By the way, I might not send you the usual red at Christmas this year. Coals to Newcastle and all that.'

That would be a blessed relief given some of the stuff he's sent her in the past. As she turns away, she almost bumps into Varvara.

'Do you have a moment? I have some news. I am afraid it is bad news.'

'Oh dear. Let's find some privacy.'

They find a quiet, shady corner in the garden and sit together on a convenient bench.

'I am sorry to tell you this but Link is no longer alive. It was announced recently on his website. Such a shame. I was still doing business with him for the jewellery website.'

'Did you find out anything about him?'

'I did. His real name was David Jones and he was constrained to a wheelchair. He injured his spine playing rugby, whatever that is. I tracked his mother down and visited her. Martha had been his carer for years.'

'How did he die?'

'COVID. Last year. He was extra vulnerable to it and did not stand a chance when it took hold. Martha blames herself for bringing it into the house.'

'Is she OK? For money, I mean.'

'She is well set up. Link – sorry – David left his mother some money and a small number of NFTs. CryptoPunks actually, rare ones. Christie's auctioned them recently for about five million. Hammer price. What do you think of that?'

She didn't know what to think about NFTs anymore. In March, an NFT incorporating a digital artwork by Beeple had realised sixty-nine million dollars at auction. Robert could well have been barking up the right tree when he started investing in digital art. If only.

*

The tour gets underway and is well received. Monty is particularly taken with the tastings, during which he buttonholes Marissa about business possibilities. Dinner in the evening is a great success, carrying on well beyond midnight.

There's not much to say about the wedding. It was a joyous affair, a memorable day for everybody and particularly memorable for

Pamela and Marissa. Before leaving, Pamela and Varvara have a quiet chat during a walk around the grounds. They talk about Robert's ashes and what to do with them. They're currently gathering dust on a shelf above the open fireplace in one of the sitting rooms.

'It doesn't seem right that he's stuck up there on the shelf, enduring the disparaging comments about the urn from most of the people who see it. I wish Grayson had stuck to the brief.'

Varvara has no idea who Grayson is.

'What do you have in your mind?'

'I'd like to bury his ashes in the grounds and plant a tree. A sweet chestnut or similar, something that can cope with the conditions. A small plaque. What do you think?'

'I think it would be perfect. Send me some pictures when it is finished. That would be good.'

One last thing.

'Are you happy now, my dear? With Dmitro, I mean.'

'Very happy. He is very much the love of my life. Again.'

'How did you find him?'

Now, there's a story.

Chapter 45

Varvara had asked for the 2022 meeting to be brought forward because of the worsening situation in Ukraine. The three women agreed to meet in London and had booked a pod on the London Eye at her request. No champagne – it hadn't seemed appropriate somehow.

As soon as they're on board and start moving, Varvara takes the lead.

'First, I want to share some good news with you.'

She proudly shows her friends her right hand. There's a gold wedding band on her ring finger.

'Yes, I am now Varvara Shevchenko. I am sorry I did not invite you but we had to move quickly. It was a small ceremony in Kiev with a couple of friends.'

She accepts the warm congratulations. There is more news.

'I have recently applied to become a citizen of Ukraine. I could be parted from Dmitro at any moment.'

'What do you mean by parted?'

'I will cut straight to the point. The military situation is bad in Ukraine, much worse than you can imagine, especially in the Donbas where Dmitro was born and where war has been raging since 2013. Do you remember the airliner that was shot down?'

They did. Back in 2014. It was denied by the Russians, a sure sign they were involved.

'Do you think Putin will invade?'

'He will this time. I was in St Petersburg recently, talking to some old friends and comrades from the army. They were unwilling or unable to tell me much but what they did tell me made it unmistakeable. There will be an invasion dressed up as something else. It will be cruel, relentless and bloody – Russians know no other way.'

'Which side will you be on?'

'The same side as Dmitro of course. He is a reservist, an artillery specialist, and expects to receive his recall papers soon. He will be on the frontline within a few weeks. There is a lot of history under the bridge so you must not forget their hatred of Russians or their ability to put up a fight. I am a proud Russian but I cannot support what is happening, believe me.'

'What do you intend to do?'

'As soon as hostilities begin, there is likely to be a mass evacuation of women and children to safe areas. The men will stay and fight, whether they want to or not. In Poland, where the hatred of Russia is even greater, they are making contingency plans to deal with large numbers of refugees. I plan to contribute in a small way. I have a plan to refurbish unused and derelict commercial buildings in Poland and relaunch them as hostels for refugees. They may be needed for some time.'

'Can we help?'

'I was coming to that. My plan has ambition and cannot be done on the cheap. I would like to liberate the cryptocurrency and put it to work in Poland. I know we said we would put it beyond reach but I cannot think of a better cause. Do you agree with me?'

Marissa and Pamela look at each other. It's all about trusting their friend. Not just a friend – somebody who saved their lives. Marissa speaks for both of them.

'We agree. Can we have a last look at the value before we shake hands on it?'

Varvara smiles and fires up her iPad. Marissa hands her the wallet. As their pod reaches its highest point, the value on screen pushes beyond a staggering two billion pounds.

[10/02/2022: 1 ETH = 2,354.36 GBP (Source AOEx): Fund value: £2.12 billion]

'Spend it wisely, my dear. Don't forget to take this with you. Just in case.'

Pamela hands her the metal plate with twelve of the twenty-four seed phrase words. She won't be requiring it anymore and is glad to hand it over. Varvara stows the iPad, wallet and plate in her rucksack.

When they leave the pod, there are hugs all round and a few tears are shed. Then, the usual promises to stay in touch although nothing is arranged this time. She's gone in an instant, lost amid the multitude of people on the South Bank.

As she passes the Tate Modern, she drops a package in one of the rubbish bins. It's a small, easily-concealed handgun – a second-hand Glock G43 to be precise – wrapped in an old carrier bag. She hadn't needed it.

Also by Paul Hirons

1997 remembered – a faux memoir

Praise for his debut novel

Acerbically sardonic – laughed my way through it!

Julie

Once you start reading difficult to put down.

Tony

An excellent novel. Can't wait for the next one.

Anthony

Plenty to enjoy in this book.

Brian

Great read. Left me wanting more.

Karen

I enjoyed the comedy elements of this book.

Angela

Available now at the **Amazon Kindle Store** or via my website at **pahirons.com**

Acknowledgements

The inspiration for this story came from Misha Glenny's *McMafia*, a compelling, fearless and, quite frankly, terrifying account of failing states and global criminal networks.

I visited the Bill Viola retrospective in Bilbao in person but I've referenced the excellent *Going Forth By Day* exhibition catalogue to ensure I got the detail right.

Thanks to John for his invaluable advice on how fine art auctions work and apologies for ignoring his valiant defence of the outrageous levels of commission.

Of the many people who have encouraged my writing, I'd particularly like to thank my hard-working team of beta readers for their excellent feedback on the manuscript. Step forward: Angela, Helen, Julie, Louise, Jonathan and Nick.

A special mention is due to Angie for her comprehensive advice on jewellery making and tools. I well remember her lining up the tools for inspection on our table at the Broadway Indian Restaurant. I can only imagine what our fellow diners thought about our loud speculation regarding their suitability as murder weapons.

Finally, a big thank you to Barbara for her continuing encouragement, professional proofreading expertise and for generally banging the drum on my behalf.

Printed in Great Britain
by Amazon

60155996R00188